PRESIDENTIAL

INTENTIONS

BY

DOUGLAS J WOOD

ISBN: 1484926528
ISBN 13: 9781484926529
Library of Congress Control Number: 2013909624
CreateSpace Independent Publishing Platform
North Charleston, South Carolina

This book is dedicated to the many people who encouraged me to complete it and helped me in accurately reflecting history and events, including my wife, Carol Ann; my daughter, Meghan (a prosecutor in Miami, Florida); my good friends Evan Smith, Michael Thompson, and Mitch Becker for their review of early drafts; Dr. John Frattarola (an obstetrician); Rear Admiral (Ret.) John D. Hutson (formerly Judge Advocate General of the United States Navy and President and Dean of the University of New Hampshire School of Law); Nancy Schulein (my assistant for more than fourteen years); Elhanan Stone (my law partner for many years, now retired in sunny Florida); and the staff of CreateSpace.

Chapter One

I am a woman, and I support equal rights. Equal rights in America, however, is not a cause only for women or for minorities or the disabled, but for all Americans. Anything less is to deny our heritage as the most prosperous, decent, caring, and God-fearing society in the world. I accept your nomination for president of the United States with equal rights as my goal, platform, and banner.

Speech in acceptance of nomination, Convention Center, Memphis, Tennessee, July 27, 2016.

September 2, 2016
Baltimore, Maryland

Samantha Harrison, Republican candidate for president, hated hospitals. The moment she walked into one, she felt the depression and suffering infecting the hallways and rooms. The clinical smells of the myriad drugs and antiseptics used to keep the surroundings clean served to create an atmosphere more of finality than a future. Adding to the sterility were the detached nurses and doctors rushing as if they were pressured to get the job done and get home early rather than provide comfort, care, and hope to patients and their families. But Sam couldn't blame them—after all, look how socialized medicine forced nurses and doctors to look at patients as numbers rather than people needing help.

Johns Hopkins Hospital was particularly clinical. It was a teaching hospital, so its agenda was to instruct interns and residents rather than care for the patients. Sam knew that wasn't true, but could think of nothing more impersonal than a dozen newly *graduated* doctors gathered around a bed discussing her husband's suffering as though he were just another potential cadaver for a classroom. Sam vowed when her time came, she would not die in a hospital.

As she walked down the hall to Ben Harrison's room, she felt tears returning as she once again succumbed to the cold green walls and linoleum floors so shiny her reflection was as apparent as looking in a mirror. She couldn't help but remember being told hospitals use linoleum floors because blood cleans off easily. She wondered if that was true.

Hesitating at the door to her husband's room, Sam dreaded what she'd find inside. Her thoughts went to the last time she came to a hospital to see a dying man.

In 1968, Crownsville Hospital Center in Crownsville, Maryland, was decidedly different from Johns Hopkins. A suburban hospital in a wealthy community, it had a better sense of aesthetics, a softer atmosphere. For what killed her father—bone cancer—he didn't need a fancy, high-tech environment. He just needed a constant drip of pain-killers in ever-increasing doses to mask the inevitable. Sam was too young to remember much, and she was thankfully spared the moments of dementia her father fell in and out of in his last days. She never had to see his bones, so brittle that lifting him from the bed would break another rib. Witnessing the fear her father had of dying and the tears he shed whenever he had a few lucid moments with Sam's mother, Elizabeth, were memories Sam had also thankfully been spared. But one thing remained as vivid as the day she saw it: the devastating look in her father's eyes, knowing death was imminent and there wasn't a thing anyone could do to stop it.

On his last day alive, Sam's father asked to separately see Sam and her brother alone. He knew he had little time left. The pain was increasing by the hour, and his lucid moments grew fewer. He told the doctors to cut off the medication during his last moments with his family so he could be as aware as possible. Somehow he'd get through the pain.

During the time Sam spent with her father, he said only a few words. Most of the time, he simply stared at her, touching her cheek and holding her hand. Sam didn't know what to say. She felt helpless. It was the first time Sam ever saw her father cry. She gave her father one last, long hug. On October 1, 1968, Sam's father died in her arms before she let go. He never did get to say good-bye to her brother.

Regaining her presence and the harsh reality she was in Johns Hopkins where her husband lay dying, Sam pushed open the door into room 397, afraid she was about to lose her closest friend with too little time left to tell him just how much she loved him, forgive all his faults, and hope he could forgive hers—even the ones he didn't know about. It was all she could do to keep her composure.

Their daughter, Amanda, was already there. At first Sam feared he already passed and she was too late. Amanda, sensing her mother's fear, stood and told Sam that Ben was just asleep. Amanda said she didn't want to wake him and drain his energy before Sam arrived.

"I'll leave you alone with Daddy."

Sam stood over the bed, feeling helpless. "Amanda, please stay. I don't know if I can handle this alone."

Amanda put on her coat and walked to the door. "Mom, it may be selfish of me, but I'm leaving. I can't bear this anymore. For the last two weeks, I've been here every day watching Daddy die. Then I go home and watch you on the evening news talking about solving everyone else's problems. I know you're doing important things, but it's been hard on me. All Daddy talks about is you, telling me how amazed he is to see you become one of the most respected and influential people in the country, maybe the world. I've said my good-byes, Mom. I'm sorry, but I have to leave."

In that brief exchange, Sam felt the sting of the sacrifices she'd made in pursuit of public service. They were costly. Perhaps too costly. Amanda left without a hug.

Sam sat down by the bed, afraid to stir Ben. He looked so serene. She put her hand on his.

The scene was not as depressing as Sam had expected. It had been a full week since she'd last seen him. Time had become precious and cut into her personal life, and for this she felt she'd let Ben down.

She knew they had stopped using medications and technology to bring him back to health. His heart wasn't getting better. He was beyond extraordinary measures and had given clear instructions that other than occasional painkillers, he didn't want anything more, so all the chrome machines and plastic tubes were gone. He actually looked comfortable. Amanda had arranged some flowers. Copies of *The Wall Street Journal* and *The Washington Post* lay neatly stacked on the floor next to Amanda's chair. She read the financial and political sections to him every day.

A nurse entered to take his pulse. The touch on his wrist woke Ben.

He smiled when he saw Sam and gave her hand a squeeze. They sat silent for the longest time.

How odd, here I am with the man who has given me so much and asked for so little, and I can do nothing.

The presidential candidate felt completely helpless. When her husband needed her most, there was so little she could give. She was just as lost as she had been forty-eight years before with her father. As the nurse left, Ben focused his attention on Sam.

"Where's Amanda?"

"She just stepped out. She figured we wanted to be alone for a few moments."

"Really? Gee, Sam, I don't know if I'm up to it right now. Besides, if the nurse walks in, it would be embarrassing. The reporters would have a field day. But it sure would get you the nymphomaniac vote."

They laughed. Ben could always bring humor into the most serious moments. It was his way of making people comfortable, and he did it very well.

Sam began to tear up, "I'm sorry I haven't been here more often, Ben." Ben squeezed her hand harder.

"It's all right, Sam. You've been here all along. I've read about you every day and watched you on the tube each night. I admit I do cringe a bit when they chant 'Sam's our man' at rallies. But I couldn't be prouder and happier for you than I am now." Sam smiled, and the tears dried as she recalled better days as Professor Benjamin Harrison's student at Stanford.

Sam and Ben knew this could well be the last time they'd ever talk, but neither wanted to say so. The last time she'd ever get Ben's advice. The last time she'd have Ben to intercede with Amanda. But saying good-bye was not acceptable to either of them. Instead they just sat together for another hour or so, talking about things of little importance. Finally Ben said he was growing tired and thought it would be best if he got some sleep. He'd see Sam the next day, if that was OK with her schedule. She said that would be fine.

As the last rays of sunlight filtered through the window and shone on Ben, now asleep, he was radiant as Sam held his hand, watching the sunset. Dusk blotted out what remained of daylight, and Ben's heart stopped. He died holding the hand of the woman he loved.

Chapter Two

My veto of this bill is without hesitation. When a child comes home and his home is empty, he hurts. When a child comes home and has no mother to talk to, he gets no help to solve his problems. When a child comes home and has only a television to keep him occupied, he loses sight of the world. The state legislature's misguided bill will require mothers on welfare to work for their weekly check, performing menial tasks for government offices. It is a pathetic piece of legislation that will only serve to increase our problems, not solve them. We need to find ways of letting our children come home to families, not cartoons. Let's do more to find deadbeat Dads rather than create dead-end Moms.

Speech from Governor's Mansion, October 1, 2011.

July 27, 2016
Memphis, Tennessee

While the tumult was typical of past Republican presidential conventions, this was a special moment. Samantha Price Harrison was the first woman Republican presidential candidate in US history. And she would be running against the likely Democrat nominee, Hillary Clinton. The question of when the country would have a woman president was over; the only remaining question was which one America would choose. The two candidates bore no resemblance to one another, in politics or appearance.

Sam, as she was popularly known, was less than a month shy of fifty-nine, a strikingly handsome woman at five foot ten with brunette hair without a strand of gray. Clinton was sixty-nine and made no secret of covering her gray. It was rare to ever see Sam in a suit, although suits were the standard for Clinton. While both were somewhat moderate within their respective parties, on key issues, the two were miles apart. Clinton was a Washington insider, having served as a Capitol Hill staffer, a first lady, a senator from New York, and secretary of state in the Obama administration. Sam had served as a successful businesswoman, a tough criminal prosecutor, a congresswoman from Virginia, and as Virginia's governor, where she enjoyed significant popularity across party lines. Both had strong foreign relations experience and understood the threat of terrorism, although how they might handle it certainly differed. Regardless, pundits on both sides of the aisle predicted a campaign on issues and records, not on whether a woman should be president.

The convention was much like others. Banners, hats, and chants. Press on the convention floor looking for sound bites and partisan politicians looking for their fifteen seconds of fame. Some might describe the scene as America at its best. Others would say at its worst.

As the applause, balloons, and hysteria reached a crescendo among the delegates, Sam let herself get lost in the moment, however short it may have been. She made history as no Republican woman had done before and earned a brief time of self-absorption after a hard-earned victory in a long and tough primary campaign failed to elect a winner. So it came down to a vote on the convention floor. Deals had to be made, and Sam was prepared to make them. While she had the largest delegate total, it was not enough to win the nomination. Her next closest opponents were Marco Rubio and Rand Paul. Sam had no interest in making any arrangement with Paul. He and his Tea Party supporters were far too divisive for her blood. And she doubted Rubio and Paul would form an alliance. But none of the other candidates had enough delegates to put Sam over the top, and she had no desire to cobble together a multicandidate coalition. She knew a deal with Rubio had to be made. A ticket with candidates from two southern states could be a problem, but she was confident the party would overcome it. Paramount in her mind was having Rubio on the ticket gave them a potential edge for the Hispanic vote. A vote Republicans overwhelming lost to Obama in the last two elections.

The Republican Party leadership made it clear to insiders Sam was the candidate they wanted. And they liked the idea of Rubio on the ticket as well. Sam knew their belief was that no male among the candidates had a realistic chance of beating Clinton. Sam's objective intuition agreed. With so many voters on various federal benefit plans like welfare, unemployment, and more, Clinton virtually owned almost half of the people who might vote if the Democrats could hustle enough voters to the polls. Based upon Clinton's inheritance of Obama's grassroots organization, it was certain there would be a high turnout of loyal Democrats. Nor did Republican leadership feel there would likely be any significant loss of loyal Republicans voting for Clinton. Certainly, conservative Republicans would never vote for Clinton. The moderates in the party would welcome Samantha Harrison despite some of her more conservative views. So they didn't worry about the Republican base. It boiled down, as it did in 2012, to the *undecided*, and whether the Republican candidate could capture enough conservative Democrats.

Sam was in full agreement with the leadership's strategy. A woman candidate trumped any lock on women voters. Rubio would help capture the growing and prosperous Hispanics. Neither Sam nor Rubio had any skeletons in their closets like Travelgate, Benghazi, and others. It meant the media bias to cover gender and race issues might actually give way to the real issues Sam cared about—leadership, integrity, and experience managing complex problems. As far as Sam was concerned, Clinton was no match to her on any of the key issues voters cared about. Sam was ready, and the Republican puppet masters were confident she could match or *better* whatever Clinton brought to the table. It was also a relief to Sam that being a woman would not be an issue with Clinton as her opponent. There would be fewer irrelevant and inappropriate questions to answer.

Sam sent Zachery Watts, her campaign manager and political mentor, to talk with Rubio's team, offering him the number two spot on the ticket. Surprisingly, he readily accepted, realizing his campaign against Clinton had little chance of victory. Sam also knew a junior senator with only a few years' experience in the Florida House of Representatives wouldn't stand a chance against Clinton's resume. Win or lose, Rubio would be catapulted further up the party hierarchy. And while he had Tea Party connections, they were not as deep as Paul's. Sam was confident she could manage any damages Rubio's Tea Party association might create with moderate or left-leaning Republicans as well as independents.

With Rubio in her camp, Sam dispatched Watts to meet with Paul's team and give them the news. Paul took it well but made it clear that if Sam and Rubio did not keep a campaign true to less government and lower taxes, they could not count on his support. Sam and Watts got the message loud and clear.

Once the alliance with Rubio and Paul was announced, the other candidates fell into place. Sam won the nomination on the first ballot. The Republican Party was united once again. At least for one night.

Two hours after accepting the nomination, Sam relaxed in her suite at the Peabody Hotel while Watts acted as the gatekeeper, preserving what little privacy Sam had left. The Peabody, steeped in tradition, was a location for reflection on the day's events with the many visitors who came by with congratulations. It was one o'clock in the morning by the time all the well-wishers had finally gone.

Watts was the first to speak. "Before we call it a night, we have to talk about tomorrow's press conference. After an acceptance speech that expansive, there are going to be a lot of questions. I wish you had let us review the speech before you gave it. Jesus, you all but threw out the platform."

"I'm the one running, Zach. If I can't express my own thoughts in my own words, I don't deserve the office. I've never understood why it seems acceptable for candidates to have speechwriters. If you can't put your own views into words, you shouldn't be on a ballot. Damn the platform. It doesn't mean a thing, and the American people know it. They need to know what I think, not the thoughts of old party farts."

Watts shook his head in frustration, knowing Sam would never toe the official party line, but he couldn't let her off easy. "Come on, Sam. You sounded more like a damned Democrat than a Republican. Even some of the delegates were wondering if they were at the right convention. Where'd all that shit come from?"

Sam acknowledged Watts had been instrumental—critical, even—to her success. But the time had come for a game change. Sam shifted on the couch, leaned forward, and narrowed her eyes sternly at her campaign manager.

"I'm facing an election campaign with the highest Dow Jones average in US history, and there's no sign of where it might go. It overshadows the unemployment figures. We're not at war. There hasn't been a terrorist attack in almost a year. Our party looked like fools in 2013 and took blame for the failure of the shutdown. In 2014, we barely held on to the House and made no progress in the Senate. Despite all the mess Obama left behind and his poor ratings, he still scores better than Republicans. What I've got going for me is the healthcare mess, the economy growing at an anemic rate, and a deficit with no plan to reduce it. But America wants social programs, and we've got to find money to fund them. I'll give you your tax cut, but I can't abandon popular programs. If I don't get elected, you and the party favorites can abandon me as just another politician who failed to toe the conservative Republican line. I'm not going to do that, Zach, because if I do, I'll lose just like Romney did."

Watts left without further comment, now used to Sam's last-minute changes and dismissals. It had not always been that way. Politics is a funny thing. Politicians rise to the top because of astute and calculated campaigns mapped out by consultants like Watts. But once they reach their zenith, politicians relegate consultants to minor roles, usually to the politicians' peril. Sam was no different. She was a seasoned politician, not at all like the neophyte Watts first encountered in law school. The pressures of the primaries and the anticipation of the upcoming campaign made moments between the two perfunctory and to the point. It was all business.

As rain began to fall, Sam fell into her own thoughts. She had attained her hard-won goal. But she worried. "Governor Ice," as *The Richmond Times-Dispatch* liked to call her, was slowly melting, missing family and friends, and feeling oddly abandoned at a time when she could have all the people anyone could wish for swarming around her. With all the success, there was an uncomfortable sense of emptiness Sam couldn't quite understand. As she dozed off in her chair, TV droning on, Sam chalked up her fears and empty feeling to the daunting challenge ahead and the heavy burdens of the office she sought to hold.

Chapter Three

Fellow graduates, today we are at a crossroads. We can either check out as so many have, or we can stay committed to making America an even greater country. We can choose to take pride in our heritage or abandon it. We can hide and hope the problems go away, or we can fight to make things right. As far as I can tell, our parents don't need to worry about us. While there are others who preach destruction and cowardice, all of us are ready for the challenge and look forward to giving America our hearts and our wills just as our parents did a generation ago.

Excerpt from valedictorian speech, Indian Creek Upper School, June 23, 1974.

June 23, 1974
Crownsville, Maryland

Elizabeth Price could not have been prouder. Her daughter, Samantha, was giving the valedictorian speech. With her seventeenth birthday just two months away, Sam was among the youngest graduates in Indian Creek Upper School's class of 1974. On top of that, she was class president, voted most likely to succeed, and winner of every writing award given by the school. If that were not enough, Sam's stunning looks and popularity fed every boy's imagination.

Crownsville was a typical Maryland suburb. Packed with successful bankers, brokers, political consultants, and lawyers, the town's property values were inflated well beyond what made sense. The high school, with its campus like grounds, rivaled the best private schools in the country. The graduating students had their choice of colleges, with over 98 percent continuing their education. The dark sides of the school—the drugs, alcohol, and teenage pregnancies—were well hidden. Crownsville liked to keep its warts out of sight.

As Sam began her speech, Elizabeth worried she'd grown up too fast. Sam's father, Andrew, a bank manager and sometimes local politician in Crownsville, died when Sam was eleven, and the last five years had been particularly tough on the family—financially and emotionally.

Andrew Price was a World War II veteran with an impressive array of medals and citations as an army captain. He preached *hard work every day*, insisting Sam and her brother, Alex, finish their daily chores and homework before play, all too often curtailing time for any play. When he traveled, Elizabeth gave Sam and Alex a break from the pressure. But when Dad was home, which was more often than not, the family was run like a military platoon: discipline with constant pressure.

Unlike Sam, Alex didn't handle the pressure well. It was his father's dream Alex serve his country in the army and then pursue medicine or law, breaking out of the Price tradition of rising no further than middle management. While he also expected nothing short of excellence from Sam, he showed less interest on where the future might take her. For all Sam knew, her father would have been satisfied if she were a secretary like her mother. Perhaps that explained why Sam was an overachiever, promising herself that she would go further and do better than any Price had ever done. While she had no stomach for medicine and little fascination for law, she was determined to have better grades and go to better schools than Alex. He became competition, both for her and the attention of her father. When Andrew Price died, Sam took it hard, never quite forgiving him for not being there when the future held out the rewards of her hard work, like delivering the valedictorian speech.

After her husband's death, Elizabeth continued working as a secretary for Douglas Sanders, a prominent Crownsville attorney, but barely made enough to make ends meet in such an expensive suburb. Most of the pension went to daily expenses and tuition costs for Alex at the University of Wisconsin. Other expenses had taken a toll on the savings, and there wasn't enough left in the cookie jar for Sam's college costs.

But that didn't matter. Sam was already accepted at Radcliff and Smith, both with full academic scholarships. But an acceptance to Stanford meant the most to Sam. She had decided the smartest and most successful businesspeople went to Stanford, and she wanted to be the best too. Besides, *US News & World Report* said it was the best school for business and economics, Samantha's choices for the future. So at the tender age of sixteen, Sam had her future mapped out to a certainty. Her father would have wanted it that way. But on graduation night, she was still anxious to hear from Stanford about a possible scholarship. Doug Sanders, a Stanford graduate himself, wrote a fine letter of recommendation and said he made the necessary calls to the university, but there was still no word.

Sam's heart raced as she took the podium for her valedictorian speech. Never before had she spoken to such a large crowd, let alone a crowd of adults. Her oral reports in class and her debate club matches had not prepared her for this. Her throat began to close, and the audience seemed to fade away in a haze. She felt dizzy. She couldn't read her notes. From what seemed like a trance, she started to speak.

When finished, the applause and the sight of people standing jerked Sam from her dizzy state. She immediately saw her mother, casting a smile wider than Sam had ever seen. Sam stood there, soaking up the applause. Finally the principal gently touched her arm to let her know it was time to sit down. She loved every moment of it.

Later, the compliments flowed like a waterfall.

"Sam, you outdid yourself," said the principal.

"A beautiful speech," said one of the parents.

"Where did you find those inspiring words?" asked a teacher.

Dinner with everyone was quick, and Sam was home by eleven. In her room, alone, she recited the prayer her father had taught her—the same prayer she had recited since she first began the nightly routine at three years of age.

"Now I lay me down to sleep. I pray the Lord my soul to keep. God bless Mommy, Daddy, Alex, and all my friends. Amen." Her father never let her recite the second sentence of the prayer, "And if I die before I wake, I pray the Lord my soul to take." He always told Sam no one was going to die in the middle of the night, and they'd all have breakfast together in the morning.

Two days later, Sam got word from Stanford. She was awarded a full scholarship. All she had to do was help graduate assistants for four hours a week. Sam was on top of the world and knew nothing could hold her back now. She was going to Stanford. Her brother only made it to the University of Wisconsin. Without a scholarship. She loved her brother, but couldn't help feeling she'd beaten him and won the approval of her father.

Chapter Four

We can no longer cater to the rights of criminals while we ignore their victims. No criminal should profit from a crime, and no victim should be ignored or forgotten by the system. No criminal should bargain for a better deal because of a system burdened by lazy judges and sharp lawyers who don't care if their clients are a menace to society. We are not in the business of running hotels and halfway houses for criminals who only repeat their behavior once set free. Jail is an unpleasant place, and creating any other fantasy only serves the interests of criminals, not our society.

Speech before the Virginia Bar Association, Bowling Green, Virginia, October 15, 1998.

August 24, 2016
Georgetown, Washington, DC

Sam, just five weeks after her nomination in Memphis, could barely remember the last time she had been at her daughter's brownstone. Amanda had stopped celebrating Christian holidays when she married Nathan, and Sam wondered if Amanda might have converted to Judaism. Not that it mattered to Sam. She had no prejudice whatsoever for Jews, Catholics, or any religion. Growing up, Sam and her family attended church only on the appropriate holidays. Ben used to kid Sam they were *Cheesters*—Christians who limited their worship to Christmas and Easter. Organized religion was not a strong issue with Samantha Harrison.

As her secret service agents watched—or secret servants, as Sam liked to call them—she rang the doorbell. Nathan answered, stepping back to let Samantha in.

"Hello, Nathan. It's good to see you again. You look well." Her son-in-law never impressed Sam. While a fine young man in Sam's eyes, she viewed him as naive and ignorant of the real world's realities. He and Amanda were married after dating only six months, not much longer than Sam and Ben. But Sam thought it was too soon.

"Thank you, Governor. You look good, despite the pressure I'm sure you're under. Please, let's go to the living room. Amanda will be down in a moment. You know Amanda; she's never on time."

Nathan, you're such a condescending twit, thought Sam.

The brownstone was something out of *Architectural Digest*. Since Amanda was a graduate of the Rhode Island School of Design, the brownstone's interior appearance made sense. And while Nathan was successful in his own right, Amanda was trying to make her own mark as a designer. Amanda would have her own business by now if she'd only accepted Sam's help. Unlike her older brother, however, Amanda never accepted help—not even from her father, a man she virtually worshipped. Like mother, like daughter.

Nathan offered Sam a glass of wine, and she accepted. What she really wanted was a stiff Scotch. Since it wasn't offered, she didn't ask. The two went into the den in the front of the ground floor.

As they walked in, Sam asked, "Well, Nathan, do you agree with Collins that the bond market will soar and the stock market decline if I'm elected president?" Horace Collins was chairman of Merrill Lynch and touted as the next logical chairman of the Federal Reserve if the Democrats remained in control of the White House. The two sat down in the overstuffed Queen Anne chairs across from the sofa.

"To be honest, Governor, I don't particularly care about the stock market. I trade bonds. Anyway, the country's choice of president doesn't really affect the bond market. It will rise or fall with the general economy, and is affected more by the world markets than by anything a president can do. I think Collins is just being a loyal Democrat. After all, he's probably given them millions and wants to be chairman of the Fed so bad he'd sell his own soul for it. It's hard to find a bigger ass in finance than Collins."

"I see," said Sam, thinking how sad it was a man could become so convinced of his opinion at such a young age.

Sam had also heard about all she could take of media crap that the presidency had little effect on the financial markets.

Jesus, if the president of the United States can't affect markets, who controls America: the people or the boardrooms?

Sam took a sip of wine, a Merlot Sam found to be rather mediocre. "I'm not sure I agree with you, Nathan. I assure you, however, I don't agree with your chairman."

"Yeah, well, I guess I shouldn't expect you to."

Nathan, you can be such an idiot at times.

Amanda entered the room. "Hello, Mother," she said. Sam and Nathan stood.

To Sam, Amanda looked vibrant. She had the beauty of Sam's youth, and none of the negative effects that years of political wrangling and compromise now showed on Sam. Sam could not help wonder how she herself might look if she hadn't made the choices she'd made, choices she believed took a toll on her appearance. She couldn't help feeling jealous of Amanda and resentful toward those who pushed Sam so hard in politics. Sam wasn't sure when she became a handsome woman and was no longer described as beautiful. The debate on what politics physically does to those who hold high office is something many do not understand. Sam understood every time she saw Amanda.

Nathan poured Amanda a glass of wine and resumed his seat in the chair. Amanda sat on the sofa. The feeling in the air was very cold. The three sat uncomfortably.

Sam broke the silence. "Amanda, you look well. I really appreciate your seeing me tonight. I know it's not exactly what you might have chosen to do." Sam was stunned by the remorse she felt at having been so distant from her daughter for so many years. She began to feel ill, knowing her daughter would show no mercy.

Amanda drank the last of her wine and held her hand out with a gesture that said, Nathan, get me another glass. He obliged. Sam couldn't help wonder if her relationship with Nathan was a loving one. Amanda seemed to order Nathan around like a lapdog, something Sam knew she never did with Ben.

"Amanda, there are important issues at hand. I'd like to find a way to put on a public face of unity, otherwise all we do is give ammunition to Clinton, handing her a presidency she certainly doesn't deserve and the country cannot afford. So can we just suspend our personal differences and make some sort of announcement of reconciliation? You can say you now understand me, and I'll say I now understand you, although neither of us really does. I wish we did."

Amanda stiffened and drank the last of her wine, again gesturing to Nathan for more. "That's not realistic, Mother. The media will tear that apart and continue to push. I always hoped we might understand each other rather than bury the differences for another day. The hypocrisy of a feigned truce will come out and only make matters worse."

Nathan fetched Amanda more wine.

If only I could tell my daughter the truth. I need you to be on my side. But Sam had long ago abandoned honesty with Amanda.

The twit again broke the standoff and spoke up. "Really, Amanda, I think you're a little out of line here. I know it may sound condescending to you, but your mother is running for the presidency of the United States, for Christ's sake. I don't think you or I am in a position not to help."

Amanda snapped, "This is not your affair, Nathan. Please let me deal with my mother on my own terms." He genuinely looked shocked.

"Fine. I'll leave you two to one another. Governor, would you like another glass of wine before I go?"

"I'll have a scotch. Macallan, if you have it. On the rocks. Thank you."

Chapter Five

Equal rights for single parents. We cannot ignore or abandon programs like daycare. Unless we provide programs to ensure equal rights for single parents, we will all become the parents of those children as they grow up under a corrupt system of welfare checks, no supervision, and crime.

Speech in acceptance of nomination, Convention Center, Memphis, Tennessee, July 27, 2016.

June 25, 2015
Fredericksburg, Virginia

Sam, no longer governor, settled into Fredericksburg, taking over the office space she opened when first elected. Virginia had no interest in keeping it and was more than happy to have Sam assume the lease. To call it an office, however, was an understatement. Built as the governor's office away from Richmond, the suite of seven rooms was spacious, and Sam's office was particularly opulent.

Today's visitor was Amanda. Amanda was pregnant.

Samantha Harrison's position on abortion couldn't be clearer: she was a right-to-lifer. Sam made a point of it in her campaign for governor and refused to back down under pressure from moderates not wanting to lose votes. Samantha Harrison believed in never backing down or compromising her positions. Or at least that's what she told herself. There were plenty of pundits who would argue otherwise.

Amanda knew she was about to walk into a firestorm but was determined to keep to her own convictions as she walked into Sam's office.

Watts was shuffling through some papers on the desk when Amanda first entered. "Hello, Mr. Watts. How goes the campaign?"

Amanda never liked Zachary Watts. As far as she was concerned, he was always trying to convince her mother to concede to the demands of the Republican political machine, the group Amanda called the Imperial Party. A group of old bureaucrats trying to hold on to ideals long ago deserving burial. Increasingly, Amanda expressed her opinion that Sam made too many compromises under Watts's pressure—often without realizing she was even doing so. All under what Amanda thought was the spell of the aphrodisiac of political power. She no doubt thought it could blind anyone. But Sam disagreed and grew increasingly tired of the constant conflict.

Watts responded without looking up. "Amanda, today there is no campaign. Right now, your mother has enough on her hands. The rest of the country will have to wait."

Amanda found a seat in one of the leather chairs in front of the desk. "Come on, Mr. Watts. Your Imperial bosses want Mom, and your job is to deliver her. So how goes the campaign?"

Watts kept looking through papers wishing he could ignore Amanda.

"Even if there were a campaign, Amanda, your arrogance about it doesn't help. Despite what you may think, you are not the center of your mother's universe." While he knew he'd never be able to say it to Sam, as far as Watts was concerned, Amanda was a spoiled brat, ever too ready to attack her mother for unfounded reasons. Watts wondered how weak Sam's husband must be to allow such an attitude to develop. It couldn't have been Sam's fault. She was too strong.

"I'm here to see my mother. Sorry, but I don't have an appointment."

"Since when do you need an appointment?" Samantha asked as she entered the room. Amanda wondered how much of the conversation with Watts her mother had heard.

Amanda stood. "Hi, Mom. Sorry to barge in." The hug and kiss were ceremonial for Amanda. Sam wished they could be more.

The office was pure Samantha Harrison. Rich with mahogany and silk, it overwhelmed you with its majesty, a place where conviction and decisiveness clearly reigned. This was not a place where the timid lasted long, if at all.

Empty caffeine-free Diet Coke cans cluttered the desk. Samantha was on a constant diet in an attempt keep her figure. Without doubt she was still the most attractive politician in America and evoked comments not appreciated by her feminist supporters. While she enjoyed the attention, she certainly never admitted it publicly. But she kept on a diet nonetheless.

Amanda sat down again as Sam found her seat behind the desk. The distance between the two, in many ways, far greater than the few feet separating them. "Where's Nathan? Is he with you? Your father and I would love to have dinner with the two of you. Is he in town with you?"

"No, Nathan's not in town and this is not a social call. I spoke to Daddy yesterday in Washington, and he thought I should come to see you myself. He refused to be my messenger. Besides, in case you haven't checked your bed lately, Daddy's in DC for the weekend. I'm afraid you're having dinner alone tonight."

"I didn't say dinner tonight. I know fully well where you father is." That was a lie. Sam thought he was coming home that afternoon. She vowed to have a word with her appointment secretary. "I don't know how to make you feel welcome here anymore, Amanda. If there is something I did to make you angry, tell me, and we'll deal with it. The mystery tires me."

"I'm sorry if I seem to be coming on too strong. In a minute you'll understand."

Amanda's glare at Watts was a clear message to leave. He was more than happy to avoid witnessing yet another fight between Amanda and Sam and quickly obliged.

"What's wrong? Are you all right? Is it Nathan?"

"I'm fine. Nathan's fine. I'm pregnant."

Samantha rose to move toward Amanda, beginning to smile.

Amanda stayed in her seat. "Stop, Mother. I'm getting an abortion."

It was as though she had hit her mother with a sledgehammer. Sam stopped cold, the blood visibly draining from her face. She fell back into her chair with a thump.

Sam stared at Amanda for a moment, looking for words. She composed herself and stood, towering over Amanda from behind her desk as she began to walk around it toward Amanda.

"Amanda, for the past thirty years I have fought against abortion despite the pressure from my colleagues to abandon the unborn. I know you well enough. You think you're making the right decision. Despite that, I cannot condone it. It is wrong. Abortion is the taking of a life. You already made your choice, and now you're pregnant, carrying the life of another being. An innocent being with no one to defend him but his mother. Please don't abandon your child. There are alternatives to abortion."

"Christ, Mother! Don't you think you ought to ask me why before you condemn me to death row?"

Sam took the chair next to Amanda. "All right. Why? Is there something wrong with the baby?"

"No, Mother, I just don't want this baby. I'm not ready."

"Not ready? Grow up, Amanda. Is it fair to tear a living being from your womb before he breathes his first breath or sees his first light? Have you thought of asking him? Do you really think it's just a game that an operation will solve your problems? He has no voice, Amanda, except the voice you alone give him. Don't ask me to condone your selfish needs. You're wrong." Sam, now towering over Amanda, locked her stare on her daughter, who was now clearly uncomfortable.

Amanda returned the stare, staying in her chair. "Who made you the ultimate authority? All my life I've heard you preaching the rights and wrongs of society. What about my rights? Where were you when I needed a mother's help? I came here to tell you only because I didn't want you to find out from the press or some other pathetic snoop. I'm not here for your approval. I've given up on getting your approval for anything I do."

Neither shifted their gaze.

"My time has never been denied to you, Amanda. All it seems I've gotten lately in return is your anger. I don't deserve that."

"I guess you never deserve any back talk, do you, Mother. After all, you were the governor. Before that, super congresswoman, rooting out all the evils of big government. And of course, we can't forget prosecutor extraordinaire, keeping our streets clean by getting bad guys sent to the gas chamber." Sam rose and walked to the window overlooking the gardens, deciding not to correct

Amanda that Virginia lets death row inmates choose between lethal injection and the electric chair.

Amanda stood. She wasn't done. "You know what it is to grow up the daughter of a legend, famed for having bigger balls than any man she met? If I had your time, it wasn't real. You lecture, never teach or approve. Even when I did something right, there was more I should have done."

Both were now standing a mere three feet apart as if they'd paced the requisite distance for the duel to begin. "When did I do this to you?" Sam held her composure as best she could, wanting to slap her daughter for insolence. But she didn't need some media hack to find out she'd hit her daughter because she wanted an abortion. The pro-choice movement would have a field day.

"Please, Mother. You've never been there for me. Where were you when I found my first boyfriend? Where were you when I had my first period? You were in Washington, voting in Congress for some law no one remembers. Dad had to tell me how I wasn't going to die and that I'd be all right. He was there, you weren't. So don't stand there and tell me how you've been there for me. You haven't come close."

"I had responsibilities I had to honor, Amanda. There were many other times I was there for you." Samantha, shaken, walked back to her desk and sat down, shielded by its mahogany expanse, protected from her daughter's attack.

"Sorry. I must have missed it, Mother." Amanda stood and walked out of the room without another word. She had the abortion that night. The media found out the next day.

Chapter Six

Equal rights for the unborn. The right to choice is one of the most divisive debates in our history. There are no simple answers, and most of our personal views are the result of our own experiences and the teachings of our parents and religious leaders. I thought about abortion just before we had our second child, Amanda. I had a new job and was selfish, not wanting any interruptions in my career. I thank God I couldn't bring myself to make what everyone told me was my choice. Then I realized I had already made my choice. I chose, rightly or wrongly for myself, to get pregnant in the first place. I already exercised my choice. Women who are the victims of crime or incest didn't make a choice and have the right to choose abortion. Where the life of the mother is at stake, we must favor her and leave our prayers to care for the lost child. But I also believe it is not the place of government to dictate the choice of abortion for any woman. It is her decision alone to choose her personal needs over a greater responsibility. If she makes the wrong decision, it is God—not us—who should be the judge. Every day I look at my beautiful daughter or even think about her, it reinforces my conviction. Every day I thank God I made the right decision. I made the right choice. Abortion is wrong.

Campaign speech, August 10, 2016.

August 24, 2016
Georgetown, Washington, DC

With Nathan out of the room and a Macallan in her hand, the standoff with Amanda continued.

"Amanda, I want to bury the hatchet. We don't need to make any public statement other than our love for one another and our respect for each other's privacy. I'm not asking you to take responsibility or to compromise your ideals. Whatever you believe will not affect my chances in the election. You don't need to appear publicly with me. I just want to know we're a family. If for no other reason, we need to for the sake of your father. His life in the hospital doesn't need more newsmongers looking to make headlines on our personal lives."

Amanda poured herself more wine.

"Bringing Dad into the picture is a low blow, Mother. When did you start caring how he felt? He's been just another piece of baggage on your way to fame. A faithful and loyal supporter. Just as if you had a lapdog."

Nathan returned, "Governor, the secret service agents are asking for you. They say it's time for you to leave to make your next appointment."

Nathan retreated from the room. Samantha thought Amanda was behaving in the way Sam found so contemptible in her own mother. Maybe it was true children eventually became whatever their parents were. *What an awful idea,* thought Sam.

"Your father deserves better than what he reads in the headlines, Amanda. Clinton's henchmen are having a field day. Let's just put it to rest."

After yet another awkward silence, Amanda spoke. "Fine. Have your precious Zachary Watts prepare my statement. I'll issue it and behave accordingly. I won't embarrass you any longer."

"Thank you, Amanda. I'm truly sorry we can't do better. I've always loved you. I will never stop loving you. I can't tell you how I regret my lecturing you in Richmond last year. You are your own individual, and I accept that."

Amanda, as ever, refused to give. "Good-bye, Mother. I'm not in the mood for more lectures. I've got a long day tomorrow—and guess you do too, taking on the world's problems. You know the way out. I'm sure Nathan would be pleased to wait with you until you finish your drink." Amanda left the room. Sam downed the rest of her Scotch and hurriedly left, unwilling to listen to more of Nathan's crap.

Chapter Seven

Equal rights for children, our most precious asset. We must prepare them to compete in world markets. We must support education to the fullest, even at the expense of other, more politically favored programs. Our teachers must not deteriorate into second-rate educators. They must meet the highest standards to have the privilege of teaching in our schools. They need our moral and financial support. They need the support of responsible and caring parents who take an active interest in their children's education, not leaving the babysitting to our schools. If we do not invest more than rhetoric in our children's future, they will have no future. All the battleships, space stations, bureaucracies, and government programs in the world will never change that.

Speech in acceptance of nomination, Convention Center, Memphis, Tennessee, July 27, 2016.

July 28, 2016
Memphis, Tennessee

The press conference the morning following her nomination was not the disaster Watts feared. Sam handled the press like a well-coached pro. The supposedly ace reporters virtually never came up with tough questions. Under years of training by Watts, Sam had been manipulating politicians and the press for years. The search for truth ended when circulation managers became editors and heads of network news. The game had become too easy. Abortion, taxes, capital punishment, welfare, health care, social security, the deficit, military spending. It was always the same. It was all predictable.

Sam knew all the hyperbole meant nothing. Politics is a fluid process of constant change. What a politician believes can always change. More important is a politician's priorities, something a smart elected official never reveals. It is within those priorities where compromises—and trades—are made. It is how pork finds its way to bills where it has nothing to do with the underlying legislation. It is the reason the expression "politics makes for strange bedfellows" is so true.

Today Sam once again played the game she knew so well. She listened carefully to the questions, and then talked about whatever was important to her. Answering a question was entirely optional, no matter how many times it was asked. All she needed was patience and balance.

Ann Compton, now one of the older journalists in the business, asked the first question. "Governor, don't you think your strident stand on abortion will hurt your campaign? Won't it hurt the women's vote for your candidacy?"

Sam could not resist. "Ann, when are you going to stop asking your questions as though you already know the answer? I find it hard to believe you know what American women think. The important thing for voters—men and women—is to know I am not afraid to take stands I believe are right and openly speak my mind. I leave no doubt how I feel. That's something you're unlikely to see from my opponent, whichever candidate the Democrats nominate." *Good,* thought Sam. *I didn't answer the question.*

Next up was Jake Tapper of ABC News. "Governor Harrison, how do you propose to raise the money to fund all the programs you spoke about last night? They all sounded nice, but you said nothing about funding. You almost sounded like a Democrat."

Sam smiled and decided humor was her best defense. "Jake, what a terrible thing to say, let alone think. Those kinds of comments could cost you your credentials. I sound like a Democrat? I can assure you I'd no more sound like a

Democrat than I'd sound like the ass they use as their symbol." The reporters laughed. Even Tapper grinned.

Good. Get in the jokes. Disarm the reporters. Just what Watts taught me. They'll remember the Democrat and the ass long after they've forgotten any of my nonanswers.

Tapper kept pushing the issue. "Can we expect more taxes? And just how far are you willing to go on spending cuts?"

What claptrap. How do you think you fund programs, you ninny? You either cut spending, tax the people, or print more money. And since the president and Congress don't control the Federal Reserve, government can only cut or tax.

But Sam had not become the first Republican woman candidate for president of the United States by falling for loaded questions about taxes.

Fed up with Tapper and anxious to get to another reporter, Sam responded with a smile conveying feigned patience. "Jake, there are many ways to stimulate the economy and raise revenue for funding. Traditionally, my opponents look to tax increases. I don't see the growth of our nation so simply. Our economy is complex and requires complex programs to assure its continued prosperity. What's more important is we keep our domestic budget balanced and our trade balance in check. With the proper balance, including possible tax cuts, the fueling of our economy can create unprecedented opportunity. There's still incredible waste in government at every level. I balanced the budget in Virginia. I did so by taking measures to bring business back to Virginia with incentives and opportunities, not taxes. In Congress, I voted more against tax increases than I did for them. Just because I back aggressive programs does not mean we'll need to increase taxes. That may be the Democrats' simple solution, but not mine."

Another classic no answer. Sam was sure Watts would be pleased. She said nothing new and created no damaging sound bite. Sam knew some of what

Watts did was manipulative, but she didn't care. The presidency was in sight, and in the end it would be her presidency alone.

Before Tapper could follow up, Sam pointed to the Carl Cameron, the chief political correspondent from Fox.

"But are you ruling out a tax increase?"

Sam was taken aback by such an aggressive question from Cameron, but should have known leaving a tax increase floating in the wind would never satisfy Fox listeners. She stood mute for an uncomfortable three or four seconds, enough time for the cameras to catch what she feared might be seen as indecision. "Carl, we all pay taxes. No one wants to pay more. I don't want anyone to pay more. I don't want to pay more. Using the tax scare for your listeners and the American public serves no one's purpose. There are issues we need to address far more important than taxes, particularly when our economy has the potential of such great prosperity—more than we've seen in any generation. As the world continues to shrink and threats to our democracy increase, taxes should be the least of our worries."

Sam pointed to a new reporter, now tiring of questions and wondering if Watts had been right about her acceptance speech. But so far, Sam knew no damage was done.

And so went the rest of the press conference. No answers. No damage. Politics as usual.

For Sam, it was all becoming too simple. She couldn't help but think the American public was smarter than Watts and all her handlers wanted her to believe. Sure, they had one example after another of one-term presidents. Lyndon Johnson, Jimmy Carter, Gerald Ford, Bush 41. All of them thought the American public was smart enough to understand complex issues and compromise—only to be gone in four years. On the other hand, Richard

Nixon, Ronald Reagan, Bill Clinton, Bush 43, and Barack Obama, for good or for bad, hid the truth from the American public from the moment they took their oath of office—for two terms. So the lesson is unsettlingly clear. Unless you want to be a one-term president, honesty is not the best policy. And Sam did not want to go down as the first woman president of the United States who couldn't get reelected.

Chapter Eight

Much has been written on gays and women in the military. Field officers, responsible for soldiers fighting on the front lines, seem overwhelmingly against sharing combat duty. Conventional wisdom says we should listen to the experts—the ones who have to live with our policy—and ban gays and women from the battlefield. I could not more strongly disagree. While the safety of our soldiers is and will always be of primary importance, equal rights have always been a stalwart principle in our republic. We cannot ignore those rights on anecdotal opinion. Until I am shown written and supportable proof that our soldiers are in greater danger because of the presence of gays or women in combat situations, I will not support legislation that discriminates against any class of America's citizens.

Statement before Armed Forces Subcommittee Hearings on Gays and Women in Military Combat, March 15, 2004.

August 5, 2016
St. Eustatius

A little more than three weeks after her victory in Memphis, Sam left the spotlight while the Democrats had their convention in Los Angeles, respecting the unwritten rule that the opposing party lies low during the opponent's convention. Sam sought her own solace on St. Eustatius, a small Caribbean island that had been her and Ben's favorite escape. She'd had enough of the barrage of the evening news reporting how well the Democrat convention was going and how the paparazzi were such dupes for all the movie stars and glitterati on the convention floor. Besides, Watts and his cronies were in full campaign-planning mode, and the best thing Sam could do was get out of their way and hide for a few days.

The Gin House had only a small handful of rooms. Owned by two former ad executives from New York, it offered the kind of privacy Sam and Ben cherished. While they brought the kids to other Caribbean locations from time to time, they never brought them here. This was their private sanctuary, where visits offered them time to stay acquainted outside the din of parenthood and politics. The occasional respites were always welcomed.

Sam and Ben walked together every evening at dusk along the roads and paths of the island, passing the occasional cotton tree and cemetery, taking in the turquoise Caribbean views along the way. They'd eventually find their way to a beach with its sand long-ago colored gray by volcanic ash. In all, they made nine trips to the island and became regulars. But this was the first time Sam had been there without Ben, and she missed him. He urged her to go to get some rest before hitting the campaign trail in full stride. He said he'd dream of her and the sandy beach while nurses poked him in the middle of the night. Ben was right; she needed time alone.

"Sam," Ben used to say as they sat at dusk on the beach each night, "how many sunsets do you think the average person watches in their lifetime? I bet it's not much more than a dozen. I intend to reach the *Guinness Book of World Records* for watched sunsets. And I won't mind sharing the record with you since you'll be there for each one." She went one sunset ahead that evening.

Solitude often breeds reminiscing, and Sam was no different than anyone else. As she sat watching the sunset, she thought about her journey to the nomination since taking a job as an associate at Wilson, Smith & Watts rather than clerking in the United States District Court for the Eastern District of Virginia.

Ted Wilson and John Smith, both Mayflower descendants and staunch Republicans, ran Wilson, Smith & Watts. Zachary Watts, while a name partner, was really just a lawyer who wanted to practice law. Caught in the maelstrom of a leading political law firm, Watts soon abandoned that ambition and joined the field of political strategists masquerading as lawyers. Over time he learned to love the manipulation that made him the consummate political manager. No one was ever sure if he was his own man or just a puppet for Wilson and Smith. To Sam, however, it made no difference. Watts was her handler.

She did well at Wilson, Smith & Watts and was liked immediately by most of the clients. There was the occasional need to politely decline the advances of the more amorous clients, but she took it all in stride. Clients seemed to think they had some sort of privilege with their lawyers they would never dream of taking with their employees or contemporaries. Sam always marveled at how sexual harassment of your attorney seemed to be a right for so many men. Testosterone seemed to bloom more than flowers every spring. Maybe it was one of the last places men could display their bravado without risking their careers. Or maybe they were just stupid. It really wasn't a big deal to her since she knew she could depend on Watts to quietly counsel any clients who went too far. He often did. In truth, he did it more than Sam knew. On December 18, 1992, however, even Watts couldn't help her.

It was a particularly good year for Wilson, Smith & Watts. Watts became managing partner at a time when the firm had more business than ever and a firm high of 132 lawyers—midsized by Virginia standards, but nonetheless more profitable than firms many times its size. All this happening when the country was in the midst of a recession and other law firms were cutting back or closing. Either Watts was a brilliant manager, or he was a lucky man. Either way, Ted Wilson and John Smith were content to let him run the show.

That year's Christmas party was in Washington, DC at the Washington Club off Dupont Circle. It was open only to firm attorneys and staff, totaling over two hundred people. Usually a stiff affair, the 1992 fete had a feeling of relaxation, probably because Watts handed out generous bonuses to everyone earlier in the day. Sam received the equivalent of 25 percent of her salary.

It must have been a good year indeed, she thought.

The Washington Club was the district's premiere location for any party that meant anything. The private club was founded in 1891 and hosted the most powerful parties in the city. Tonight was no exception. Wilson, Smith & Watts partners were among the power elite. Like all true power brokers, however, they kept their public image quiet and reserved, leaving the hot discos and more public lobbying efforts to the naive.

"So, Sam, what do you think of this private practice of law?" It was Ted Wilson asking one of his mundane questions. He was an adequate lawyer, but everyone at Wilson, Smith & Watts was more than just adequate. Watts saw to that. Wilson was a short man, perhaps five foot six, with thinning gray hair. His protruding belly and usually slovenly appearance belied the power he held. Known to drink too much, Sam could never figure out why Wilson had such a powerful political base. She suspected it must be his money, because it certainly was not his intellect. Nor was he a smooth politician or diplomat like John Smith or Zachary Watts.

"Well, after receiving my bonus this afternoon, I can certainly say it's a profitable business. Congratulations on a good year, Mr. Wilson, and thank you for your generosity." Sam desperately hoped someone would rescue her before the ordeal became unbearable.

Where is Watts?

Wilson, swaying, spilled Scotch from his glass. "We've never talked about your political views, Mrs. Harrison. Do you consider yourself a Democrat or Republican?" It was obvious Wilson had too much to drink as he slurred half his words. But everyone knew he always had too much to drink.

Sam certainly didn't think of herself as a Democrat, although she admired many of the things the Democrat Party stood for and still believed John F. Kennedy was an inspiration. She wished she had seen him at an age when she might have appreciated his genius. And she had problems declaring any allegiance with a party that had the likes of Richard Nixon among its members. This was not, however, the time for honesty or an indecisive answer. Indecision would only make Wilson probe more.

"For the most part, I guess I'm a Republican." Sam waited for Wilson's reply as he stood in front of her, contemplating like most drunks do when they aren't listening and need time to absorb what little they heard.

Wilson's glazed eyes looked at Sam. "For the most part, you guess? Come on now. You can't guess. That might be the diplomatic response for the outside world, but not me. It would be better to say you're an independent than guess you're a Republican. And if you're an independent, fine. Provided, of course, you're conservative and vote Republican!" Now drooling, he roared in laughter at what he thought was a very funny comment. With his outburst, a crowd began to gather, sensing yet another memorable show from Wilson.

Sam didn't recall that being an independent was an alternative offered by the question. Now it was probably too late to take that route.

Sam hoped to calm the moment as she saw Wilson's face growing red. "While I've always voted Republican, sir, I try to keep an open mind." A few in the crowd snickered, which only caused Wilson to press on. Sam knew she was digging a hole for herself.

Where is Watts?

"An open mind is not what this country needs right now!" Wilson was beginning to get even louder, and worse, belligerent.

Jesus. Since when is an open mind something this country doesn't need?

Sam was not about to stand down to someone like Wilson. Other young associates in the crowd were mumbling for her not to take any grief from him, urging her on in hopes of some real fireworks. As she would soon learn, such youthful exuberance came with a price.

Sam stiffened and resolved to stand her ground. "With all due respect, Mr. Wilson, I think open minds are exactly what we need. It was a closed mind that brought us Watergate and the Vietnam War. Only an open mind can question authority and ensure a well-debated decision. Isn't that what democracy and the Constitution are all about?"

Wilson seemed caught off guard by such an imprudent comment. He continued to sway as he considered his response, looking as if he'd drop his glass at any moment. "Young lady, you've got a lot to learn. If it weren't for your good looks, someone would have taught it to you by now. This is not a game we're playing. You have to take positions. And listening to you, I imagine yours are mostly horizontal."

The slap across Wilson's face was automatic. It was the first time Sam had ever struck someone. Wilson's drink went flying, wetting a good half of the crowd that had gathered and now scrambled for distance. The glass shattered on the floor. The entire room fell silent. Watts was there before another word was spoken.

Where have you been, goddamn it?

Red faced, Wilson bellowed: "You little tart, you're through! Don't even think of coming in tomorrow except to clean out your desk. Handle it, Watts." Wilson glared, waiting for Watts's dutiful response in support. Watts simply took Sam by the arm and led her away.

Watts was uncharacteristically upset, grabbing Sam's arm until it hurt. "Whatever possessed you to do that? What could he have possibly done?"

"Let go of me." Sam yanked her arm away. "Wilson deserved it, and it's probably long overdue. No wonder you keep me and every other female associate away from him. And maybe that explains why there aren't any female partners too. He's a fucking pig."

Now in the corner of the room, no one dared to come near them. Watts calmed down as he spoke to Sam. "You don't get it, Sam. He meant what he said. Yes, he's a fucking pig, but he's always been one. Despite that, he somehow brings in millions. He will never change. He's going nowhere."

Sam was naively shocked. "How can that be, Zach? How can a firm like Wilson, Smith & Watts tolerate him? The firm has your name in it too, Zach. Doesn't keeping assholes like him make you just as bad?" Sam regretted the last statement.

Watts put her questions aside. "I'll do what I can to help you, but Wilson is in more control than you know. He holds a lot of keys to closets better left closed. Without his support I can't manage the firm. Maybe that makes me a hypocrite in your eyes, but I'm responsible for a lot of peoples' livelihoods. Clients come to me because they think I've got the same connections he does. The truth is I don't. But Wilson lets them all believe I do. So he avoids dealing with anyone he'd prefer to ignore. As hard as it is to believe, he calls a lot of the shots. The only reason he leaves me alone is I keep making him money. If I ever stumble, he'll kick my ass out too. And probably with full support from Smith."

Sam couldn't believe what she was hearing. A name partner in a prestigious law firm had just harassed her publicly and received the slap he deserved. For that she was about to lose her job. And her mentor, Zachary Watts, was a part of it all. As she escaped into the ladies' room, she felt helpless. She began crying and threw up in the sink. The only solace she received came from the bathroom attendant. Even the other woman lawyers kept their distance. Sam freshened up as best she could, said good-bye to Watts, and took a taxi home.

She said nothing to Ben. At that point, she didn't want to hear a single piece of advice from any man, even though she was confident Ben would support her. But there was nothing he could do at this point, so burdening him with the problem before she had a planned solution wasn't worth it. Sam always had a plan before she sought anyone else's advice.

Cleaning out her desk the next day, her anger grew. For years she'd been told she was a rising star. She was assured she'd make partner one day. Just stay the course. Keep up the good work. Keep working ridiculous hours. Keep sacrificing your family life. Keep screwing up your marriage. After years of loyalty to the firm, she was dismissed because a partner had sexually harassed her. And he was still in control. Nothing in the system was supporting her.

As she boxed the few things she had in the office, John Smith called and asked her if he could have a moment of her time in his office. Sam was tempted to tell him where to go, but she took the walk anyway, asking her now ex-secretary to put her box of belongings in the lobby so she didn't have to come back to her office again. It struck Sam that her secretary, who she assumed had some loyalty to her, was entirely void of any passion in following Sam's order. How could Sam not have seen this chauvinistic atmosphere in the years she'd been at the firm? Was there anything these men didn't control?

Smith's office had the trappings of his elite status as one of Washington's most powerful lawyers. His corner office had a breathtaking view of the Potomac River and was adjoined by its own conference room and private bathroom. The bar was always fully stocked and on display, replete with the customary fine crystal glassware and decanters. The antique furniture and paintings were priceless. It was a place where political careers were not only planned, but also made and broken. It was the first time she'd officially been in his office, although all the young attorneys snuck into his office out of curiosity late at night when Smith had left for the evening, occasionally stealing a shot or two of his fine brandy. It was all part of the game.

Watts was with Smith, sitting on one of the ornate chairs in front of Smith's mahogany desk. Smith sat behind his desk in a leather chair given to him by Dwight Eisenhower, a fact he was known to tell just about anyone who visited his office. Smith motioned Sam to sit in the chair next to Watts. Obliging, she already felt intimidated, looking at Smith across the wide divide of his desk and seeing Watts relegated to no better a seat than hers.

Smith began. "Samantha, what happened last night is regrettable. But there's nothing we can do about it. Unfortunately, we cannot allow you to stay, even though I'm told Teddy may have been out of order. The firm needs to continue on an even course, and Teddy is an important part of it all. I am truly sorry."

She glared at Smith. "Mr. Smith, you can't really expect me to accept that. Regrettable? May have been out of line? What do you want me to say? 'Don't worry, Mr. Smith. I understand. Anything for the firm'? I'm out of a job, pissed, and in no mood for soothing words from you or anyone else at this firm. I think it's best I just leave and do whatever's right for me." Her glare moved to Watts as she stood to leave.

Watts gently put his hand on her arm.

"Just hear us out. We're not finished yet." Sam sat down, once again taking an order. She mentally noted what appeared to be an inability to simply leave on her own terms.

Smith leaned back and looked out on the Potomac, as if he was about to deliver a sermon from the mount. "You are among the most talented associates we have. While you may not be aware of it, I have followed your progress closely. You have conviction and drive. Your future is bright. This episode will not hurt it."

Fuck you. Look at me when you're talking to me, asshole.

Watts picked up on the tension mounting in Sam. Sam refused to even look at him. "Sam, Mr. Smith has arranged for you to be appointed as a commonwealth attorney, working directly for the Bowling Green County prosecutor. A top slot. It's a great opportunity, but not a cakewalk." Watts actually sounded sincere.

Sam turned her head, now with a look of disdain. "Fuck you, Zachary." Sam couldn't believe how crude she was. "A criminal lawyer? Where do either of you get off thinking I want to be a prosecutor, much less get me the job before I even decide what I want to do? I'm an economist and a corporate lawyer. I'm not interested in trying jaywalking cases. What is this anyway, an offer to buy my silence so I won't embarrass the firm? Don't worry. I'm not stupid. I know if I take on the venerable Wilson, Smith & Watts my career is over. It's the nature of the beast. You win. I move on."

Smith swung his chair around and faced directly at Sam. His reaction was formal and now devoid of any paternalism. "Miss Harrison, don't you think we know that? You pose no threat to this firm whatsoever. You are a minor player in a game you won't understand for years. Maybe never. But you have talent, as raw and undisciplined as it is. You can decide to waste it at some other white-shoe firm, or maybe on your own, fighting for great causes and forever seeking revenge against the likes of Ted Wilson. You may even win a few cases and become rich while chasing your windmills, but adding nothing to the greater scheme of things. So if you want to just walk out, fine. Or you can take a real opportunity being offered to you. Get experience. If it's not what you want, then leave. But I hope you're not so foolish."

His stare was as penetrating as any Sam had ever seen. Sam felt glued to her chair even though she wanted to leave. Even though she felt manipulated. Smith had been well served by his six terms in the House, a close Senate defeat in Virginia, and an ambassadorship to Japan.

Sam regretted her imprudent speech and tried to regain her composure. "I'm not about to challenge anything you're saying, Mr. Smith. Far too much has happened to me in the last two days. I'm still trying to absorb it all. I'll take my time to think through all of it. And while I sincerely don't think I owe you or this firm the courtesy, I'll consider seeing the prosecutor. But if I do, I intend to make it clear to him I want no favors. Wherever I get my next job, I'll earn it on my own, not because John Smith was my benefactor. With all due respect, sir, I will not be indebted to you."

Smith smiled. "You're not indebted to anyone. At least not today. But know this, someday you will find yourself indebted to someone. We all do. It goes with success."

Watts stood, obviously the sign it was time for Sam to leave. He showed Sam to the door. After Sam left, Watts returned to the chair.

"She's quite a young lady. She'll do well," Smith quipped.

"Thank you. She is a real talent, and I hate losing her over one of Teddy's damn outbursts. But a commonwealth attorney? That may be a bit of a stretch."

Smith treated Watts no differently than he did Sam. He didn't have conversations with people. He lectured them. "I've called a lot of these things, and I feel right about this. Placing her in that job will fetch a nice political profit for us in Bowling Green County. And don't worry; she's tough. Between you and me, I'll put a wager on it that she'll be one of the top prosecutors within three years. And even better, whether she knows it or not, if she takes the job, she just may become a red-blooded Republican."

John Smith never did favors for anyone unless there was something in it for him.

Chapter Nine

Equal rights for those injured by shoddy products. We cannot allow cheap foreign products to poison our children and endanger our welfare, nor can we let our own manufacturers lower their standards of excellence to meet foreign competition. We've got to stop second-class products from ever entering our commerce. We've got to charge not only the companies that expose us to those risks but their executives as well. But we cannot at the same time allow fat-cat trial lawyers to prey on these companies with massive class actions that have no foundation and are nothing more than blackmail. We need a balance.

Speech in acceptance of nomination, Convention Center, Memphis, Tennessee, July 27, 2016.

August 6, 2016
St. Eustatius

The knock on the door snapped her out of her sleep, and the scents of the Caribbean once again filled the air, making a harsh awakening a little easier to bear.

It was Richard, the hotel's messenger. There were no telephones in the rooms. Sam liked it that way and refused their offer to install one for this visit. Her demands for privacy drove her new secret service agents up the wall.

For Sam there was something perverse about it.

It's funny, here they are in my little piece in the world, and the tight-suited secret servants can't relax. What was so secret about them anyway? You could spot them a mile away; Brooks Brothers clowns sent to paradise to protect a presidential wannabe.

"Sorry to bother you, Governor, but there is a fax at the front desk."

How nice, Sam thought. By not bringing it with him, she could have politely avoided seeing it until she was ready. Fearing it might be news about Ben, she put on her robe and hurriedly followed Richard along the balcony overlooking the turquoise sea. It was shortly after sunrise, and she took note of the beauty and tranquility she feared would soon be left behind.

The not-so-secret servants were waiting in the lobby, if you could call it one. It was an open area adjoining a wide veranda of multicolored tiles surrounded by palm trees gently swaying in the soft breeze. A few guests sat at one of the tables eating breakfast, and while they recognized Sam, proper decorum dictated they not interrupt her privacy and only whisper of her presence. Sam wondered whether the secret servants would break their arms if they did acknowledge her. Not good publicity for the morning. Besides, the hotel made sure all of its guests understood her privacy was paramount on this visit.

As Sam passed her federal protectors, they all nodded and said, "Governor." Sam wondered if they knew how to say anything else. Maybe they should call her Madam Candidate. She never did understand why politicians were always addressed by whatever last office they held. Sam like to joke how glad she was her last office wasn't Virginia's dogcatcher. Would she have to correct them when she became president? Probably not.

The fax was from Watts. He was arriving on the next afternoon's flight. Sam knew he wouldn't stay away long; her campaign meant too much to him and his future. He had so much to do and only twelve weeks to do it in. Tomorrow it was time to get back in the fight. Sam was grateful she at least had a few days away from the political furnace, but deeply regretted the one place she and Ben had was now going to be invaded by Watts. It was bad enough secret servants had now become a part of the memories.

That night Sam ate alone in the small gourmet restaurant across the street from the hotel, under the distant and watchful eyes of the secret servants. The meal was divine but lonely. She indulged herself first with a Chopin vodka martini, neat, and the better part of a bottle of Napa Valley Silver Oak, one of Ben's favorite wines the restaurant stocked at his request. Unfortunately, neither the wine nor the ever-attentive waiters could fill Sam's empty feelings without Ben.

After dinner, as the sun was setting, Sam went for a walk, hearing the quiet footsteps of her keepers following from a safe distance behind.

Is this what it means to be president? Never left alone? No privacy?

Her mind wandered between thoughts about the daunting challenges ahead, Ben, her children, and her future. She could have walked all night, but as the light faded, one of her assigned detail suggested it might be best to get back to the hotel.

Sam slept well, as she usually did, even in the most pressured moments. For some reason, whenever she went to bed, her tensions faded and sleep came quickly—always preceded by the silent rendition of the prayer her father taught her.

Chapter Ten

Equal rights for the homeless and the disenfranchised city dwellers who have given up or can no longer care for themselves. If we continue to turn our eyes away from their homes on the street and in the gutters, we only add to the crime in the streets, our image of a callous society, and the deserved damnation of a civilized world.

Speech in acceptance of nomination, Convention Center, Memphis, Tennessee, July 27, 2016.

February 3, 1993
Bowling Green, Virginia

When Sam started her career in the commonwealth attorney's office in Bowling Green, it was not exactly love at first sight. Robert Morgan, Bowling Green County's aging but colorful commonwealth attorney, was as tough on staff as he was on criminals, whether accused or convicted. Sam's first meeting with him was typical Morgan.

"Well, Mrs. Harrison, I can't say I'm thrilled about the pressure to hire you, but I need another body, and I've heard you've done well in the interviews with my assistants. You should know there are some lawyers who would give their eyeteeth for this job. Lawyers who really give a damn about criminal law and prosecution. Do you?"

Morgan truly cared about criminal law. A no-nonsense lawyer, his conviction rate was the envy of every prosecutor and politician in Virginia. Many wondered why he never sought higher office. While a few people knew he eventually hoped for a judicial appointment to the federal bench, most thought he'd end up in politics.

The Bowling Green office was relatively small, with only a half dozen assistant prosecutors. While they all had different responsibilities, everyone reported to Morgan.

Sam was still stinging from her experience with Ted Wilson and the empty retribution he received. "I'm sorry if I seem less than committed, but I want to be honest. John Smith got me here. I know that. But everywhere else I turn is a dead end, and I can't just start off on my own."

Sam had tried for over a month to find a new position, telling Ben she'd had enough with a big-firm world and wanted to look at other options. While she could tell Ben didn't believe she was telling him the whole truth, she knew he'd simply let it go, thinking she probably messed up a case or pissed off a big client. Sam decided it was better Ben not know what happened. Why, she didn't know. She just didn't want to confide the Wilson incident with Ben despite knowing he'd understand, as he always did.

Sam, now resigned to the reality the job as a commonwealth attorney was the only real option she had left, decided to respond honestly. "I'm sure this is as uncomfortable for you as it is for me. I do not want Mr. Smith to be the reason I work here or make any advancement. I want to do it on my own. I can promise you I'll work harder than any assistant in this office. I won't be afraid to ask for help and will give it whenever I can." In truth Sam was having a little difficulty even believing herself. She couldn't help wonder if Smith had worked behind the scenes derailing every other job prospect to make sure she worked where he wanted her to.

Morgan stood and looked out his office window.

Sam couldn't help asking herself, *what was it with these people, they always look out windows whenever they think they're about to say something profound.*

"Mrs. Harrison, I don't care if you're here because of Smith or not. Sure the bastard's got a lot of power. But he doesn't run my office, and I can assure you this is the last time you will be able to count on him. He's given you a chance to work in the best damn prosecutor's office in the country, and if you so much as screw up once, I'll kick your ass back to the streets. If you want to, you now work for me. No one else. Now why don't you see my secretary, Ethel, for the details."

Sam could feel a knot growing in her belly. *Not again,* she thought.

Morgan sensed her discomfort, showing real regret for his words. He sat down again at his desk, putting both hands on it as he faced Sam. "Look, I'm fully aware of what happened and why you left Smith's firm. But I'm not another Teddy Wilson. Hell, he's a good old Southern boy who never got himself out of the back woods. Some say that about me too. I'm gruff at times and miss the nuances of political correctness. So forgive me. I apologize if I offended you but warn you if you work for me, I'll offend you again. It seems I offend everyone sooner or later. Just get out of my office and see Ethel. That assumes, of course, you want the job and can get started on Monday."

Sam had no idea how to respond to such offensive comments. She needed a job. The period of silence seemed forever before Morgan spoke again.

He softened. "May I call you Samantha?" She nodded. "Samantha, I have enough young assistants who stare at me, and I'm not surprised to receive the same from you. If I offend you with my words, I again apologize. If you want to work for me, get used to it. Or sue me. But for now, as I already said, why don't you go see Ethel. You can let her know in the morning if you want the job. Personally, I hope you take it. And if you decide to do so, I strongly suggest you find a way to express yourself with something other than a blank stare."

He stood and walked toward the door. Ethel was waiting on the other side as if she'd gotten some kind of cue once Morgan started for the door. Rather than waiting for Sam to come to her, Ethel walked in and gently took Sam by the arm, frowned at Morgan, and escorted Sam out. The door closed quietly behind them.

"Relax, Samantha. Your blood will start flowing again at any moment. Just count yourself lucky you're not a criminal—I mean alleged criminal. Mr. Morgan sees no difference. But for some reason, I scare him. And God only knows it looks like he's staying forever. So I guess we're a pair. Let me show you your office, if one can call a cubicle an office."

"I don't think I want this job. And please call me Sam." Sam was still confused by exactly what had happened

"Yes, you do," responded Ethel. Sam knew Ethel was right.

On the ride back to Arlington, Sam's head was filled with planning. She knew she'd take the job. Upon reflection and reassuring words from Ethel, something told her it was the right thing to do. But it meant moving, and Ben's commute from Bowling Green to the district was too far. That's when she saw the exit reading Historic Fredericksburg, knowing it was less than an hour from the district on a good day. And since Ben's hours were flexible, he could choose when he left for GW so he could avoid the traffic. Sam took exit 126 and spent the afternoon with a real estate agent. The agent found Sam the perfect place, much larger than the house in Arlington and surrounded by beautiful countryside with good schools for Amanda. Four bedrooms, three baths on over two acres. And one of the bedrooms could be converted to an office for Ben. She knew Ben would love it, and he did. They closed on February 27 and moved in on March 8. The house in Arlington sold for $710,000 two weeks later. And since Ben paid cash for the house in Fredericksburg, a mortgage application didn't slow anything down.

Morgan was true to his word. After a few weeks of orientation, Sam started at the bottom in arraignments. Each day Sam spent hours in court while a parade of criminals pled not guilty, got their bail, or went back to the Bowling

Green Peumansend Creek Regional Jail or the Caroline Correctional Unit 2. The occasional woman went to the Central Virginia Correctional Unit for Women. Sam thought the whole process was silly.

What am I doing here anyway?

She barely had to speak except in rare instances where a senior prosecutor marked a file with a "no bail" notation. On those occasions, Sam got the opportunity to tell the court how awful the defendant was or that the alleged criminal was sure to run and hide, even though the defendants were people she had never seen before and would never see again, nor knew how letting someone free on bail might put Virginia's citizens at great peril. If the defendant was white, bail was set and he was released. But if he was black or Hispanic, even if bail was set, the defendant rarely had the money to post it. They went back to a cell. Unless the charge was for a capital crime with a potential life sentence, women always got bail. All too often, they were the only ones at home to care for their children. The fathers had long since vanished. And if the Caroline Department of Social Services wanted to move the children, that took time, and judges thought it better to leave the status quo alone while the system worked through the process.

Chapter Eleven

Dear Mom, I'm not sure I like being a prosecutor. The work is challenging, but I have to look at the worst side of life every day. I think I'm losing my compassion for those accused of crimes, even those who might be innocent. I see so much trash in court, I'm beginning to wonder if I can tell good from evil. Looking forward to Christmas. Love, Samantha.

Letter to her mother, October 12, 1999.

April 14, 1993
Bowling Green, Virginia

Sam had been working at arraignments for nearly three months. She wondered if Morgan wanted her to give up and leave or whether he even knew who she was anymore. While it was all boring Sam, she would be damned if she let Morgan win. As Sam sat bobbing up and down with each arraignment, she thought of the advice Ben gave her a few nights before as they lay in bed.

"Either drop this job, Sam, or get into it. I'm no lawyer, but I just don't see why arraignments are as unimportant as you make them sound. Besides, you're the new kid on the block at the bottom of the heap, so live with it or get out. To be honest, since you started on arraignments, you've not exactly been fun to be around."

Ouch, it's not like Ben to speak to me that way.

"I'm sorry. You're right. I think my problem is I don't know why I'm doing this. I'm thinking of quitting. Maybe I'll do that tomorrow. Why do I want to be a criminal lawyer anyway?"

Ben seized on the moment to urge a change. "That's a question I've been asking myself. Not that you couldn't be a good criminal lawyer, but your heart sure doesn't seem to be in it, and sooner or later, you're going to screw up. So you're just wasting your talents. Until you took this job after leaving Watts's firm, I thought you were on track. Now I don't know where you're going. But at this point, I don't much care about the reasons." Ben took Sam's hand, gently squeezing it. "I'd just like to have you back."

She smiled and gently squeezed Ben's hand. She both loved and hated these moments with Ben. She loved them for the affection and support he showed even when being critical. She hated the moments because she never knew what to say. She just wasn't as romantic as Ben and never really stopped being his student.

The next night Ben took a taxi and met Sam in Bowling Green for dinner at a favorite restaurant. He'd worked that day out of the house, so the trip was an easy one. As the two went to get Sam's car after dinner, they saw flashing lights.

Usual police activity, Sam thought.

They stayed on the opposite sidewalk as they walked north toward the lights.

As they got closer, the scene took form. A car had smashed into the light pole. An expensive Mercedes. A man (Sam guessed the driver) was in the backseat of a police cruiser. An attractive woman was talking to the police. *Maybe the wife*, thought Sam. As they got closer, Sam saw two yellow outlines of bodies on the street. The bodies were gone. One large. One small. Whoever they were, an ambulance or coroner had taken them away, reducing them to yellow tape, the police department's own form of street graffiti. Sam and Ben continued past the scene.

Ben's only comment was, "I guess you'll see the guy in the cruiser in court in arraignments tomorrow."

"I imagine so," replied Sam.

The next day's arraignments started off as routine as ever.

"All rise. This court is now in session. The Honorable Martha Dickerson, presiding."

The morning droned on, Sam doing her usual bobbing up and down with each plea and being bored stiff. Martha Dickerson, a magistrate judge with hopes of rising to a full trial judge, was a no-nonsense jurist. If you appeared before her, you better be prepared.

Earlier that morning, Sam asked Ethel for an appointment with Morgan and was assigned three o'clock. She'd resolved to quit. One more morning of arraignments, and she was out of there. "Back on the streets," as Morgan would put it.

As the guards brought in the last defendant, Sam noted the file had no warnings against bail and no special note from Morgan or any of his assistants.

Another routine arraignment, she said to herself.

All she had to do was stand up and sit down a few more times. At that point, where she and Ben were going for dinner to celebrate her freedom was more important than the latest defendant the Commonwealth of Virginia wanted incarcerated.

"State versus Jonathan Scott. Charge: vehicular homicide." The charge was a routine criminal offense when someone died in an auto accident. There would most likely be a not guilty plea and a later deal to a lesser charge, particularly since the accused was white.

Scott's lawyer spoke before the judge even said a word. "Your Honor, my name is William Silverman, and I am representing Mr. Scott. He pleads not guilty."

Dickerson stared down at Silverman. "Mr. Silverman, I know who you are. I'm sure everyone in this courtroom does. It speaks well of Mr. Scott that he can afford you. But I do not recall asking you how your client chose to plea or asking you to say anything at all. You would be well advised to let me run my courtroom."

Silverman smiled as sat down. "Sorry, Your Honor."

Reputed to be one of the best criminal defense lawyers in Virginia, Silverman tired quickly of the arraignment routine and tried to move it along to ease the pain. He yearned for the battle of a trial or negotiating a deal for leniency. Sam knew his reputation and had heard many prosecutors talk about defeats across from him. This was the first time she'd met him.

Sam was struck by how handsome he was. Impeccably dressed with a youthful, innocent appearance belying his twenty-five years defending criminals. The few gray streaks in his hair only made him more handsome. She immediately understood his allure with jurors.

Too bad I'll never see you in court.

Given his reputation, Sam thought it was odd he was even at an arraignment and hadn't sent one of his lackeys. Whoever Scott was, he must be important. There was never any glory at arraignments, and William Silverman always went for the glory.

The judge went on. "Since you have given us a preview of your client's plea, Mr. Silverman, we will dispense with the need of you repeating yourself. It is also clear to me that there is adequate probable cause of your client's guilt to continue this matter. So for now, I'll hear from the people on the issue of bail."

"Your Honor," Silverman, now standing again, started before Sam could even begin. "My client is president of Ekels Industries and has been a pillar in his community. He serves on the board of the American Red Cross and is known nationwide for his philanthropy. Certainly there is nothing in this case warranting more than a release on his personal recognizance. I can assure this court he has no intention of fleeing the jurisdiction."

Sam wasn't listening, observing the nice job Silverman did cleaning up Scott for his day in court. He had no resemblance to the drunken bum in his mug shot. Clean shaven and adorned in a blue Armani suit, crisp white shirt and Hermes tie, Scott looked like the quintessential American tycoon and community icon. Sam wondered how Scott pulled it off in a holding cell. Scott sat stoic with an almost regal look on his face.

You coach your clients well, thought Sam.

Silverman continued the verbal defense of his upstanding client, giving Sam time to take more than her usual passing glance at a file. The more she read, the more she regained her focus on her job and not dinner with Ben.

True to Ben's prediction, Scott was the man in the police cruiser from the night before. There wasn't much in the file. Blood alcohol was .11, and the accident caused one death, with one more in the hospital. Suspended license for driving while intoxicated. At least two previous charges of DUI, both dismissed without any indication why. Seven speeding tickets. By all counts, a fine driver indeed! And apparently quite the drunk.

This man is a menace. But so what? I shouldn't care. I'm quitting.

There was no notation on the file indicating the case deserved treatment different from every other white executive who screwed up. He'd soon be free to go, regardless of the amount of bail, assuming the court would even entertain requiring it. Sam looked again at Silverman as he bantered with the judge and couldn't get it out of her mind why someone like Silverman was here. Sam wondered if there might be more to this than met the eye. Her curiosity and growing nervousness made her look at the file more closely while Judge Dickerson and Silverman continued their dialog.

The judge's words caught Sam's attention. "Mr. Silverman, you never cease to amaze me every time you appear in my courtroom. Contrary to what you may believe, you do not represent the people of the Commonwealth of Virginia. That is the prosecutor's job, and I would appreciate your letting her at least take a stab at it."

Silverman seem almost condescending. "My apologies, Your Honor. I'm sure Miss Harrison will do her job just fine. I've no doubt she is as qualified as all of Mr. Morgan's assistants."

Mrs. Harrison, you putz. Wife of a man with twice your reputation or money. Asshole.

"Enough, Mr. Silverman! Sit down." Judge Dickerson clearly did not find the last comment Silverman had made amusing. "Mrs. Harrison, may I hear from the people?"

Later Sam would wonder what got into her mind over the next half hour.

Sam stood, and unlike her norm of stating her case from behind the prosecutor's table, she walked to the dais in the center of the courtroom as if to add importance to what she had to say. "Your Honor, if Mr. Scott is a pillar of society, he is certainly a shaky one. The arrest report shows Mr. Scott's blood alcohol level was .11 when he killed Susan Walker. Mrs. Walker's twelve-year-old daughter, Sarah, is in critical condition after being flown to Children's Hospital in Richmond." Sam kept flipping through the file. "Furthermore,

Mr. Scott was driving on a revoked license because of a past conviction for drunk driving. In fact, if I read this preliminary record correctly, Mr. Scott has at least three past charges of driving under the influence, has lost his license twice, and on at least one other occasion hit a pedestrian with his car. I can't clearly tell from this file what injuries that person suffered. No doubt Mr. Scott paid handsomely in settling that case. And he's also got a basket full of speeding tickets. He's clearly a deadly menace to anyone on Virginia's roads."

Silverman was on his feet, beet red. "Your Honor, my client was convicted of DUI only on one occasion. The other accusations resulted in dismissals."

Sam wasn't about to back down, her adrenaline pumping furiously. "No doubt because you represented him." Silverman's glare was piercing. Sam wanted to sit down, but Judge Dickerson had no intention of letting that happen. And while the courtroom's laughter at Sam's last comment was hard to ignore, it did not amuse the judge.

"Sit down, Mr. Silverman. The court will hear you when it's ready, not when you feel like having an outburst. Mrs. Harrison, please continue." Judge Dickerson had grown tired of Silverman and was clearly curious where Sam was going.

Sam continued. "The point, Your Honor, is Mr. Scott killed someone while driving drunk, exhibiting behavior he had shown before on numerous occasions. I have no doubt he will appear for trial. That is not the people's concern. A conviction is certain. When convicted, there is a virtual certainty he will serve time. He's already shown he has no respect for the law by driving without a license. He'll undoubtedly do it again. How many people will we let him hurt, or worse, kill? To put him back on the streets is tantamount to giving a murderer a loaded gun and sending him to Main Street in Bowling Green. Virginia's criminal law §19.2-120 allows the denial of bail where a court believes there is probable cause to believe a defendant constitutes an unreasonable danger to the public. Release him, and there is clearly probable cause to believe there will be a predictable result. Someone else will get hurt, or worse, die. Nor can we take his or Mr. Silverman's word he won't drive. He's already driven countless times after two suspended licenses. And we still don't know that Mrs. Walker's daughter won't die as well. She remains in critical condition. Your Honor, the people oppose bail in any amount."

Oppose bail? With a rich white guy, no less? Am I crazy?

Sam felt her legs giving way, making it more difficult to settle herself. She returned to her table and sat down.

Silverman made no effort to control his anger, once again interrupting before the judge could say a word. "Your Honor, Miss Harrison's theatrics are without foundation or merit."

Theatrics, thought Sam. *What theatrics?*

"Mr. Silverman, please address the prosecutor as Mrs. Harrison. You should know better."

Thank you, judge, it's about time someone scolded the bastard.

Silverman ignored the criticism, "My client serves as a director of countless charitable institutions. He is a deacon in his church. I can assure you he will not violate his right to drive again. As it happened, he found himself stranded at a dinner in his honor when his wife, Sharon, took ill and had to leave. There was no one else to drive the car. Mr. Scott foolishly decided to drive home. It was the first time he had driven since losing his license. Certainly that is not enough to remand him to jail without bail. I should also remind the young prosecutor the days of the inquisition are past. We believe people are innocent until proven guilty."

Judge Dickerson was beginning to find the debate entertaining, and she wasn't about to let Sam give up. It had been ages since Dickerson presided over a juicy arraignment, and she was enjoying herself. She turned again to Sam, her expression inviting Sam to contribute to the circus.

Sam stood. "If it pleases the court, let me be clear. As I said, it is not the people's position Mr. Scott will flee. We can certainly expect him to be in Virginia at the time of his trial. That is not the point. The point is Mr. Scott chose, yet again, to drink for hours and get behind the wheel of a car when he knew full well he had no right to and was in no condition to do so. A man of his position could certainly have called a cab. Instead, he chose to drive. There's no question he hit these people. The result is contemptible, and this court should not allow him to be free to do it again. The conscience of the court should not allow it."

Scott was frantically whispering in Silverman's ear. Silverman put his hand on Scott's shoulder to calm him down as Silverman again rose to his feet. "Your Honor, I object. I see no reason for the people to be carrying on like this. It is as though my client was being arraigned on a murder indictment. Let me also remind the court and prosecutor of Mr. Scott's long support of the police and their worthy causes. You simply do not deny bail for a man of such stature when the prosecutor agrees there is no risk of flight. The argument by this prosecutor, which I seriously doubt is supported by Mr. Morgan, is ludicrous." Silverman was now virtually screaming. It was unlike him to lose his composure. The judge loved the show.

It was too late to let up. Sam was in the fight to win. She was actually excited to be in a real fight for a change. Sam's mind was racing.

Is this what being a prosecutor all is about?

"That is precisely what he should be charged with, Mr. Silverman: murder. I can assure you the people are indeed serious. Your client is a killer, and he will get what he deserves regardless of how easy it is for him to post bail or afford your fees. And if keeping him off the streets means getting a murder indictment, that's precisely what the State will do."

Silverman lost it. "My God, Your Honor, where does this rookie prosecutor get off with that kind of lunacy, that kind of threat? She's out of her mind."

Someone in the gallery watching the battle yelled, "Book 'em, Danno!" The court burst into laughter.

Judge Dickerson, gavel pounding, took back control of her courtroom. "That will be enough from both of you. Mrs. Harrison, this court is capable of reading the record, although it is refreshing to see the commonwealth attorney's office occasionally reads it as well. And I will admit all of this does not bode well for the defendant. I am also persuaded, Mr. Silverman, your client is indeed a menace. He has certainly proven that. I am granting the people's request that Mr. Scott be held without bail, but only for three days. If the people are so certain Mr. Scott is the criminal the prosecutor believes him to be, they have those three days to get an indictment. There is a grand jury sitting now in courtroom twelve, taking up other indictments Mr. Morgan would like to pursue. He can now add this one to the docket. Otherwise Mr. Scott will be released on his personal recognizance. If an indictment is returned, we'll address the issue of bail at that time. Mrs. Harrison, I wish you luck with Mr. Morgan. This case is adjourned until four o'clock on Friday or sooner if the grand jury returns an indictment."

Everyone rose. As Judge Dickerson left the courtroom, she ignored Silverman's pleas for her attention. While denial of bail was appealable, Silverman knew three days would probably pass before he convinced another judge to overturn Dickerson's order. So his client was most likely stuck in a cell for the next three days. Once Dickerson closed the door to her chambers as she left the courtroom, the mood turned somber for everyone.

After a few words with his attorney, Scott, obviously bewildered, was handcuffed and led from the courtroom by the bailiff. His wife was in tears. Silverman gave Sam a chilling stare and stormed out of the courtroom. Sam stood there, not sure what to do next. She knew Morgan would not take this well. A Virginia judge had just challenged the commonwealth attorney to deliver on the words of one of his newest prosecutors—a prosecutor whose entire short career was on arraignments. As the court stenographer walked by, Sam heard her say, "I hope you know what you're doing."

So do I.

Sam avoided the office the rest of the afternoon, having lunch alone on a bench in a park across from the courthouse. She was confused. On the one hand, she had convinced herself she was going to resign. On the other hand, she had just taken a stand and couldn't back down now. And by not backing down, she'd gotten herself in a fine mess. She knew regardless of whatever decision she made, there would be no peace until she faced Morgan.

Chapter Twelve

My Dearest Amanda, it's your tenth birthday! I can't believe how quickly you've grown. And while I'll give you lots of hugs later, I wanted to send you this note as something to keep as a memory of my love. I love you, Amanda, with all my heart and soul.

Sam's Birthday card to Amanda, July 26, 1995.

April 14, 1993
Commonwealth Attorney Offices

Three o'clock arrived. As Sam climbed the steps of the commonwealth attorney offices to see Morgan, she found herself surrounded by the press. They were screaming questions, all of which seemed to meld into one long tirade.

"How long will you put Scott away for?"

"Have you made a deal yet?"

"Will Morgan really go for a murder indictment?"

"Did Morgan know you'd take that position?"

Sam couldn't get to the office door soon enough despite her fear of what lay behind it.

When Sam entered Morgan's foyer, it was obvious he was waiting for her. Sam had hoped to have a few moments alone with Ethel, but that wasn't going to happen.

She barely had a chance to say hello to Ethel when Morgan stormed out and grabbed Sam by the arm, pulling her in his office. His grip actually hurt and made her think of the grip Watts used at the Christmas party, but Sam was not about to show any weakness by objecting. He virtually shoved her into a chair. He sat on the edge of his desk across from her, eyes squarely focused on her.

Morgan spoke firmly but not loudly, clearly trying to control his anger. "Harrison, I put you somewhere I thought you could handle without controversy. Get your feet wet. Get to know the ropes and the judges. Instead you appear before one of the most militant judges in Virginia and have her challenge my ability to get an indictment. It's bad enough Scott's represented by one of the best lawyers in town who gives the PBA at least twenty thousand a year."

Sam's voice was level and confident. "I came upon the accident last night. I saw what Scott did. I couldn't stand there and ignore what I saw."

Morgan began pacing around the office as if he were circling Sam for the kill. "Oh, so now you're a witness, too? Have you ever seen a murder site? Have your ever seen the pools of blood left every night on our streets by thugs who could care a lot less about the value of a human life than they do about their next fix? OK, Scott's a scumbag. So what? You could have sought an indictment without holding him in a jail. Did you ever think of house arrest? How about daily reporting? Or an ankle bracelet. How about anything other than sending this idiot to hell for three days while we jerk off trying to think what we'll do with a grand jury?"

He moved to his chair and sat down, still anything but calm. "It's been said a good prosecutor can get an indictment on a ham sandwich, and we probably can, but not in three days." With a look of indignation, he waited for Sam to answer.

Sam sat straight up, as though she was sitting at attention during a court-martial. "I'm sorry, but I was trying to do the job you sent me to do. If that means I do only what the file notations tell me to do and don't bother to read the file, you might as well hire a robot for the job. But there weren't any notes. So I read the file, as thin as it was. The more I read, the angrier I got at Silverman's arrogance and the angelic face put on someone I consider a cold-blooded murderer. I believed Scott was wrong and knew what he was doing. I had an obligation to press the court."

Morgan rose and again began pacing. "Well, you made your bed, and now you get to sleep in it. Since you so fervently believe Scott is a murderer who belongs behind bars, you go get the indictment."

Sam was shocked. "I've never been before a grand jury, Mr. Morgan. I don't even know where the jury sits."

Morgan now stood in front of Sam, arms crossed with a cold a stare. "Well, you have three days to find out. I guess you'd better get started. It's just too bad the other assistant DAs are so busy. It looks like you'll have to do this one all on your own." As he walked back to his chair, the grin on Morgan's face was one of perverse satisfaction, as though he'd just found a way of ridding himself of a pest.

Sam felt cornered. Not moving from her seat, she asked, "What if I don't want to go further? What if I just leave?"

Morgan spun around. "No, Harrison, that would be too easy. You're not running anywhere to hide. Right now nothing would please me more if you left. It wouldn't surprise me if you made the appointment with me today for that very purpose. But somehow I doubt you're out of my life. Something tells me you are my living nightmare. So go do your job."

We'll see about that. Sam left the office.

She couldn't quit now—at least not until she got the indictment. Or at least tried. Now she wanted to beat Morgan even more than she wanted to beat Silverman.

It didn't take long for her to find where the grand jury sat. And there were plenty of other commonwealth attorneys ready to help. Ethel saw to that.

Chapter Thirteen

Everyone loves to talk about balancing the budget and reducing the deficit. It's all common fodder for Washington to debate the pluses and minuses of tax increases, tax cuts, or spending controls as ways to achieve the goal of intelligent fiscal management. Yet Washington is incapable of behaving in a fiscally responsible manner. Why? Because the House, Senate, and administration are corrupted by self-interests. They've been bought by constituents who will never see eye to eye or agree on who should pave the way, either by paying more taxes or getting fewer entitlements. Until our leaders in Washington face the issues honestly, there will be no solution. The status quo is unacceptable. I urge you to place fiscal responsibility first in your mind when casting your vote. If the candidate asking you to trust them can't be trusted to be honest, don't vote for them. And think hard about reelecting any incumbent. Clearly the incumbents have failed. If they want to be reelected by you, make sure they make promises they'll keep, not the empty ones they've made so far.

Campaign speech in first House election bid, July 4, 2000.

April 17, 1993
Grand Jury Room

Early Thursday morning Sam presented her case to the grand jury. In Virginia, unlike most states, grand juries are small. Only five to seven jurors sit for weeks at a time hearing one case after another. While grand jury duty was largely boring for jurors, most took the duty seriously, even thought they were stuck in a stuffy room day after day, hearing from only the prosecutor and occasionally a few witnesses.

The grand jury system is a curious exercise. Only the prosecutor presents his or her case. The state can call witnesses but doesn't have to. Jurors are permitted to ask questions but usually don't. The defendant never appears. They are just a name. No defendant to watch. In short, it's all a one-sided proceeding where securing an indictment was almost always certain. With a lot of help by fellow assistant prosecutors, by the time Sam walked into the jury room and faced the jurors, her confidence was absolute. It was a lot simpler than she thought. It certainly didn't hurt that Mothers Against Drunk Driving was demonstrating outside the courthouse. Sam didn't ask how the event was orchestrated, let alone who organized it. *Thank you, Ethel.*

She presented her evidence. The police record. The coroner's report. The photographs. Surprisingly, the jurors had many questions, and Sam suspected they read the press and knew what a wonderful citizen and philanthropist Scott was. They all seemed to know Scott was a Bowling Green hero, not one of its bums. Of more concern to Sam was she knew most people drove even when they'd had a few too many. The idea of seeing it as murder was difficult for them. So Sam concentrated more on the habitual behavior of the defendant and the consequences to the victims, one dead and one near dead.

After two hours, she left with her indictment: murder, second degree, and attempted murder, second degree. As Sam made the walk back to her office, she felt euphoric—more than she'd anticipated. Her victory was sweet. Now she wanted to try the case, but knew Morgan would never stand for it.

As Sam approached the steps to her office building, she again saw the reporters. She didn't see Sharon Scott, the wife of the newly indicted defendant, waiting among them.

The scene quickly turned ugly. The reporters were intrusive, and Mrs. Scott was on the attack.

One reporter shouted, "Did you get the indictment?"

"It's not appropriate for me to comment. You'll all find out in due time."

Sharon Scott pushed her way past the throng of reporters, yelling: "You fucking dike! If you had any compassion or did half of what my husband does, you'd be worshiping him, not crucifying him like a bitch after headlines. What's next? Do you want to indict me as an accessory?"

Maybe I should. After all, you let him drive.

Sam froze, staring at Mrs. Scott, whose eyes showed nothing but contempt, deep red from days of crying. Yet Sam felt oddly relaxed.

Sam spoke calmly. "I assume you are the defendant's wife. For that you have my sympathy." She turned toward the press, clearly unhappy about being confronted but still calm. She decided to hell with confidentiality and Morgan's rule of not speaking to the press. "Make no mistake, her husband is going to jail. He is a killer, and that is where he belongs. He and perhaps his wife may be able to live with that, but the victims cannot. Don't blame the Commonwealth of Virginia or the innocent woman Mr. Scott killed and the little girl who lies in a cold hospital in Richmond because of his decisions." Sam turned back to the wife. "Wake up, Mrs. Scott. Wealth will not shield your husband from justice."

The slap from Scott's wife connected well, but Sam barely flinched. Perfect timing by a *Washington Post* photographer caught it all on camera, ready for the front page. The press remained silent. Mrs. Scott sat down on the steps and wept. Sam walked on.

Morgan watched the circus from his window. The phone rang behind him. The conversation was brief.

Sam walked past Ethel and directly into Morgan's office, intent on taking command.

"Mr. Morgan, this is my case, and it's mine to try. I'll win. Don't even think about taking it away from me. I won't stand for it."

Morgan, sitting at his desk, replied softly. "Sit down Samantha. I'm not going to take the case away from you or fire you for talking to the press. That would be too easy."

You're not?

"It's yours to try. So win or not, you do it on your own. Let me know who you'd like to assist you in second chair, and I'll see what I can do. Now if you don't mind, I've got other matters pressing for my attention." Morgan dismissively motioned her to the door.

Bewildered at not having the battle she was ready to wage, she stood quietly for a few seconds until Ethel broke the silence with the suggestion that Sam may not want to continue blocking the door. As Sam walked by Ethel's desk, she noticed Ethel's call log. Zachary Watts called twice in the past hour.

Judge Dickerson set bail at a quarter of a million dollars. Sam put up little resistance. Scott easily posted it and was home for dinner. The next day the headlines read: "Scott Indicted. Prosecutor Promises Prison Next, Leaves Wife Weeping." The article said Sam had ice running in her veins when she encountered Mrs. Scott, remaining calm and in total control, barely reacting to the slap. The papers all reported Sam was someone to contend with and another example of the high commitment of the prosecutors in Morgan's office. Up until that last point, Sam thought the article was fine. She just couldn't bear the compliment given to Morgan. He didn't deserve it. In Sam's eyes, he was just another political chauvinist like those she'd encountered time and time again. He was someone to be neither trusted nor admired.

On October 15, six months after indicting Scott, Sam got her conviction. Five weeks later Scott was sentenced to five years. With good behavior, he'd be out in two. The case made national headlines.

Within a week following the sentencing, Morgan transferred Sam to the criminal trial division. She began trying cases, enjoying the job more every day.

Her rise after the Smith trial was spellbinding. She won case after case, including two more against Silverman. In fact, Sam never lost while in the criminal trial division. Sure she took pleas, but every time she tried a case, the jury found the defendant guilty. On February 15, 1995, Morgan appointed her deputy commonwealth attorney. Young attorneys flocked around her for the opportunity to work with the woman the press began describing as—next to Morgan—the most feared prosecutor in Virginia. She could dissect a case with investigative skills admired by even the most hardened investigator in the police department. She was Virginia's new crusader against crime. She loved the attention.

Morgan left her alone, knowing she was as competent as they came—maybe even the best he had ever seen. He knew he could do no better. He and Sam rarely spoke, and when they did, it was never something one would describe as a cordial conversation.

Chapter Fourteen

The respect for lawyers in our society has never been lower. Lawyers are blamed for the failures of Congress because most politicians are lawyers. They are blamed for the rising costs of auto insurance because lawyers represent the people who receive millions of dollars for their injuries. They are blamed for the crime on the streets because the judges who release the criminals are lawyers. Listen to some critics, and you'll begin to think lawyers are the root of all our problems. Our job as commonwealth attorneys is to regain the respect our profession once had and still deserves. Politicians aren't lawyers; they're just men and women, many of whom happen to have a legal education. Car insurance doesn't cost more because of lawyers; it costs more because the laws passed by politicians put no limit on the generosity of a sympathetic jury. It is not the lawyers who keep crime on the streets. It's the lack of jails and stiff mandatory sentencing that keeps criminals on the streets. Be proud of our profession and never let anyone tell you lawyers are the cause of their problems. Indeed, above all else, we must protect everyone's freedoms and be certain to never let our government, or any government, take them away.

Address to new commonwealth attorneys at swearing-in ceremony, January 16, 1996.

July 13, 1997
Criminal Court

The headline in *The Washington Post* read, "Icy Prosecutor Enters Last Day of Trial."

Peter Vasquez was a rapist and murderer. And of a cop, no less. A hardened criminal who had been arrested three times for robbery and assault, he'd already served ten years in Virginia prisons. Under pressure from party bosses, Morgan let Sam take the case. He really wanted this one, but knew his own political career was under the control of the Republican Party machine. A machine wanting something to keep Sam visible. It had bigger plans for her. Morgan was told she needed the press to reinforce her reputation as one of the toughest prosecutors in the country and a clear candidate for national office. Morgan was told he'd remain a county employee.

On June 27, 1996, Peter Vasquez brutally raped, tortured, murdered, and dismembered police officer Janie Silvers. Pieces of her body were found in shallow graves in four of Bowling Green County's remote areas. Vasquez showed no remorse, insisting on his innocence despite the evidence. His hair follicles were found under the victim's fingernails, a knife was in his apartment with Janie's blood still on it, his DNA was found on the victim, and there was testimony from neighbors that he bragged about his little escapade.

The press release from Sam's office said she was trying this case because it involved a cop, and a guilty verdict would allow for the death penalty, something Sam knew Morgan had every intention of insisting upon. While it wasn't the first death penalty conviction Morgan's office had sought, it was the first Sam had personally tried.

After picking a jury on June 10, the two sides made their opening statements on June 25. It took barely two weeks for Sam to win a conviction. The defense tried to persuade her to take a plea. Sam refused. Morgan would have no part of that. The defense tried to get the press to buy into a story that Sam was only trying the case as a public relations stunt to support a bid for Congress. The press didn't bite, however true the allegation may have been. Vasquez was a scumbag, pure and simple, and was convicted in the press long before the jury found him guilty of aggravated first-degree murder, a conviction supporting the death penalty. Now Sam needed to convince the jury that Vasquez deserved to die with a needle in his arm rather than rot in prison for the rest of his miserable life.

A week later when the death penalty phase of the trial began, Sam was torn apart. Philosophically, she was dead set against state-sanctioned executions. As she saw it, Sam could no more condone a murder by execution than she could a murder by abortion. No one doubted Sam was true to her convictions, whatever they were. But now she had a job to do. She had to convince herself it was not for her to second-guess the desires of a bloodthirsty electorate and an uncivilized legislature.

What bothered her most was the feeling she'd sold out and admittedly tried this case to get press on the eve of announcing her run for Congress. At times she wondered if she was too hungry. She worried she might be starting down a road that led politicians to lose sight of their convictions and sell out to whoever gave them the best shot at office. Those worries, however, didn't stop her. She had now retained none other than Zachary Watts as her political advisor. Watts had left Wilson, Smith & Watts and was now a full-time consultant with an impressive list of victories for congressional districts throughout Virginia.

Watts would often pontificate, "Politics requires you compromise some of your ideals to get the opportunity to do those things you think are for the greater good."

How trite.

On the day she retained him, Watts told her: "I know you'll end up in Congress or maybe even higher up the ladder. Whether you know it or not, you've been on this road from the moment you left John Smith's office. So why don't we both cut the crap and get on with the program. I believe in you, Sam. A lot of people do. I think you can get somewhere and do something significant. But if you're not ready for the compromises and the heat, including putting someone like Vasquez in the ground where he belongs, get out now and save my time."

While withdrawing from politics might still be an option, it was far too late for Sam to withdraw from sending Vasquez to his death. So her concern about compromises she might have to make in the future took a back seat to the death penalty.

"OK, Zach. But I'll tell you this: while I'll uphold the law, I'll never endorse it when I think it's wrong. Once this trial is over, I don't want the subject of the death penalty brought up again."

"Sure." Watts had trouble swallowing the word. He really did believe in Sam. There was something pure and good about her he couldn't put his finger on. She was honest and aggressive, a believer in herself, however against the grain some of her views might be to staunch Republicans. She was his greatest challenge yet.

At the penalty hearing, Sam began her summation as she had so many times before, standing at the dais in front of the jury box. "Ladies and gentlemen of the jury, you have sat diligently and heard testimony and proof in one of the most heinous crimes in memory: the rape, torture, murder, and dismemberment of an innocent off-duty police officer. You have watched the defendant, Peter Vasquez, sit coldly while the victim's parents wept. He never once showed a sign of remorse or regret. You took only thirty minutes to convict him of aggravated first-degree murder. Thank you. And as you announced your verdict, he still sat there without a sign of remorse or regret." She allowed her voice to quiver. "He continued then and continues now to sit there like the animal he is."

Sam paused, feigning an effort to regain composure. She walked around the dais and stopped in front of the jury, being sure to look into the eyes of each juror as she spoke. "I'm also sure all watched the defendant as he sat through this trial without emotion or remorse."

She kept her stare on the jurors. "Did Vasquez really think he was going to get away with it? Did he really think his lawyers would dupe you into believing the evidence was all circumstantial and you couldn't convict him simply because the Commonwealth of Virginia told you to? You answered with a decided no and convicted him for the crime he committed." Sam backed away from the jury box, staying in eye contact, stopping ten feet away. She had orchestrated this dance many times. Keep the jurors looking at you with eye contact and movement, pausing between key arguments.

She could hear Watts in the back of her mind: "*You're doing good, Sam. Now go for the kill.*"

"Now I must ask you to complete your job. For you this is the toughest part of all, for the burden on you is now greater than any asked of you before. I want you to agree to put Mr. Vasquez to death. Don't do it for Janie Silvers. Don't do it for her family and friends. And definitely don't do it for me or the Commonwealth of Virginia. Do it because Peter Vasquez deserves it."

Sam walked directly in front of Vasquez, staring at him with icy eyes for a few seconds. She pointed at Vasquez and looked back at the jury. "He is an animal. That, you have already determined. His crime was one of utmost violence, premeditated and horrifying. We can only wonder how much poor Janie suffered while this animal thrust his crimes upon her. How many times do you think Peter Vasquez thought about the crimes he was committing? How much remorse do you think he displayed each time he raped Janie, even when she was unconscious—maybe even dead? Did he think it was wrong when he savagely sliced apart Janie's body and buried it, piece by piece, in shallow graves? If you don't return the death penalty, how much remorse will he feel as he lies in prison for the rest of his life, laughing at how he beat the system and became a ward of the state?" She again approached the jury, putting her hands on the edge of the jury box. "Do not buy into the defense's argument Peter Vasquez deserves your leniency. He deserves your wrath. He deserves only one thing more. A sentence of death."

Sam leaned in toward the jury. "In the name of decency and in the name of what he deserves, I ask you to deliver that sentence. Thank you." She slowly panned the jury, one by one, looking into the eyes of each as if looking for approval.

Sam returned to her seat. As she sat down, she sickened inside. She had played her role to the best of her ability. She knew the public defender Vasquez had for his attorney didn't have a chance. While he gave a valiant try, at times even impressing Sam, it took the jury less than two hours to return the death sentence. She'd won, and she knew the headlines would hype her chances at a bid for Congress. Just what Watts ordered.

After a few weeks of perfunctory motions and courtroom wrangling, the judge entered the death sentence. Naturally appeals stayed the execution.

CHAPTER FIFTEEN

Equal rights in health care. We must not become a society of socialized medicine. Democrats are taking us there, and it is not the answer. Yet we cannot ignore the ever rising costs of health care and the outright denial of it to those who often need it the most. We must gain control of the skyrocketing costs of insurance, medical equipment, and drugs. Otherwise all the breakthroughs and technology in the world will serve only the rich and affluent while denying basic health rights of all those who support our country and who most need our help. Healthcare must be brought back to choice and competition now before it's too late.
Speech in acceptance of nomination, Convention Center, Memphis, Tennessee, July 27, 2016.

September 9, 1975
Stanford University

Stanford was all the experience a seventeen-year-old could hope it would be. One of the most beautiful campuses in America, it was an idyllic place to learn, a think tank of eager minds, hand-picked from among the most brilliant pool in the country.

Sam did well her first year. Dean's List. Her mother could not have been prouder. Sam delighted in her own success, sharing in her mother's pride.

But it was not until her second year that Sam was certain she had made the right choice. That was when she met Professor Benjamin Harrison.

Applied Econometrics was a required course for all business majors. Professor Benjamin Harrison had a reputation for being tough. His course weeded out the weak. Only 50 percent passed. At thirty-five, he was a young professor, and his tough image seemed out of place, like a defense to prove his wisdom. Becoming one of Stanford's younger full professors at the age of thirty, he was also one of the most respected.

He was a wealthy man in his own right from his investment prowess—or maybe luck, as jealous others liked to put it. He inherited a few hundred thousand dollars from his mother when she died in a car accident. His father died many years earlier. He invested in such stocks as IBM, Apple, Intel, Capital Cities Communications, and others before they became the investment community's favored stocks. He balanced his holdings with astute moves in and out of the bond market and investments in foreign equities and emerging companies. It was said he never lost in the market, although he had on more occasions than he cared to admit. But overall, he was ahead. Way ahead. No one including the most experienced educators at Stanford doubted his ability to analyze and predict a business trend. That's why he was already on a dozen boards and an economic advisor to many leading Republicans. He routinely consulted with then presidential candidate Ronald Reagan, a man Ben greatly admired.

How he taught became clear the first day. The assignment from the night before was one hundred pages on macroeconomic theory, the first concentration in the course. Sam had found the reading vague and a little too theoretical. It wasn't at all like the hands-on approach to business she expected as a business major. She had a hard time believing such theories applied to the operation of a business, which really ought to be more a matter of common sense. While she read the assignment, she knew she didn't understand it and nervously came to class.

Professor Harrison came in five minutes late and sauntered to the podium at the front of the classroom. He was strikingly handsome in a professor sort of way. At six foot four with dark-brown hair and hazel eyes, he towered over most students. Even in his role as a disheveled professor, he looked like someone out of *Gentlemen's Quarterly*.

"Good morning. My name is Benjamin Harrison. Undoubtedly you have heard of me. I will not bore you with some homily about looking at the person on your right and realizing one of you will not pass this class. The person on your right is the one who has a chance of passing. It's the person on their left who will probably flunk."

No laughter.

"Christ, people. That's a joke. Lighten up."

Still no laughter.

"Fine. It's too early for humor anyway. Let's get on with the massacre." He picked up the class list. "Mr. Abrams, this is your bad day. It's the price you pay for being first on the list with a last name beginning with the letter A." Harrison looked up, "Mr. Abrams?"

Aaron Abrams tentatively rose from his seat.

"I guess your parents really did you in, Mr. Abrams. It's bad enough your last name hits the top of the list, but your first name gets there too—unless, of course, your brother's first name is Aardvark."

The first laughter.

"I see," said Harrison. "This class finds its humor in personal attacks. That's good because we'll have plenty of those."

Abrams was still standing.

"Well, Mr. Abrams, it's good to see you're patient. Now why don't you tell us about macroeconomics in twenty-five words or less?"

Abrams looked blankly at Harrison.

Sam's thoughts were logical. *Tell us about macroeconomics in twenty-five words or less? What kind of question is that?*

It was the first day of class with only one reading assignment behind them, and this professor expected poor Aaron Abrams, a man cursed by the alphabet, to explain what half this course was about.

Has Stanford gone mad?

Abrams remained silent.

"Sit down, Mr. Abrams. Do I have any volunteers?"

A few hands rose.

Brownnoses.

There were some in every class. The problem was they always seemed to get the better grades. Sam vowed she'd never be a brownnose and preferred to earn her grades the honest way.

Harrison pointed to a hand in the back. The student rose.

"Your name, please," asked Harrison.

"Michael Summers, sir."

"Ah, a man safely within the middle of the alphabet. Well, Mr. Summers, are you prepared to tell us about macroeconomics in twenty-five words or less?"

Summers responded, thinking he'd be safe taking a humorous route in responding. "It seems to me, sir, that you should be telling us about macroeconomics. If we had the answer, we wouldn't need this class. After reading one hundred purely boring pages from an ancient textbook, I think I learned as much about macroeconomics as I know about molecular physics. What I did learn is macroeconomics relies on theories based on past practices and applies them to today's needs without regard to changes in the business climate. Frankly, it's lost on me."

Summers sat down with a smug smile.

Whoever you are, you're crazy. But at least you're not a brownnose.

Sam vowed to herself to meet Michael Summers.

You could hear a pin drop. Harrison stood silent.

"Mr. Summers," Harrison finally intoned, "would you please come down here?"

Summers rose again and came to the front of the class, no longer displaying any of the bravado he'd exhibited only a few minutes earlier. As he came down the aisle, Sam thought she was about to witness her first public execution. How would Harrison do it, with one shot in the back of the head? Maybe he'd just strangle him.

Summers stopped in front of the first row.

"No, no, Mr. Summers. Come up here with me, right here in front of the class."

Summers stepped up onto the podium.

"Mr. Summers," said Harrison, "the class is now yours."

Harrison stepped down and sat in the first row.

Summers stood speechless. He looked to Harrison, his eyes pleading.

"I'm sorry, Professor Harrison. I spoke out of hand. It's just that your reputation scares us, and I foolishly thought if I took a humorous approach, I'd gain your respect." Summers didn't know he had actually succeeded.

Harrison remained silent, letting Summers stew in his own juices. Two agonizing minutes later, Harrison rose and resumed his place on the podium alongside the now trembling Mr. Summers.

"You may resume your seat. You see, class, Mr. Summers is right, although his sense of humor could be improved. Macroeconomics is hard to make sense of, much less in twenty-five words or less. It's as hard to understand as any theory in science because economics is a science as old as math itself. Do any of you honestly think something new can happen in economic theory just because you think you're smart? I can assure you, none of you is smarter than the economic theorists of the past. And you are all fools if you think macroeconomics has no application in real life. You will never understand microeconomics, let alone business, unless you have a full understanding of macroeconomics. Since the show is over, let's get into the assignment."

Wow. Forget Summers. I want to meet Professor Benjamin Harrison.

Samantha's attraction to Benjamin Harrison was purely academic at first. He intimidated her, as he did every student. The more she attended class, however, the more she became infatuated with him. She promised herself she'd take every course he taught.

Chapter Sixteen

Equal rights for the elderly. How soon we forget our older citizens. Why, unlike societies of the past, are we so ready to discard those who know so much and who can give us wisdom unmatched by any contemporary? If we deny equal rights to our elderly, we deny our history and are destined to repeat our mistakes.

Speech in acceptance of nomination, Convention Center, Memphis, Tennessee, July 27, 2016.

October 21, 1976
Stanford University

Benjamin Harrison finally noticed Samantha Price in Experimental Economics, a course she took the first semester of her junior year.

He gave Sam her first D on an exam, one she had known she hadn't done well on. She was not, however, prepared for a D.

When class ended Sam approached Professor Harrison and asked if she could speak to him about her grade.

"And your name is...?"

Sam's heart sank. This was the third course she'd taken with Harrison, and he didn't even know who she was? Granted, Sam was not active in class participation and never volunteered answers, but he called on her at least a dozen times from that infernal class list he kept close at hand.

She took a deep breath and responded: "Samantha Price, sir. I was devastated by my grade on the last exam and wondered if you had some time to discuss it with me."

"You failed the test?"

"No, sir. You gave me a D."

"And you're devastated by a D? What would you do if you got an F, cast yourself into the mouth of a volcano? I hardly think a D should devastate anyone. After all, it's only one test and a passing grade."

Sam wasn't interested in just a passing grade. "Maybe you think a D is no big deal. But I'm not personally satisfied with anything less than an A, and the lowest grade I have ever received at Stanford is a B. This is my first poor grade. I'd like to go over the test and understand what I missed so that it doesn't happen again. If you're too busy, perhaps you can assign one of your teaching assistants to help me."

He smiled and gently touched her shoulder. The touch caught her off guard, and she could feel her cheeks reddening, her heart speeding. For some unexplainable, almost childish reason, this was the first time a man had affected her that way, particularly one that seemed more intent on insulting her than helping.

"OK, Miss Price. We'll go over your exam. My office hours are seven to nine every morning. Be in my office tomorrow at seven thirty."

He grabbed his briefcase, turned, and left without saying anything more.

That night Sam couldn't sleep. She stayed up until two going over the test and reading the assignments. The more she went over the test, the more she thought she had answered the questions reasonably well. Certainly there wasn't anything in her answers admitting she'd done anything wrong. Her class notes shed no light on the problem.

She'd heard stories of private meetings with Harrison. If you left alive, it was a miracle. He was even known to lower grades. He demanded the best of his students, and if you had the nerve to go one-on-one with him, he demanded even more. He expected you to be as good as he was. Remembering poor old Michael Summers, Sam decided to fight fire with fire and stand her ground.

At 7:35, she knocked on the door and entered without waiting for an invitation.

Harrison was at his desk, feet up, reading *Mad* magazine. When she entered, he simply stared at her.

"May I sit down?" asked Sam.

He nodded and put down the magazine, still leaving his feet on the desk. "You're late. No good morning professor?"

"Sorry. Good morning."

"And a fine one it is, Miss Price. So let's get right to it and have a look at your exam." His feet came down, and he took the exam from her. Harrison browsed through it for about five minutes while Sam looked around his office.

The office was far more organized than she'd thought it would be. She pictured the stereotypical absent-minded professor with books and papers strewn everywhere. Sure, there was some of that, but very little, considering. What fascinated her most, however, were the pictures on the walls and credenza. They were photographs and drawings of every sort of political leader. There was Churchill, Calvin Coolidge, Stalin, Marx, even Castro. The more she looked around the room, the more she realized most of the photographs and drawings were of communists or socialists.

My God, there's a photograph of Adolph Hitler. What is Harrison, anyway? A Fascist? Or worse, a Nazi?

"OK, Miss Price. Let's talk about your answers." Harrison got up from behind his desk and came around to the front and sat in the chair alongside Sam. As soon as he got up, Sam's heart began to race. It pounded so hard she wondered if he could hear it. Sam feared it had nothing to do with nervousness over what Harrison might say about her exam. She felt her stomach tighten. The nervous sweat only made it all more emotional. She feared she'd never get through this without embarrassing herself like some schoolgirl.

"You're a junior, right?" continued Harrison. "Next year, if you stay at Stanford, you will finish your degree with courses that teach you more in one year than you learned in your first three years combined. To take advantage of the opportunity, you must begin to think, not regurgitate words from text-books or notes from class. That was fine the first couple of years when you had to learn the basics. Now you have to become an expert."

Sam stared at the exam in Harrison's hands, deathly afraid to make eye contact. Harrison continued, "I gave you a D because you walked through this exam, as did most of your classmates. In fact, only one student received an A, one got a B, and only two out of the thirty-four in the class got Cs. You received one of twenty-four Ds."

No one got an F? So I'm one of twenty-four idiots with a D? Is that supposed to make me feel better?

Harrison, expecting some sort of response from Sam and hearing none, went on. "While it is refreshing you're here fighting for a better grade, something none of your classmates has the courage to do, you received what you deserved." Harrison reached his hand back to his desk, shuffled through some papers, and picked up another exam book.

"Here, Miss Price. Take a few moments and read this answer. This is the student who got the A. I made a copy just in case some student was brave enough to come see me. If after you read the exam you think you deserve anything near his or her grade, I'll be happy to hear your arguments. Otherwise I suggest you use this answer to open your mind to original thinking. And if you have the chance, you can also feel free to let your classmates know how truly disappointed I was with their performance on this exam."

Sam barely heard a thing he said. She was mesmerized by his voice. The way he towered over her while sitting in his chair. The way he smelled. How much she'd like to see him again, outside the classroom or his office. The vision in her mind had nothing to do with economics. She blushed, hardly the response Harrison expected.

"Are you all right, Miss Price?"

Sam snapped out of her daze. "Yes, I'm fine. Is it hot in here?"

Harrison smiled, suppressing a laugh. "I'll open a window."

As he rose, he placed his hand on her forearm. Sam thought she'd faint. How could he have such an effect on her? She felt like a fifteen-year-old on a first date! She had to get a grip on herself if she hoped to leave the meeting with any sense of dignity.

They spent the next hour going over the two exams. He asked her questions challenging basic theory, wanting to know how she thought, not what he or others had told her. By the time they finished, she knew far more about how to deal with the academic in Harrison and was intent on learning more about him outside the classroom. She just wasn't sure how.

Sam rose. "Thank you, Professor. While I'm still upset about the grade, I think I know what you're looking for, and we'll see how I do next time. By the way, who got the A, if I may ask?"

"Barbara Peterson. And her fiancée, Michael Summers, got the B. They're two of the brightest students at Stanford and have become my friends. But the grading is anonymous, so don't get any ideas. The three of us are having drinks at Rudy's Pub tonight, and if you'd like to join us, please do. It should be a lively debate on why Barbara is smarter than Mike—at least this time."

Sam's expression gave away the obvious.

Harrison cleared his throat. "Miss Price, I'm not asking you for a date. I just thought you might like the conversation."

Sam was mortified, and not being able to remember what she said when she left the office complicated her emotions even more. She headed straight for the ladies' room, where she promptly left her toast and coffee breakfast in the first stall.

She must have changed her outfit ten times before she settled on a pair of Levi's and her favorite green silk blouse. She always felt it highlighted her brown hair and green eyes. The Levi's had the mandatory tear in the left knee. She let her hair down rather than leave it tied in a ponytail as she usually did. She took one last look in the mirror. *Not bad*, she thought. The truth was she was a lot better than "not bad." Put simply, she was stunning even in as simple an outfit as jeans and a blouse.

She arrived at eight o'clock and saw Harrison sitting with Barbara and Mike in the corner.

Rudy's Pub was a popular hangout for Stanford students and some of the professors. While it was typically noisy, as were most college spots, the tables were far enough from the bar to afford some privacy and allow for conversation without shouting over the crowd.

She went straight to the table. The conversation froze.

"Hello, Professor Harrison. Hi, Barbara, Mike. I hope I'm not intruding."

Barbara spoke first. "Ben, close your mouth. It's not becoming of a professor at Stanford to be staring at a co-ed that way."

Sam was breathtaking, and Harrison's expression barely hid his appreciation.

Barbara continued. "Sam, please sit down. Ben here told us you might join us, and we were kidding him about how he couldn't describe you to us. How he can be alone with one of the brightest and sexiest students on campus and not remember what she looked like is typical Benjamin Harrison. Well, by looking at his expression now, he's woken up."

The look between Sam and Harrison was a nervous one, both trying to fight off too obvious a blush.

Is he really blushing? I like that.

"Barbara, you're embarrassing me," said Harrison. "And besides, this morning was official. Now we're all off duty and can relax. Miss Price, please sit down. And if it's OK with you, please call me Ben."

"Most people call me Sam."

"Best-looking Sam I ever saw," Mike contributed.

"Stop, Mike," said Barbara. "I have no intention of marrying a chauvinist pig, and if you want to find out why you got a B, clean up your act."

Everyone laughed, and the tension of the moment faded away.

The night was fantastic. Conversation went from economics to politics, from sports to movies. Everyone was thoroughly enjoying themselves and drinking more than they knew, except for Ben, who drank club soda and an occasional cup of coffee. Benjamin Harrison was always in control.

By evening's end the four were the only ones left, a habit Sam later learned was not uncommon for Ben. He was often the last customer of the night as he regaled some late-night students on economic theory. People wondered if he ever slept.

The owner came to the table. "Professor, I'd like to close before breakfast, if you don't mind."

"Very well," Ben responded. "But I will tell you this, Rudy, as I have told you countless times in the past: that attitude will never turn this pub into a McDonald's money machine."

"If I'd wanted to own a McDonald's, I'd be wearing a clown suit. Right now I just want to go to bed."

Ben smiled as he rose. "Then we're off. May I walk you back to your dorm, Sam?"

"I'd like that."

Barbara couldn't resist. "My God, Mike. We've just witnessed the first flight of the new lovebirds!"

Mike looked shocked. "Barbara, you're the pig, not me. Let's go home before you get both of us in trouble."

"Yes, dear," responded Barbara condescendingly. "After all, I am smarter than you in economic theory. So how do you feel about having some wild sex?"

Barbara and Mike left, mumbling polite insults to each other neither Sam nor Ben could hear.

"They're a nice couple," Sam said to Ben as they left.

"Yes, and I think they really are in love. At least as long as they keep their focus on mutual business interests. Time will tell."

Sam and Ben walked silently for most of the mile back to Sam's dorm.

Sam broke the silence. "Can I ask you something?"

"Sure. But beware. If asked a question, I answer it. So be prepared."

Undaunted, Sam asked, "Why do you have photographs of people like Marx and Hitler in your office?"

Ben stopped and looked at Sam. "Ah, a great Stanford debate. The truth is, I have them on my wall to remind me how misguided so many thinkers were in this world. When I think I've gotten an answer, I remind myself they thought they had answers too. It keeps me from getting too caught up with myself. The funny thing is many on the faculty believe I'm some sort of communist or Fascist maniac. The pictures are to keep me in focus. Now let me ask you something."

Sam returned his look at her. "I can't promise you I'll answer. I'm not as blunt or confident as you are." Sam was always the consummate politician. The two struck a nice balance.

"Blunt, no," noted Ben. "But confident, yes."

"Your question, Ben?"

I called him Ben? I like that.

"Do you have a steady boyfriend? I know it must sound silly to ask these days, but I'm curious. Someone as attractive as you must surely date someone seriously."

Sam felt like an excited teenager, talking to a new boy she wanted to date. "To be honest, I haven't had much time for men. Stanford has kept me preoccupied, which is the way I've wanted it."

"Oh."

Sam was quick to catch the dejection in Ben's response.

"At least until now," Sam blurted out, and with some embarrassment, slipped her arm under his as they again continued to walk. "And you?"

"I haven't found a female Lenin yet."

They both laughed, and their love affair began.

Chapter Seventeen

Equal rights for democracy, the foundation of our society. We cannot allow a reversal of the world's progress toward democracy. Too many countries continue to be at war with their citizens and those who would deny them their freedoms. We must support their causes with money, machinery, and manpower. We must remain the most powerful country in the world and stand as a shining example of democracy and success. We cannot succeed if we become a secondary military power. We no longer need to outspend rivals who have no concept of their citizens' needs, but we cannot cut our spending as far as some in government want us to. We cannot let the ignorant few destroy our country's commitment to support and protect democracy worldwide.

Speech in acceptance of nomination, Convention Center, Memphis, Tennessee, July 27, 2016.

August 25, 1978
Crofton, Maryland

The romance between Ben and Sam was fast and furious. They kept it as quiet as they could, but it became common knowledge by Sam's senior year. Ben gave Sam a B in any course he taught. He always knew which exam was hers by the little flower she drew on the lower right-hand corner of the first page. And she never deserved anything less than a B. Sam and Ben had agreed giving her no better than a B was a good idea to prevent unnecessary questions. It didn't hurt her grade point average enough to matter. She was guaranteed to get a job with her grades.

The wedding was a simple affair at Maryland's Walden Country Club two months after graduation—at least as simple as the opulent surroundings allowed.

The Walden Country Club, located in Crofton, was the exclusive enclave of affluent Maryland bankers, lawyers, and luminaries. Douglas Sanders, Sam's "sponsor" to Stanford, was dating Sam's mother on a regular basis, and arranged the affair. Elizabeth Price could never afford the Walden Country Club. It didn't matter. Ben was more than able to pay for the wedding. Sam's mother was happy, and Sam was ecstatic.

Not many from Ben's family came. Both his parents were dead, and he had no brothers or sisters. Two of his uncles, four cousins, and some professors from Stanford attended. Most of the people attending on Ben's side were mutual friends of Sam and Ben. What made the evening most exciting, however, was attendance by Wyoming Senator James Black, minority leader of the Senate Finance Committee and a politician who conferred regularly with Ben on economic matters. A staunch conservative, Black was touted as a potential presidential candidate, and everywhere he went, he was always "on" in the political sense. He and Ben were close friends.

Alex, Sam's brother, gave her away at the wedding. Sanders offered to do so and was disappointed when Sam declined his offer. But he was ever the gentleman and fully supported Sam's decision to have Alex attend to the honor.

For Sam, walking down the aisle was more difficult than she expected. She felt a true loss not having her father at her side. Sam had long come to realize, particularly with Ben's constant reminders, that most of what motivated her in college and probably in life was a need to know she made her father proud. She never understood how she could love someone so much when he had been dead most of her life. For Sam, her father never left her side, silently urging her to win and win again. She missed him as she prepared to walk down the aisle.

Alex could feel Sam's sense of loss.

"I know I can't substitute for Dad, but I know he'd be proud of you today. I'm sorry he died when you were so young. You really didn't get to know him. He was a proud man who loved you more than you could know. You were the jewel in his life. When we walk down the aisle together, he'll be leading the way."

She hugged her brother, crying. For the first time, she regretted not knowing him more closely. Unfortunately that was the price of sibling rivalry: you often found out too late what your petty behavior growing up cost you in relationships with those closest to you.

Alex gave her his handkerchief. "You've probably spent the better part of the day putting on makeup. We can't let it be spoiled yet. I don't want to face Ben if I've made you look as though I slapped you around or something. He may be older than me, but no doubt he could kick my ass."

Sam smiled. "I wish you and I had gotten to know each other better. You're my brother, but I've probably spent more time with casual friends than I have with you. Promise me we'll change that."

"We will. But first let's get you married. Mom can't afford to face the neighbors if this thing doesn't go off as scheduled."

They laughed. It did them well. Deep down, Sam knew her relationship with her brother would never change despite what he promised. For Sam, that was all right. They had just shared a memory that would sustain their love forever. For the first time in their adult lives, they had been together with their father.

The main dining room of the club where the reception took place overlooked the golf course with its floor-to-ceiling windows. It was raining, and the view from the windows reminded Sam of one of her favorite restaurants in Washington, the Lafayette in the Hayes Adams Hotel. She had only been there twice and never with Ben. It was beautiful.

The conversation at the reception was classic Benjamin Harrison. Halfway through the reception, with the heated debates on politics, the economy, and crime, one would have thought by the reception's conclusion all the world's problems would be solved. The best debate, however, was between Sanders and Senator Black.

Sanders, a liberal Democrat, never made it in his five bids to become mayor of Crownsville. A truly dedicated and accomplished lawyer, he was cursed with a practice in the middle of Maryland's Republican stronghold of financial executives, none of whom would ever countenance the idea of supporting a Democrat. Nonetheless, Sanders was an excellent debater and every bit as good as Black. Even before the wedding, Sam and Ben knew the conversation would be lively. They only hoped everyone would still be friends by evening's end.

Sanders started the debate. "The real problem our county is facing, Senator, is a lost generation of young people who have no commitment to improving the system, making the world a better place. Instead all they're interested in is business and law degrees and high-paying jobs. Things they should be doing while they're still young are being forgotten. Worse yet, they've all lost faith in our government. If it's not Watergate, it's some other corruption. We've got to get our youth back into politics."

Black accepted the challenge. "I regret you insist on continuing Democrat dogma that long lost its legitimacy. Our problem is not too few young people involved in politics. The problem is young people have removed their rose-colored glasses and come to realize the operation of government is a serious matter, and handouts and free lunches are over. What we don't need is a return to the absurd programs of the past like the Peace Corps or CETA. They're a waste of taxpayers' money and do nothing to help our economy."

"I could not disagree more," responded Sanders. "The Republicans will cut the guts out of public support programs if they have their way. It's a huge mistake. We can't ignore the needs of our poor."

Black seemed amused by this amateur politician from Crownsville. "Please stop the emotional merry-go-round and get down to reality. President Reagan has given us back our respect. He's taken a realistic approach to government, not an open-bank-account attitude so many of the Democrats espouse, particularly Carter. Where Carter ever thought he'd get the money to support all his programs is beyond me. He certainly didn't get the congressional support he needed. In truth, he failed because he was an outsider. Outsiders can't win or operate in Washington."

Sanders focused his stare on Black. "But that's exactly what we need, an outsider to clean up the mess. How can we justify giving aid to dictators all over the world while we have people starving in Appalachia? Reagan doesn't have a clue on how to run a government. I have no doubt Reagan will not be re-elected. I can't say who will get the nod from the Democrat Party, but whoever gets it will win in the next election. America wants to put a Democrat back in the White House so government can be given back to the people and not remain the playground of big business and fat-cat lobbyists."

A few of the guests gathered, entertained by the aggressive banter. Sensing his audience, Sanders continued: "But we have strayed from my point about youth in government, Senator. I shouldn't be surprised; Republicans are artful in dodging the issues. You say the problem is not that there is no youth in government but that the youth just doesn't see the world through the eyes of a Democrat. I must beg to differ."

Sanders waited for a response. Not getting one, he continued. "The statistics and surveys clearly show today's youth is disillusioned with what they see in Washington and at state capitals. Government has lost credibility, and I fear we are parenting a lost generation who will care only for material things and lose sight of the value of giving before taking and supporting those in need at home and throughout the world. If we do not stay with the original ideals of our democracy, we will decline and find ourselves overtaken by the Japanese and Germans and—mark my words—the Chinese. We can't let that happen."

"Oh, come now," Black finally responded. "It isn't that bad and we don't need hysteria. If I'm not mistaken, youth has traditionally been dissatisfied with government. In the fifties, we had as many protests as we did at the end of the Vietnam War. We just didn't have the media exaggerating them like it does today. During FDR's terms, students protested nationwide. There is nothing new about youthful disdain for government. In fact, I wouldn't trust any kid who thought government was good. But that is not the point. I do not stray from the original question. You cannot look at youth in a vacuum. History shows what we are going through with our youth today is no different from any period in our past. We cannot lose the lessons of our past. More importantly, we must not jump to conclusions and ignore history. If we go down that path, we will indeed repeat our mistakes. That's something even you Democrats don't want to do."

Sanders couldn't help but laugh. "I'm beginning to appreciate why you're a senator and I'm just a practicing attorney. You are blessed with the silver tongue of a politician. I guess you and I will just have to agree to disagree. But mark my words, Senator: a Democrat in the White House will soon reawaken America's youth to government."

Black turned to Sam. "Sam, you've been uncharacteristically quiet. What do you think of Mr. Sanders's comments? You are the youth he speaks of? He thinks you're disillusioned with government. Are you? Have you given up on the old farts in Foggy Bottom? Is your business degree more important than getting involved in the political process?"

The senator's questions caught Sam off guard. It was one thing to listen to a debate between two seasoned combatants, but it was quite another thing to be cast in the arena like a lamb to slaughter. She knew any answer would only prolong the debate and immerse her into a no-win situation.

Ben, seeing the growing group across the room, came to her rescue. "No way are the two of you going to get my bride involved in any debate. She'd chew you both up, a decidedly ugly way to culminate our reception. Besides, I hate to see grown men cry."

Ben had given Sam an out. But she didn't want out just yet. She wanted to get herself out of the situation on her own terms, not on terms determined by Black or a rescue by Ben.

"It's OK, Ben," said Sam, taking Black's bait. "I think I'd like to respond to the senator."

Ben stared at Sam quizzically, not understanding why she would enter a conversation where she was being set up. Ben knew Black all too well and knew better than to get into debates with him. Even if Sam agreed with him, he would attack her on some other issue. He loved the battle. He could not leave a conversation without defeating an opponent. That's what made him so effective in the Senate, and why Ben knew politics was one place he preferred to remain an advisor, not a participant. Ben wasn't sure how to help Sam out of a dilemma where she was only digging herself a deeper hole. It was obvious, though, she didn't want his help.

Ben decided a graceful exit was best. He had no interest in witnessing the impending carnage. "Suit yourself, Sam, but don't say I didn't warn you. I think I'll have that dance I promised your mother. Good luck."

Black brought Sam back to focus. "Now that your husband has deserted you on your wedding day, would you care to entertain us with your thoughts?" The senator smelled blood, and he was intent on going for the kill, convinced Sam would support Sanders and give the senator the chance to cut both of them down to size.

Sam began, "I've only voted in one presidential election in my life. As a senior at Stanford, I never had time to think too much about the political process. Stanford doesn't give business majors the leisure to think about politics. We're there to learn economics and business, not political science. I will say this, however. Listening to the two of you, I think politics is not much different from basic business. Two sides square off for their self-interests and eventually come to a compromise serving their mutual needs but not necessarily the needs of the business community as a whole. For example, it may make a lot of sense for two giant corporations to merge and achieve great efficiencies. It may even bring down the costs of goods to consumers. But in the long run, it may destroy competition and, by destroying competition, stifle innovation and raise barriers to entry for new market participants. Most businessmen—and apparently most politicians—seem to have the short-sighted view on both sides of the aisle, as you politicians like to say."

Both Sanders and Black looked stunned. A few more guests started to gather around the trio. Sam continued: "The issue has nothing to do with youth being disillusioned with government. I really don't know if we are or not. I can't speak for my generation. No one can, particularly you or Mr. Sanders. I hope you both forgive me, but however much I respect you both as people and businessmen, you are presumptuous to think you know how my generation feels—or worse, to think we all behave as one. If I am disillusioned, it is not with government but with the inability of Democrats and Republicans to reach agreement on basic policy. Government has become a business run amok in claptrap and self-interests. To tell you both the truth, I don't much care whether we have a Democrat or Republican in the White House. I just want someone with fresh ideas. Someone who will cut through the debate and bring the two sides together. If government continues as it is, we will have nothing but a stalemate while the competition passes us by. It's really a simple matter of good business. What Washington is doing is bad business. Now if you'll excuse me, I must return to the guests. I still owe a lot of thank yous. Please carry on, gentlemen, and when you've found the answer, let me know. We could all use it." Sam took a gracious exit.

My God, thought Black as Sam walked away. *She won the debate.*

He didn't know he never had a chance. Sanders was equally taken aback. This youngster had just shut up a US senator and a prominent attorney with a two-minute colloquy, leaving before either of them could respond. And she did it with poise and great aplomb. Both were impressed, although a little bruised.

After the reception Sam and Ben didn't speak about the incident with Black and Sanders. Sam knew Black had talked with Ben about it, but Ben was not volunteering anything from the conversation, and Sam wasn't asking. It was their wedding night, and both had other things in mind.

Chapter Eighteen

I'll rock you in your cradle until you sleep
I'll hold you in my arms whenever you weep
I'll chase away your fears
I'll wipe away your tears
I'll never let you go
Without a good-bye
And you'll always have my love
Until the day I die.
Sam's poem written for Jeremy, February 24, 1986.

February 24, 1979
Stanford University Hospital

This Lamaze stuff is a whole lot of bullshit.

Sam lay in the maternity ward of Stanford University Hospital. There she was, in the middle of her MBA studies, having a baby just after starting her new classes for the winter semester. Ben was no help. He'd become so preoccupied with his job and Black's constant attacks on Democrats that he missed most of the Lamaze classes. Barbara Summers "subbed" for him. Nothing could have been more absurd than having someone sub for you in a Lamaze class. When the time came, Sam thought it was like going to the second-string rookie when you needed a home run in the ninth.

Or something like that.

Sam was having difficulty keeping focused. She was in pain, not sure she'd made the right choice with natural childbirth. She should have done what her mother did: get knocked out and wake up with a baby. The only moron right now, as far as Sam was concerned, was herself for putting up with this pain. She felt another contraction coming on, barely ten minutes from the last one. She tensed up in anticipation of the pain.

"I guess I should have attended more of the classes. I really feel lost here on how to help you," Ben volunteered.

"No kidding, Sherlock," Sam responded through the increasing pain. "You're no help right now. To tell you the truth, I'm not sure it would have mattered. This hurts so much. All the training in the world wouldn't help. Oh God, here it comes."

The pain was excruciating, and each contraction was worse than the last. At least it seemed that way to Sam.

Puff, puff, blow. Puff, puff blow. Shit, this Lamaze stuff just doesn't work.

"Is there anything I can do to help?" Ben felt helpless. In reality, he was useless at the moment.

"No. Just stay with me. And don't let me forget how painful this is. Make sure I don't do this again. One child is enough. We'll adopt any others you want."

Ben tried to lighten the mood. "I read someplace that as soon as a baby is born, a mother's attitude changes, and she's ready for another. If true, women are totally out of touch with reality. If you only want to have one child, I can see why. Let me get the doctor to see if there is anything he can do to help."

Sam was comfortable again. She knew in a few minutes the pain would be back. Somehow she had to overcome it, but she had no way of knowing how. What would her mother have done? Grin and bear it, probably.

But Mom took the easy way out. I should have listened to her.

Ben came back with the doctor.

"Sam," said the doctor, "I understand you're in quite a bit of pain. Your screams did not go unheard down the hall."

Good. I hope I kept everyone awake.

"You have some options," the doctor explained, as clinical as ever. "We can wait and let nature take its course. My guess is you're less than two hours away from giving birth. Second, if you want, I can give you some medication intravenously that will ease the pain and relax your muscles, but that may slow the process, and I'd rather not do that. The baby is in fine shape, and the pain is not going to kill you. Drugs may make you feel better, but they're not necessarily good for the baby. Lastly, we can perform an epidural. You may remember when we spoke about that. If you want one, we inject an anesthetic in your lower back that numbs the nerves. But we cannot make childbirth painless with an epidural. We have to let it wear off as we get closer so you can help us by pushing when we need you to. Otherwise, we may have to use forceps to deliver the baby. And while forceps are not generally a problem, the more we depend on apparatus than nature, the greater the potential risks."

What? Why is he even offering me an option that would hurt my baby?

Sam wanted to tell Dr. Green his biological apparatus must have also left off some of his brain as well. She was beginning to dislike this man.

"The decision is yours, Sam."

Decision, my ass.

Sam determined then she would go to a female obstetrician in the future. Preferably one who had ten kids.

She virtually jumped out of the bed on the next contraction. She was not doing well with the pain, and it made her angry. She realized this was her battle, and all the propaganda about Lamaze and having your husband there to help was a load of crap. Giving birth was clearly something very alone for a woman. She asked Green to give her an epidural.

Green returned and began to fill a syringe. Another doctor entered the room.

"Wait. I don't want it. I've come this far, and I'll see it through. I doubt if I'll die. And if I do, I'm certain Ben will sue your ass off. So let's stick to the original plan."

I'm not taking the easy way out.

"Are you sure? It won't hurt the baby."

What? Now you're in a hurry?

"Sorry, Doc. You'll have to wait to tee off. I'm going to have my baby on nature's schedule and on my own terms."

I can do this alone.

"Very well. To tell you the truth, my golf game hasn't been good lately anyway." Sam didn't appreciate the humor. "Hang in there. It will be over before you know it."

It took four hours, not two. After three hours, Ben suggested reconsidering the epidural. Sam responded she'd have no part of it. Ben observed that her stubborn streak might someday come to bite her.

When it was over and Sam held young Jeremy in her arms, his body still covered with her blood, she forgot the pain. Jeremy left her amazed. How she could have created this little creature was more than she could comprehend. It hurt when they took him away to clean him up. She missed him already.

CHAPTER NINETEEN

This is what government must do: ensure equal rights, not special rights to well-connected interest groups in Washington or in our state capitals.
Speech in acceptance of nomination, Convention Center, Memphis, Tennessee, July 27, 2016.

June 5, 1980
Stanford University

Graduating with an MBA was quite an affair. Stanford made sure graduate degrees came with pomp and circumstance. Ben convinced the dean that when Sam came to the podium to get her MBA diploma, Ben would hand it to her as a surprise. While rarely done at Stanford, Ben was a well-known professor, and even the dean wasn't about to disagree with him. Indeed, when Ben asked the dean if he could give Sam her diploma when she earned her bachelor's degree in 1978, the dean said no. But Ben refused to give up and the dean, weary of the never-ending harangue from Ben, put up no battle when it came to the MBA.

Sam didn't know Ben had arranged his little surprise, and when he handed her the diploma, her tears were spontaneous. It was also the first time a graduate kissed the professor giving her a diploma. If Sam had her way, it would have been more than a kiss. As it was, it was clear to everyone the kiss was a serious one indeed.

The day was glorious—eighty degrees with a light breeze under a cloudless sky. The quadrangle was awash with the traditional black gowns, hoods, and tassels of the graduating students. The professors' robes were replete with their ceremonial vestments denoting the many degrees they held. It was like a costume party.

The speeches were inspiring, although a bit predictable. Sam regretted she did not have the opportunity to speak. This time she didn't graduate at the top of her class. She did well, but as a student-mother, the pressure was crushing. She was proud of how well she had done.

Sam had already accepted a position at the International Monetary Fund in Washington, giving her a chance to be closer to home. Ben had arranged a teaching position at Georgetown University. He was sure he'd get some lucrative consulting fees from fat-cat politicians in Washington as well. Not that it mattered. At this point Ben had managed to amass quite a fortune from their investments, and neither of them needed to work for the money. Sam knew they had money, but the truth was she didn't realize just how much they had. It wasn't that Ben kept it from her. She could see whatever financial records she wanted. It just didn't interest her. Ben took care of it, and that was fine with Sam. She had other things she wanted to do.

At a small party in their Stanford apartment that night, Sam and Ben celebrated the day. It was curious to people who knew their wealth why Sam and Ben lived in such a simple apartment. But it was close to campus and convenient. With two bedrooms, it was fine for the three of them, and besides, it was easy to keep clean. While they did have a babysitter each day to take care of Jeremy, Sam refused to hire a cleaning lady. She felt it inappropriate for a Stanford professor to carry on that way. Ben didn't care. He wouldn't have known the difference between a dirty and a clean apartment anyway.

Senator Black was at their party. He had delivered a speech at graduation after receiving an honorary degree. Over the years Sam had come to dislike Black as a politician, but did find some of his political positions appealing. She also felt President Reagan's policies were on target in other ways. The truth was, discussing politics bored her. But with Black in the room, it was unavoidable.

"Congratulations, Sam. Are you ready to enter the real world?"

Why was it even a compliment from Black rubbed Sam the wrong way?

"Thanks. But living with Ben has given me just about as much touch with the real world as I want. I've decided to take a job as an analyst with the IMF. And God knows the IMF couldn't be further from the real world!"

Her attempt at humor hadn't hit the mark with Black. Maybe he'd rather hear a sexist joke or ethnic slur. Black was noted for this dark sense of humor. Sam assumed you needed one to survive in politics.

"The world needs more young executives like you, Sam. I'm sure you'll set the IMF on its ear in no time. Maybe you can help them figure out what to do with all their third-world debt. It's eventually going to crush them."

"Senator Black, I'm not sure they'll listen to me just yet. I don't even know what area I'll be working in. We go through a six-week training period first. It's as though I have to go to school again. That part I'm not looking forward to. But like Jeremy, I guess I have to crawl before I walk."

Black smiled. "Speaking of Jeremy, how will you take care of him? Are you and Ben going to finally part with some of your riches and hire a nanny?"

That's none of your damn business, Senator.

"Ben and I have been discussing that. My mother has volunteered to move in with us if we get a large enough place. Ben likes the idea, but I'm not so certain. I'm not sure Mother can handle it—or I can handle Mother."

"So you're not sure you want your mother around so much?"

You don't know my mother.

Sam really disliked Black. He was a pompous oaf; but he was also right. There was no way Sam was going to have her mother live with them. She wasn't about to come home to Mom each night after a day at the IMF. This time they would have a full-time, live-in nanny. She just had to figure out how to save face with her mother. Ben was no help and said anything Sam decided was fine with him. At one point he'd even volunteered to be a Mr. Mom and stay home, watching Jeremy and their investments—an attractive idea to him, but something Sam would have nothing to do with. While she loved Ben with all her heart, the thought of him bringing up a child was frightening. Jeremy might become the youngest financial genius in history, but he'd grow up the sloppiest human on earth, and Sam would have to pick up after two men in her life. One was enough.

"You may be right, Senator," Sam responded. "I don't think she's up to it. She'll be living close enough to visit as often as she likes. We plan on buying a house close to Crownsville, where Mom lives. It will be nice to be close to family again. As you know, Ben doesn't have any family, and I think it will do us both good to get out of the rarefied air of Northern California and back to basics in good old Maryland."

Black nodded, "Yeah, but think of all those jokes you'll have to put up with living near the crime capital of the world, Baltimore, Maryland," laughed Black. "And how can anyone forget the beautiful sights along the beltway? Baltimore is back to basics all right. Be smart. Get Ben to part with a few more bucks and get a place in the district. If you have to move east, Washington is the most exciting place to be. Everywhere else is like a graveyard when it comes to being aware of what is happening around us."

"Maybe," said Sam, "but for a baby, the city would be overwhelming. And it's a dangerous place."

Black didn't hide his feeling that Sam was naïve. "Don't get caught up in the press you read. Sure, Washington's tough. But it's not as unsafe as they say it is. Shoot, Houston's a lot worse, and Los Angeles is no better. No, if you've got to go east, go where the action is."

"Senator, in case you've forgotten, we're only moving east because I got the job with the IMF. We're lucky Ben got his appointment at Georgetown, but whether he had gotten it or not, we were going. As for his political aspirations, you know he has none. He wouldn't want to get himself mired in lunacy. He prefers to tell the politicians how to do it. When they don't listen, he can tell them he told them so. Don't you think he's good at that?" Sam would have liked to end the question with "you twit."

Black backed away, knowing he may have crossed the line with Sam. "I apologize if I offended your feminist sensibilities. I seem to do that more often than I'd like. Yes, indeed, you are going east to pursue your career. I just think a talent like Ben's is a sin to waste. I only wish I could motivate him to get into political life. He's got the brains, humor, and looks it takes. And besides, he's got good ideas. And money. Maybe we should figure out how to get you in politics and have the best of both worlds—an aggressive and talented businesswoman backed by a brilliant economist and thinker. How about it, Sam?"

"In your dreams, Senator."

Politics. What a joke.

No, she was going to make her mark in business. Sam had no interest in chasing the kinds of rainbows that hypnotized people like Black. Besides, she stunk at lying, and lying was something a successful politician needed to be able to do with aplomb. In fact, she believed the great failing of successful politicians was that after a while they started believing their own lies. By the time they reached influential office, they had lost all touch with reality, consumed by their lies and hunger for power. Sam would leave her speechmaking for shareholder meetings and conventions, not political rallies.

Black refused to take that as a conclusion. "We'll see. I think you're more interested in politics than you want to admit. Either way, though, I'm sure the IMF won't know what hit them. And change is something they sorely need."

Ben finally arrived to save the moment. Sam was desperate for a way to leave the conversation.

"Well, since neither of you are bleeding, I guess I've come in time," volunteered Ben. "Might I risk my life and ask you what you've been talking about?"

Sam took Ben's hand. "Senator Black was telling me how we must move to Washington, buy a big apartment, and hire a live-in nanny. If we move to Baltimore, the senator figures you, Jeremy, and I are destined to be together less with my commute and long hours. The sad part about it, Ben, is he may be right. Maybe we should move to the district."

Ben seemed shocked. "If we do, your mother will never move in. She won't leave Maryland."

"I know." Sam had found her way to save face. She just hated the fact Black gave her the opportunity.

Chapter Twenty

Equal rights for our workers. When we began the last century, we were a country in the beginnings of industrialization, often putting our workforce in conditions no better than sweatshops. Our unions changed all that and brought about a field of fair play. While there has certainly been abuse over the years, the concept of collective bargaining is sound and right and something we cannot and will not abandon.
Speech in acceptance of nomination, Convention Center, Memphis, Tennessee, July 27, 2016.

August 12, 1980
Arlington, Virginia

Sam found just what Senator Black had ordered, but not in the district. She and Ben bought a beautiful colonial-style home in Arlington, Virginia, less than fifteen miles from the center of Washington and even further from Crownsville. It had three bedrooms, three baths, a full-sized kitchen, maid's quarters, living room, dining room, and den. It was on a dead-end street in one of the most desirable neighborhood in Arlington. At a cost of $600,000, it was even a bargain. They paid cash, and for the first time, Sam understood just how much money they had and how good Ben was at managing it. Ben didn't believe in tying up debt on home mortgages. He only tied up money when it gave either an immediate return or was a wise long-term investment. Ben never trusted the real estate market where ready sellers and buyers were too hard to find. *God bless him,* thought Sam. After living in Crownsville for two months with her mother, Sam was more than pleased they found the house.

Sam hired a decorator to help furnish their new home. She knew she was being extravagant, but she and Ben enjoyed making their new home something special. She and Ben had simple tastes and stayed with a traditional colonial look, buying most of the furniture from a local Maryland furniture store where Sam's mother knew the designers. In many ways the house looked like Sam's home in Crownsville. It also had the same warmth and comfortable feel.

After seemingly unending interviews, they also found a nanny. Caitlin Brady, age nineteen, moved in on the first day Sam and Ben took up residence in their new home.

Caitlin was from Northern Ireland and wanted out of the political mess. Her childhood made for fascinating and poignant conversations. Caitlin's only brother was the victim of a car bomb in Belfast, and her parents had died years earlier, leaving her to be brought up by an aunt who, while a caring person, was not up to the task.

Caitlin's first love was children. She didn't want to rush her life or make any school or career decisions just yet. She wanted time to breathe and relax, something she certainly never was able to do in Northern Ireland. While it appalled Sam's mother that a nineteen-year-old who didn't know her own future should have Jeremy's daytime affairs in her hands, Sam and Ben had a good feeling about Caitlin.

Ben started at Georgetown, teaching a graduate course on economic theory. He also landed a consulting contract with Salomon Brothers, a relatively small investment house just beginning to offer something called junk bonds through a hotshot broker named Michael Milken. Sam met Milken at a party in New York City but was not impressed. She thought he was sleazy and not to be trusted. Ben thought the same and reassured Sam that he wasn't dealing with Milken much.

Sam's job at the IMF was more challenging than she had originally thought. They put her in the International Investment Group, and she worked for some of the highest-placed executives at the Fund. While they hardly noticed her, she learned new things every day. She marveled at how little the academic life had taught her, something she loved to bring up with Ben whenever she could. She wondered how Ben knew so much having stayed in academics. She was quietly learning, and that suited her just fine.

A play at the Kennedy Center or a concert at a local venue was a regular Wednesday-night outing, usually with friends. On the occasion when Michael and Barbara Summers came to town, the four would dine at the Four Seasons. On weekends, Sam and Ben—with Jeremy and usually Caitlin in tow—took off to the Virginia wine country in the fall and spring or the Outer Banks in the summer. Winters were usually spent at home. Neither Sam nor Ben liked snow.

Sam was now assigned to Richard Lawner's team, a group managing the Fund's Eastern European loan portfolio. The assignment gave Sam the opportunity to travel internationally. It was a heady time taking the Concorde to Paris or London, doing a deal over a couple of days, and returning the same way. She was dealing with some of the top investment bankers and lawyers in the world as they cobbled together loans and financial deals for developing countries, and she liked the company she kept—Barings, Warburg, and Lehman Brothers, to name a few. Every day she learned a little more about the investment world, and when she returned home, she had her own private lessons from Ben, always helping to keep her head attached.

Sam and Ben kept up the tradition of their yearly trip to the Gin House, and October 1984 was one of the best trips yet. Michael and Barbara joined them after just taking HospiData, a private equity-backed venture they'd started shortly after graduating, through an IPO that made them millions. The four couldn't have been more excited. Ben entertained them with private classes in economics every day while the four sipped their rum punches under the palms.

Everything Sam and Ben had counted on was coming true. What they hadn't counted on was Sam getting pregnant again.

She was furious with herself when she found out. She knew exactly when it happened. It was at the Gin House on October 24, 1984. She and Ben had a few too many rum punches in the afternoon and shared a bottle of champagne with Michael and Barbara over dinner, followed by Benedictine and brandy to finish off the night.

Sam didn't take birth control pills. Not that she was against birth control; she just didn't like what she'd read about the side effects. So they either watched her time each month or used a condom.

That night Ben didn't use a condom, and Sam wasn't sober enough to figure the timing. While she wondered about it the next morning, her concern faded with the tranquil weather and a new batch of rum punches they all drank to ward off their hangovers.

It was on November 19 when she first felt sick in the morning. She knew the feeling from her months carrying Jeremy and immediately went to her gynecologist, Ruth Meyers. Sam had kept her vow when Jeremy was born, and her physician was now a woman. At ten thirty the next morning, Sam called and received the official word from Dr. Meyers.

"Are congratulations in order, Sam?" asked Ruth.

"I'm not sure. I know Ben will be happy, but this really doesn't fit in now. I just got promoted at the Fund and have been doing a lot of travel. We didn't plan for this."

Dr. Meyers picked right up on the unasked question. "Well, why don't you tell Ben and relax on it for a while. There are always alternatives."

"I know," replied Sam, "but I've never had to deal with the issue personally before. I just never thought I'd be a woman actually thinking about having an abortion."

Dr. Meyers tried to keep Sam focused. "Until you have to make the decision, no woman knows how difficult it is. If you like, I can give you the name of a counseling group. They're really quite good and don't necessarily try to convince you to do anything. They just talk you through it. Just give me a call."

"Thank you."

Sam hung up the phone. The next call would be difficult. She tried to dial Ben but hung up time and time again. She decided to wait until the two were home that night. She was leaving for Paris in the morning and could use the afternoon to think about it.

Lunch that day was difficult. It was with lawyers from Skadden Arps, usually a meeting Sam looked forward to attending. She ordered her usual glass of Chardonnay. She took one sip and remembered she was pregnant. The realization her life had just gone off track from her professional plans brought a knot to her stomach and a focus that could not have been further away from the subjects discussed at the table. She was thankful no one called on her to contribute.

Back at the office, Janet Rush, a coworker on Lawner's team, asked Sam if she was all right. "You seemed out of it at lunch today." Janet had been with the Fund more than seven years and knew Lawner better than anyone. Some said Janet knew Lawner in more than a business way, but Sam had no way of knowing if the rumors were true. Lawner, married, had three kids and never showed any attraction to Janet in public. Besides, Janet had become a good friend to Sam, and she really didn't care who she was sleeping with.

Sitting at her desk, Sam responded: "I'm pregnant. I just found out before lunch. It really hit me when I realized I couldn't have my wine. I was out of the conversation from that point on."

Janet sat down across from Sam, letting out an uncomfortable sigh. "Why do I get the feeling you're not too happy about this development? I gather it wasn't planned."

"It's just not good right now. Everything is in order as planned, and Ben and I are having the best time of our lives. Jeremy is adorable, and Caitlin is a godsend. Ben loves his teaching job at Georgetown and is really having fun consulting with Salomon. He thinks he's even teaching them a thing or two, although they won't listen to him on this junk bond business."

I just don't want this baby. Not now.

"Whoa, Sam. Being pregnant isn't the end of the world, you know. Shoot, I'm not even married yet. You've got a great head start on me."

"I'm sorry, Janet, no offense intended. I don't mean to say I never want another baby. Just not now. I'm starting to make a name for myself at the Fund, and a leave now will definitely hurt me. You and I both know that."

Janet nodded in agreement. "True. I doubt Lawner, the chauvinist pig he is, will hold on to you very long after you take your maternity leave. Oh, there'll be another job for you when you get back, but it will probably be loan analysis in third-world nations and sub-Saharan Africa since they'll figure you're intent on breeding rather than banking." Janet could always make Sam laugh.

The laughter helped, but what Janet said was true. Lawner had asked Sam on more than one occasion how large a family Sam intended to have. She assured him one child was all she and Ben could handle. She'd believed it when she said it. Now he'd think she lied all along.

It made her angry. The law she thought was on her side was really no help at all. Janet was right. The Fund would make sure there was another job for her when she returned, but the good old boys would peg her for a family girl, not a career woman. She'd be finished. And they'd get away with it.

"Look," suggested Janet, "why don't you take the rest of the day off. I'll cover for you. If Lawner asks, I'll tell him you have a case of PMS and no one would be safe around you. He'll buy that. Go home and have yourself a good cry. Deal with it in the morning."

Caitlin and Jeremy were out when Sam got home. It was a cool day with a little rain but a nice wind, so Caitlin had told Sam and Ben that morning she and Jeremy were going to the park to fly his kite. That worked out just fine for Sam.

After packing for her flight to Paris the next day, Sam called Ben at Georgetown and left a message with his secretary. Ben was teaching his last class when she called. He wasn't scheduled to be at Salomon until five, so he had some time to kill between appointments.

It delighted Ben when Sam called. It was rare treat. But when he saw she called from home, he became concerned. Then he remembered she was going to Paris the next day. Dinner at a local bistro in Arlington had become a regular event the night before Sam went on a business trip. Ben figured she went home to pack and wanted him to meet her at the apartment rather than the restaurant, as was the usual plan. He called Solomon and cancelled his appointment before he called Sam back.

"Hi, babe. Decide to pack early for the City of Lights?"

"Ben, can you please come home? I have to talk to you."

Ben's voice rose with concern. "Are you OK? Is it Jeremy? What's the matter?" It was not like Sam to talk that way.

"Everyone is fine, Ben. It's just really important I see you now." She broke into tears and hung up the phone.

Ben paid the cab an extra ten to get him home fast.

Ben froze when Sam told him, knowing by her emotional state the news did not please her. Ben, on the other hand, had a hard time concealing his delight. He had been an only child and wanted a sibling for Jeremy. He hadn't pushed because he figured he and Sam had plenty of time to plan for it.

"I don't want this baby, Ben. Not now." They were sitting on the couch, Sam's head on Ben's shoulder. Sam told Ben about Janet's prediction that Sam would return to the IMF to review third-world country loans in countries probably exporting diseases more than natural resources. This time it wasn't funny.

"I don't know what to say," replied Ben. "I know the choice is yours, and I'll support whatever choice you make, but I think this is too emotional a time for you to decide anything. To hell with the IMF. You don't need that job, and we'll find another position with someone who understands a working mother. Besides, Caitlin is certainly capable of helping out. She's even said herself she has time on her hands."

"No," Sam replied firmly. "I've decided. I want an abortion, and I am taking care of it as soon as I get back from Paris." Sam knew her decision was selfish and, in her heart, wrong. But she simply could not face an interruption in her career.

Ben realized it would do him no good arguing with Sam at that moment. Further arguments would have to wait, but Ben was set against an abortion. He was beside himself, knowing how much he wanted another child but wanting to support Sam all the same. But she was wrong. He resolved to put off any more discussion until she returned to Arlington. Maybe after five days in France, Sam would change her mind. When Sam had time to reflect after a rushed decision, she often did.

That night they skipped dinner.

Chapter Twenty-One

Enjoy Paris. You are my world. There is nothing we can't work out together. I love you.
Note left in Sam's luggage by Ben, November 21, 1984.

November 23, 1984
Paris, France

Ben had no way of knowing if his plan would work. He only knew he wanted Sam to know she could make her decision knowing Ben loved her, and things would work out fine if she decided to have the baby. He was even ready to solemnly swear he'd attend all the Lamaze classes this time.

Ben was not a seasoned international traveler. He had heard of Boyer's Chateau Les Crayeres in Reims—France's Champagne District—from Sam, who had a business meeting there a year or so earlier. Sam told Ben someday they'd have to spend a night there and feast on a three-star Michelin meal at its restaurant, Le Jardin. But reservations took a month to get unless you were staying at the hotel for at least two nights, so Ben booked two nights just to get the dinner reservation. Janet Rush had helped Ben arrange it all. Janet told Lawner there was a very special occasion and he'd better not interfere. He agreed, knowing Janet would pay him for the favor in her own way or make it cost him more than it was worth. He could do without Sam for a day or two.

Ben was standing beside the limo as Sam came out of the bank, Lawner and Janet at her side.

"Madam, may I offer you a ride to dinner?"

Sam was stunned. She was also a little embarrassed since she was standing there with Lawner.

Sam looked confused. "What's going on, Ben?"

Lawner eased the tension. "It's all right. Janet told me you and Ben are celebrating something tonight. Enjoy yourselves. I'll see you back in Washington." Lawner and his entourage scurried away.

"I thought you might need a break from the rat race and would enjoy a weekend in France," said Ben, his soft eyes melting Sam's heart. "Besides, I was getting tired of TV dinners."

Sam dropped her bag and put her arms around Ben, telling him how much she loved him. It was her first happy moment in days.

"But why a limo, Ben?"

"It's a two-hour ride to Reims, and I didn't want to walk."

Chateau Les Crayeres describes itself as an elegant turn-of-the-twentieth-century residence run by the Boyers family. One critic described the property as a rare combination of a luxurious private palace with superb cuisine, charm, and warmth. It was converted into an exclusive hotel in 1972. The restaurant was added in 1973 and quickly rose to some of the highest praise in France. The chef and his wife tended to their guests like shepherds guarding their sheep. When you booked dinner, the table was yours for the night. You were never rushed. Nothing was too much for a guest to ask.

When the limo passed through the gate to the hotel, Ben immediately knew why it had fascinated Sam. The quarter-mile drive to the front entrance was lined with manicured pine trees. While the temperature was cold, the scenery was spellbinding.

A bellman met the car immediately and escorted Sam and Ben to the registration desk just inside the front entrance. It was classic European, with its intimately small frontage and the petite young lady tending to the task of registering their special guests. And that's precisely how a guest immediately felt: special.

Sam and Ben were shown to their own villa, one of six in the complex. With living quarters downstairs and the bedroom on the second floor, the room was something out of a storybook: rich fabrics and a smell that brought back memories of family and friends. Ben immediately knew he would add it as another annual pilgrimage along with the Gin House in St. Eustatius.

The porter had barely left before Sam came to Ben, put her arms around him, and gave him a long, deep kiss. The rest was always natural for the two. Lovemaking was something Sam and Ben never found routine. It was always a gentle adventure. Always fulfilling. This time especially so in such a romantic place.

When Sam awoke, it was already eight, and dinner was reserved for nine. She woke Ben, thinking jet lag had probably taken over and he'd not be much of a dinner companion. To her surprise Ben awoke refreshed, saying he didn't understand what all the fuss was about jet lag anyway.

Just wait, it will hit you soon enough.

She pictured Ben passing out in his pâté. The thought amused her.

Dinner was marvelous. The French had seized on a simple idea. They permitted a sampling of various items on the menu, giving guests the opportunity to try a variety of courses throughout the night. The price was high for the luxury but well worth it.

After a night of pâté, duck, lobster, and venison, Sam and Ben topped it off with a chocolate mousse unlike any they had ever had, served in the bar in the tradition of Le Jardin.

The bar was an experience in itself. Rich in green fabrics and mahogany, it had an English feel. But the food and service were decidedly French. While conversation over dinner centered on the meal, the talk during dessert was more to the point of why Ben came to France.

"Sam, I want you to know I'll support whatever decision you make about the baby. But I would be less than honest with you if I didn't tell you I hope you'll decide not to have an abortion. You're young, and a break now will not hurt your career. Shoot, the IMF isn't the end-all anyway."

Sam was not surprised by the sudden turn in the conversation, feeling it took the beauty of the evening down a few notches. But she knew it was coming and had prepared herself to respond. "I know how you feel, Ben. It's just not the time. I've got an agenda and want to keep to it. Maybe we can have another baby in a few years when I'm in a position to call my own shots. Right now is not a good time. Our hands are full with Jeremy and our careers. A new baby can wait."

Ben hadn't traveled thirty-eight hundred miles to give up so easily. "Our hands aren't full, Sam. We can afford it, and you should take some time off. Maybe even go back to school. Is the work at the Fund all that challenging? Sure, places like this are exotic. But I can't believe you find it fulfilling. You're working for a twit who is screwing one of your best friends, and who understands women in the workforce about as much as Jimmy Carter understood foreign affairs. Give it up. Even if you don't have the baby, go back to school. I don't know, maybe you should become a lawyer. I know it was never in your plans, but why not? You've always wanted to make a real difference, and you never will as a banker. Maybe as a lawyer you can. Being an investment banker just doesn't cut it. Investment bankers are becoming parasites with their junk bonds and leveraged deals. Sooner or later it's all going to implode. Get out now and find another way of leaving your mark on corporate America."

A lawyer?

Sam never thought about being a lawyer. "I don't know." Sam was more shocked by Ben's damnation of investment bankers than his desire for another child. "I'll admit the IMF has not fulfilled my wildest dreams, but I've learned a lot. And I'm certainly playing in the big leagues, something even you would admit is the only place to play. That's why having a baby doesn't fit right now. Neither does law school. Christ, the thought of studying for another exam runs shivers down my spine. I'm not ready for either the classroom or the maternity ward. For now I want the boardroom."

"Sam, will you at least go to counseling with me?" asked Ben. "This decision has more of an effect on me than you might think. The little life you're carrying is part of me, too. To take it now is to take a little of me. I love you, and I want to understand. I always thought of myself as an enlightened husband, someone who would never interfere with your personal decisions. I want to support whatever you do. But this decision has me stymied. With God's help, we created something between us. Letting it go is really hard for me."

Sam had never seen Ben so vulnerable. It scared her. It also reinforced why she loved him. He was a simple man who wore his heart on his sleeve. This time was no exception.

"OK, we'll go to counseling. Maybe I'll just become a homebound mother. Who knows? Maybe we'll have another mouth to feed."

Don't get your hopes up, Ben.

Ben smiled and raised his glass, "Here's to a hearty appetite."

They went to counseling. It was there that Sam was gently persuaded to the cause of the right-to-life movement, although she concluded the choice was for her and not something a politician in Washington should dictate. She was never sure if she would have come to the decision on her own, but she became certain in her own mind that her decision was right. As she came closer to term and felt the life within her, she often wondered how she could have ever considered abortion.

How could any woman consider it?

Chapter Twenty-Two

We have become a government of favors. A government of PACs and lobbyists. The good old boys' club. Well, I'm here to close that club.

Speech in acceptance of nomination, Convention Center, Memphis, Tennessee, July 27, 2016.

July 26, 1985
Johns Hopkins Hospital

This one made Jeremy's birth seem like a vacation. Ruth Meyers, Sam's obstetrician, put it in perspective. She was six hours into a very painful experience, one contraction after another, but no real progress. Meyers was considered among the top obstetricians in the nation with particular expertise in difficult deliveries.

"As we've known all along, Sam, the baby is large," Dr. Meyers explained. "That's common in second pregnancies. While we can deliver the baby naturally, there are risks in doing so. Or we can do a cesarean."

"What kind of risks?" Sam asked, petrified at the possible answer.

"Well, it's a bit technical but in layman's terms, with a large baby, delivery can sometimes become difficult. The baby's shoulders might get stuck behind the pubic bone if there's not enough room for a smooth path to delivery. At that point, we don't have too much time to deliver, and if it becomes problematic, we might have to break the baby's clavicle. If we do, it will heal. The worst scenario is an emergency cesarean if things go very wrong. An emergency cesarean will leave a much more noticeable scar since we probably won't be able to do a bikini cut if we have to cut vertically."

"I guess that means no more two-piece bathing suits," Sam tried to joke as the next contraction started.

"Maybe so," replied Meyers clinically, seeing no humor in the statement. "You've got maybe an hour or so to think about it, no longer. I'll leave you and Ben alone."

"What do you think, Ben?" asked Sam.

Ben tried to keep it light. "I never have liked the way other men look at you in bikinis anyway. So as far as I'm concerned, you should do whatever makes sense to you. How's that for a wimp response?"

"Ben, you'll never change. I was just about to say you're no help." Sam tried to laugh through the pain. "It looks like this baby's starting out as a challenge. I think I'd like to try it naturally. If things go wrong, I can always sacrifice my wardrobe. As long as Ruth knows it's her call in the end, I say we go with a natural birth. Is that OK with you?"

Ben seemed to be losing his patience. "I said the choice is yours, Sam, and I meant it."

The next contraction took Sam's humor away. Through the pain, she somehow managed to continue the conversation. "To tell you the truth, this whole affair was not really my choice, despite your insisting it was. While I don't regret our decision to have this baby, please don't patronize me with this 'your choice' stuff, Ben. You can't deny you were part of the decision, and I want you to be part of this decision as well." Even Sam was surprised by the harshness of her comment. She excused it as something caused by the contraction and not her heart.

"All right. Let's not argue about choices right now. I think either way is fine, although the safest way for the baby seems to be a cesarean and to not put you in an emergency situation. But I'm not going to tell you what to do. It's possible a natural delivery will go fine and your recovery will be better for it. And I suppose doctors today can handle any contingency." Ben's conversation and the next contraction weren't making Sam's decision any easier.

"Why is it," asked Sam through a grimace of pain, "in matters of personal choice you give me so little help? You always tell me the choice is mine. Do you think I ask you for advice because I don't want your opinion?" Sam was again surprised by the tone she was taking with Ben. It was not like them to let discussions become tense. The truth was Sam still had some resentment over the pressure Ben had applied to persuade Sam to have his baby. In Sam's now pain-induced logic, Ben turned a practical issue into a romantic adventure, making it impossible for Sam to apply the kind of logic she used in situations of choice. She was resigned that she made the right decision but felt tricked into it. She could see she'd also hit a nerve with Ben.

"Fine. If you want to push it, I think you should have a cesarean. It's safest for the baby and you."

"No," blurted Sam as the pain came again. "I'm doing it naturally. It's my body." Sam could see the frustration in Ben's expression. She could clearly see he wanted it to be over and done. So did she.

"What the hell's going on here, Sam?" replied Ben. "Is this some sophomoric way of taking revenge on me for pressuring you to have the baby? I don't think that's a healthy way to look at this."

Ben's remark took the air out of Sam's bravado. "It's not revenge. I'm sorry, Ben. I don't know what to do. I'm scared. Delivering babies is not one of my favorite pastimes. Pain is not a pleasurable experience, and I'd just like this to be over."

They both began to calm. "Sam, go ahead and try it naturally. Otherwise you'll think you compromised, and compromise is not in your nature. But be sure you're doing it because it's what you want."

Dr. Meyers returned, sensing the tension. "You're close, Sam. I just need to check some signs. I don't mean to interrupt."

"What is the full risk to the baby if things go wrong during a natural delivery?" Sam asked her.

"That's hard to say. The risk to you is possible complications from emergency surgery. That kind of surgery is not pleasant. As for the baby, there is some evidence that after a broken shoulder at birth, the baby's arm could develop Erb's palsy if we injure the nerves in the shoulder or arm. We can adjust our approach to minimize that possibility. But I cannot totally discount it. Many women have an uneventful delivery under these circumstances."

"But there is little risk to the baby?" Sam tried her best to stay focused as the next contraction began, each getting worse than the last.

"There is always a risk to the baby, but I need your decision."

You're about as helpful as my husband.

"These kinds of decision are always difficult, Sam. But I'm afraid you don't have much time left. If we're going to do a cesarean, we've got to do some preparations."

Decision time.

"No," concluded Sam. "We're going to do this naturally."

Things seemed to happen fast once the decision was made. Sam was rushed to the delivery room. The labor was more intense than with Jeremy, and Sam refused drugs, just as she did her first time. It was her way of defiance against something she couldn't identify. Giving in to drugs was a defeat in her eyes. She certainly thought her father would have never accepted such a cop-out. It was really quite a paradox. Here she hated pain, yet refused to do anything for it.

Ben stood to the right of Sam's head, and Ruth announced everything as it happened.

"Things look good. Here's the head. Don't push too hard. It looks good so far."

So my decision was right.

Sam felt rewarded. She started to relax.

"Hold it, Sam, DON'T PUSH." Meyer's voice strained as she barked orders to the other attendants. Sam's eyes were riveted on Ben, suddenly filled with fear.

"The shoulders are broad, and the room is very tight. Sam, try to relax."

Relax? Are you serious?

Ben took Sam's hand and whispered something to her Sam didn't hear. She was petrified. Meyers was barking out orders neither Sam nor Ben could understand, laced with more than a few four-letter words.

"OK. OK. You're doing fine now, Sam. Just push a little and try and relax," Meyers reassured her. She then told her assistants in the OR, in what Sam thought was a very clinical manner, "Make sure we check the clavicle as soon as we can." As if on cue, the baby was born.

It took their new daughter no time to start screaming—and for good reason, being born with what might be a broken collarbone. While they say babies don't feel pain at birth, Sam didn't believe that for a moment. When Sam looked up, the appearance of the baby's arm shocked her. It seemed as if it hung oddly by her side. She regretted looking up. Ruth quickly wrapped the baby tightly in a blanket, making movement impossible. The baby stopped crying and calmed down. Ruth gave the baby to Sam, explaining the baby's collarbone, if broken, would heal fine. She did not believe there was any nerve damage. Everyone would just have to be gentle when picking her up for a couple of months.

The rush of emotion Sam felt was indescribable. She started to cry. So did Ben and just about everyone else in the delivery room.

"I'm sorry I hurt you," she said as her first words to her new daughter.

"You didn't hurt the baby," assured Meyers. "If anyone did, I did. And I promise you the baby will be fine and never remember. One of God's greatest gifts to us is our lack of memory of our births. Your baby is no different."

Little bubbles came out of the baby's mouth as Sam held her. She simply stared at the baby in wonder how she could have even considered not having her. She vowed to herself this baby would have all the love she needed from Sam.

Ben touched the baby's forehead, reminding Sam he was there too.

"I'm sorry if I gave you grief earlier, Ben. Isn't she beautiful?"

"Yes, she is. Thank you for understanding me."

Meyers interrupted. "I've got some cleanup to do here, so let's have the baby back and get this show on the road." She instructed the delivery nurse to get the baby to the pediatric orthopedist stat.

Ben asked, "Why the orthopedist?"

He and Sam would never know that but for Meyers's years of experience in difficult births, the baby would have been paralyzed for life. Many of her four-letter words were directed more at Sam for what she thought was a selfish decision than they were for her assistants or the difficulties during birth.

"We want the orthopedist to take a look just to be safe, Ben. Don't worry. For now, congratulations to both of you. What's her name?"

"Amanda Caitlin."

Chapter Twenty-Three

Even equal rights for the prosperous and rich. We cannot deny that the prosperous and rich support much of our country's industry, arts, and culture. If we increase their tax burdens, fail to defend their rights, or continue to demean their success, we only hurt ourselves. There is no union for the rich, but there are those who would seek to take advantage of their generosity. William Boetcker, a Presbyterian minister, explained it best in 1942. Allow me to repeat his words, "You cannot bring about prosperity by discouraging thrift, strengthen the weak by weakening the strong, help the poor man by destroying the rich, further the brotherhood of man by inciting class hatred, build character and courage by taking away man's initiative and independence, help small men by tearing down big men, lift the wage earner by pulling down the wage payer, keep out of trouble by spending more than your income, establish security on borrowed money, or help men permanently by doing for them what they will not do for themselves." Washington needs to learn those lessons. But we cannot ignore those among the prosperous who instead of feeding society, feed upon it. There can be no more robber barons and raiders who plunder, not to save businesses but to personally profit at the cost of jobs, families, and homes.

Speech in acceptance of nomination, Convention Center, Memphis, Tennessee, July 27, 2016.

August 27, 1985
George Washington University Law School

It was shortly after Amanda was born that Sam warmed up to the idea of going back to school. Being a mother at home was beginning to appeal to Sam, but she didn't want to feel she stopped advancing or challenging herself in the business world. She desperately wanted to find success as both mother and executive.

Law school appealed to her because it gave her alternatives upon graduation. The so-called "mommy track" had just come into vogue at some of the big law firms. Sam thought she'd have a chance to decide whether a full- or part-time position suited Ben and their lifestyle when she graduated. She figured she could always hang out her own shingle, not realizing at the time how naive she was.

She hoped to get into Georgetown. But even with Ben's contacts, it didn't work out. She and Ben joked she didn't make the cut because of some unsaid policy at the law school banning spouses of faculty in the student body. The truth was there was a political motivation of sorts in rejecting Sam. Ben had become somewhat controversial within the business community and on the faculty. His public stance against the junk bond business and resignation from his consulting position at Salomon made all the morning talk shows, only adding to his reputation as a maverick, something Georgetown loathed on its faculty. While not pleased, there was little Georgetown could do about it. Ben had tenure. If Ben or Sam ever knew how political her rejection was, Ben would have probably resigned from Georgetown in protest.

She was accepted without any problem into George Washington University, prestigious in its own right. Centered in the historic Foggy Bottom neighborhood of the district, it was a beautiful setting. In the afternoons the neighborhood filled with strollers, and street vendors sold watches, ice cream, and unfortunately, drugs. It was all part of the Washington scene. At night the area became illuminated with one building after another shining in the light. During some of the winter months when it snowed, Ben and Sam loved to stroll along Georgetown's cobblestone streets and enjoy the area's warmth. It was one of the few places still safe to walk in after dark, largely because university police closely patrolled the area.

The school itself was sterile in appearance and quite cold in its atmosphere. The experience proved to be far less enlightening for Sam than college. While she was certainly learning interesting—and at times, complex—principles, it was all too easy compared to Ben's economics classes or Stanford's MBA program. Sam had little trouble and made law review in her second year.

It was during the first semester of her second year she met Zachary Watts.

Watts was an adjunct professor, teaching an advanced course in securities. Adjunct professors are lawyers who practice full time, usually in leading Washington law firms, and who teach courses in the evenings. Watts's course was an elective Sam took in her second year, even though it was generally restricted to third-year students. She petitioned the dean to let her take the course, noting her MBA more than satisfied the prerequisites she needed. She also wanted to take the course to get a better understanding of securities law so she could discuss the securities business with Ben on more even ground. She hated the way she felt personally intimidated by Ben's control of any conversation relating to securities. He didn't intentionally dominate the conversation; it was just that his obvious grasp of the situation was so overwhelming, anyone around him tended to listen in silence, realizing there was little they could add. It was usually Sam who tried, each time receiving a clear, albeit polite lesson in economics. She envied the day when she could truly go toe to toe with Ben on securities issues. She thought Watts's course would help. Besides, Watts had a reputation as one of the better adjunct faculty. Too many of them were not the best instructors, however proficient they might be as practicing attorneys. Watts was an exception.

Unfortunately, Watts's course bored Sam, and she again felt unfulfilled. She chalked it off as just another disappointment in her law school experience, as she had come to call her little adventure at GW. She refused to call it an education.

The day she first met Watts outside the classroom, Sam and Janet Rush were having lunch at a popular local pub on a cold February day. Snow was in the forecast, and it was one of those days portending harsh weather with a sky of overcast gray. You felt the cold down to your soul no matter how many layers of clothing you wore. The Irish coffees helped. Sam and Janet were in the middle of a conversation about the IMF when interrupted by Watts.

Watts approached the two of them. "I'm sorry. I hope I'm not intruding, but I wondered if I might ask you something, Mrs. Harrison."

"Oh, hello, Professor Watts," replied Sam. "Janet, this is Zachary Watts, a professor I have at the law school. He taught the securities law course I told you about. Professor Watts, this is my friend Janet Rush. Janet is with the IMF. Please sit down."

Watts waived away the waiter, declining anything to drink. Janet's eyes couldn't leave Watts.

Where have you been all my life, sweetcakes?

"Actually, I'm a vice president at the Fund."

"A second vice president," corrected Sam.

Watts smiled, sensing Janet's need for attention. "Whatever title you have, Miss Rush, working at the IMF can't be all wrong. What area are you working in?"

"I'm in Richard Lawner's international finance group."

"Then it's a small world indeed. I know Dick well. I do some legal work for him and the Fund on occasion when they run into government roadblocks. Please tell him I said hello." Watts sat down.

Sam piped up, "I thought you were a securities lawyer, Professor, not a lobbyist."

Watts smiled. "How about we call each other by our first names? I'm not much older than either of you. I go by Zach to my friends and colleagues. And in reply to your comment, Sam, the truth is in private practice, you do a little of everything. Securities law and lobbying go hand in hand more often than you might think. Besides, it's always fun trying to root out obstructions to business within our bureaucracy. I do apologize again for interrupting, and I can only stay a minute. I was wondering, Sam, why you didn't sign up for the second half of my course. I thought you did quite well last semester, and it's a pity not to take the full course."

Sam didn't realize Watts knew anything about her. She was taken aback that Lawner had been Watts's client for years.

"To be honest, Professor—"

"Please call me Zach."

Sam continued: "To be honest, Zach, I didn't find it all that challenging last semester, but don't take that personally. I haven't really found anything in law school very challenging. Even law review is boring, and frankly, I'm thinking of dropping out of school entirely. In fact, I was having lunch with Janet today to discuss some of my alternatives and possibly going back to the Fund."

Watts seized on the suggestion. "Don't do that, Samantha. It will be a disappointment to you. No offense, Janet, but I don't think Samantha's talents belong at the IMF. I think she'd make a better lawyer than a banker."

"Please call me Sam. And it's a bit presumptuous to suggest you know what's better for me, let alone insulting my friend about her job," replied Sam, taking offense at the insult to Janet. "How can you possibly know what's best for me after one course in which I barely participated?"

Watts was not one to let a confrontation back him off. "Forgive me for my honesty. I mean no offense. But Sam, you don't give lawyers—or for that matter, me—the credit we deserve," replied Watts. "Since you have no reason to know me, I can forgive your rejection of my advice. But I would hope you'd know better about yourself. You're bored in law school for the same reasons I bet you were bored at the Fund. It's not enough of a challenge. Dick Lawner alerted me to you as soon as he found out you were going to GW. And your memory is not the best, Sam. We first met two years ago at the Fund on a transaction between France's Alcatel and Lawner's team. That's when I first met you, too, Janet. We were all pretty quiet at the meeting, but both of you certainly made an impression on me. I obviously didn't make one on you. Sorry."

Sam did not remember the meeting. "Is that why you waived the prerequisites for me last semester?"

"Let me just say I didn't object when the dean asked me if I agreed with his conclusion. It just disappoints me you don't want to take the second half. There's still time to come into the course, and I know you can add another course to your schedule. I checked with the registrar."

Janet, feeling left out, interjected: "Well, Sam, it seems you're being recruited, and you haven't even finished your second year. Whatever you do, hold out for the corner office."

The laughter eased the moment.

"Do you promise me a challenge, Zach?" asked Sam.

"Sam, I'll do my best, but securities law is hard to turn into a challenge of the type you want. I don't think you'll find the challenge you want until you're out in the real world practicing with the rest of us grunts." Watts rose, obviously calling an end to the conversation. "But for now, I've got to go. It was nice meeting you, Janet, and perhaps we'll see each other again. Good-bye, Sam. I look forward to seeing you in class."

Watts left, saying hello to a number of people as he walked out. He was one of the most frequent patrons and very popular with the pub's crowd.

Sam turned to Janet, "What do you think? Should I take him up on the challenge or just drop out and take care of my babies?" As if that was a choice.

"I think you should stay. Besides, he's not wearing a wedding ring, and I want you to get me a date with him."

Sam smiled. "Just because he's not wearing a wedding ring doesn't mean he's not married."

"So? Who cares? It hasn't stopped me in the past. Who knows? Maybe I'll be lucky this time. God knows I'm due for a stroke of luck. Besides, the batteries are getting too expensive for the vibrator."

Again Janet made Sam laugh. "Janet, you're unbelievable at times. But OK, just because you're my friend, I'll stay in school and take Zach's course. And if it turns out I get bored, the first thing I'll do upon graduation is sue your ass for false promises and make you pay my tuition."

"Sue whatever ass you want, Sam, but just get me his."

The lunch conversation turned to the goings-on at the Fund and Ben's newfound public fame. He was now ABC's financial expert and a regular on *Nightline*. Sam was married to a celebrity. She had to admit that combined with her pride in Ben, there was a little jealousy too.

Chapter Twenty-Four

Equal rights for the poor. Unless we eradicate poverty, we will ensure ourselves nothing more than an unending group of unemployed parents with welfare children and grandchildren. Poverty drives crime, disease, and loss of hope. That is intolerable. A government that is unresponsive to the poor is a government that is contemptible, along with any of its leaders who remain silent witnesses to the travesty of poverty.

Speech in acceptance of nomination, Convention Center, Memphis, Tennessee, July 27, 2016.

May 17, 1988
George Washington University Law School

The rest of law school was a breeze. If not for Watts getting her involved in some local political campaigns, she probably would have dropped out. Graduation in May, however, put all the boring days of classes behind her. Sam was graduating with honors. Sam's mother and Ben couldn't have been prouder. Jeremy understood it was an important event but was unhappy at losing his playtime on such a sunny day. He didn't understand why he couldn't just stay home with Caitlin rather than come to a stupid graduation. Amanda, now three, was oblivious to it all, just having fun with her grandma, who spoiled her rotten—much to Sam's chagrin. It was as though Sam's mother was trying to flood Amanda with the attention Sam felt her mother hadn't given her when she was a child. In a way Sam was right. Ben always told her not to worry, though. A little spoiling from grandma was all right. Besides, the kids only had one grandparent since Sam's father and Ben's parents had died years before.

"When is this over, Daddy? It's boring," asked Jeremy.

"Jeremy, this is an important day for Mommy, and you'll just have to hang in there for a little longer."

"How much longer?" complained Jeremy.

Caitlin stepped in. "Shush, Jeremy. Or you'll miss when they call out Mommy's name."

As if on cue, "Samantha Price Harrison, magna cum laude," boomed from the podium. Sam, replete in her graduation robes, rose, stepped across the stage, was hooded, and accepted her diploma. Zachary Watts, who by now had become a friend of both Sam and Ben and had been dating Janet for about a year, also rose from the faculty on the stage and shook Sam's hand. To everyone except Sam, Ben, Elizabeth Price, and Watts, the whole event was of little importance. Jeremy couldn't have cared less, and Amanda had no idea what it was about.

After a commencement speech by Lewis Thomas, president of the Memorial Sloan-Kettering Cancer Center, the whole affair ended with Sam, Ben, Mrs. Price, Watts, and an assortment of guests adjourning to Morton's Steakhouse for a celebration.

"Well, the boredom is finally over," said Watts as he accepted another martini from the server. "Admit it, Sam, it was worth it. Now you've got another pretty diploma to adorn your walls. And just in case you don't know it yet, that's what lawyers live for, certificates with their names on them to hang on walls. It helps feed our egos."

Sam smiled and reached out, touching Watts's arm. "Zach, you're right as always. Now I finally know why I put up with the likes of you for three years at GW. If I'd only known then what I know now, I would have volunteered for the diploma design committee. Maybe some backdrop of the Mall might have been nice. Or maybe a lawyer chasing an ambulance would have been an appropriate touch. Who knows? I should probably just let Amanda have at it with her crayons. Then it would really be a piece of artwork worthy of framing."

"I don't know," joked Watts. "How are we going to explain you to Judge Erwin? I don't think he knows the clerk he may be getting."

Amanda and Jeremy began to argue over the cookies, and Sam went to intervene, scolding Amanda for biting Jeremy.

Ben joined Watts. "So Zach, how come you're here without Janet? Sam tells me you and Janet are a hot item within the halls of the IMF."

Watts shrugged his shoulders. "I'm afraid she's in France again with Lawner on one of the Fund's fishing expeditions. Jesus, she must spend half her time in Paris. She might as well declare French citizenship and avoid US taxes. I'm surprised she still remembers English."

Ben couldn't restrain himself. "You do not sound like a happy camper, Zach. Why not make her an honorable woman and marry her?"

Watts stepped back, acting as if he were shocked at Ben's suggestion. "Marry her? I don't think so. Anyway, I can't be sure she isn't still with Lawner, even though she swears that's over."

"Why not ask Sam, Zach? Janet's close enough to her that Sam's sure to find the truth."

"Ben, if Sam heard that suggestion, she'd have you singing soprano for the next month. I want no part of putting Sam in any compromising position."

Ben gave up. "Suit yourself, Zach. I just thought we boys could help each other out occasionally." Ben went off to corral John Russell, another professor at

Georgetown, to attack Russell's latest paper defending the junk bond business as a healthy investment to keep America on the rise.

Watts grabbed another martini.

Chapter Twenty-Five

Competition is at the foundation of a healthy economy. The ability to compete freely and excel above the competition is the motivation pushing industries and entrepreneurs to lead the world in technology and invention. Yet repeatedly we see our foreign competitors protected by their governments from the very competition that makes open economies the leaders of the free world. These controls are seen as a way to protect the jobs and livelihoods of their local citizens. In truth, such policies only serve to drive down their citizens' standard of living, keep innovation outside its borders, and cost all our economies untold millions lost in support of inefficiencies. We must drop our trade barriers and persuade world governments to drop theirs as well. If the world market is not a market of open competition, we will all be forced to replace lost competition with protectionism, a result that hurts all people throughout the world. Let us lead the way.

Campaign speech, October 5, 2016.

June 1, 1988
Washington, DC

A week after graduation from GW , Sam was faced with a tough decision—whether to accept a one-year clerkship with Federal Judge Kenneth Erwin, a controversial trial judge in the United States District Court for the District of Columbia, or to accept the offer from Watts to join his firm, Wilson, Smith & Watts.

Federal courts hear some of the hottest cases in the legal profession, and clerkships are not easy to come by. On the one hand, Sam knew serving as one of Erwin's clerks was a rare opportunity. Erwin was an outspoken opponent to mandatory sentencing, had a no-nonsense approach with lawyers, and had absolutely no patience in civil rights cases or where the police exceeded their powers, particularly since they usually exceeded their powers against minority defendants. Sam knew she certainly wouldn't be bored. On the other hand, an associate position with one of the leading firms in Washington, if not the country, was hard to come by as well and might not be available when she ended her clerkship. The nice thing for Sam was it wasn't about the money. The starting salary at Wilson, Smith & Watts was more than three times the salary of a Federal District Court clerk. But with Ben's fortune, at least she didn't have to factor money into her decision.

Watts told Sam he was concerned with the clerkship, fearing she might get pulled into being a public defender after she left, or worse yet, a lawyer for the American Civil Liberties Union. Sam was more amused than concerned since the ACLU was an organization that probably loathed Watts as much as he loathed them.

Sam believed in the ACLU and its mission to jealously guard First Amendment rights, regardless of who exercised them, whether they were civil rights activists or members of the KKK. While Sam appreciated Watts's view that the ACLU often appeared too political, she also suspected they hated the idea of a talent like Sam carrying water for cases handled by Wilson, Smith & Watts. Erwin had been an ACLU lawyer. Watts warned Sam not to let the liberal tendencies of Ken Erwin spoil her.

When she interviewed with Erwin, he did not appear impressed by Sam's desire to be his clerk. While he offered her the job, he was a very practical judge, and warned her offers for plum jobs like the one offered by Wilson, Smith & Watts are not to be taken lightly.

Sam recalled the advice Erwin gave her when she asked him about his philosophy as a judge.

Erwin answered her question in a deliberate and somewhat cold tone. "Mrs. Harrison, courts operate under a system of compromises. You have to accept that. It's necessary to be successful and to move society down a reasonable path. There may be the occasional special case where a judge can make a difference, but that is a rare occurrence. Most cases are just run-of-the-mill controversies about a minor mistake by a company that makes a potful of money for an enterprising attorney. It may be hard to accept, but that's how our system works. The sooner you learn none of us can alter that, the better off you'll be."

His answer both shocked and disillusioned Sam, apparently naive in her view that courts did make a difference in every case—or at least more often than not.

Erwin caught Sam's disappointment in her expression and changed his tone to a softer, paternalistic one. "Samantha, if I hadn't been doing this for so long, I might still have the starry-eyed perception of justice you do. But you can't take on all the wrongs in one place. A court has a responsibility to many people. I made many compromises to get where I am today. Every lawyer who puts on these robes has done so. While I may even regret some of those compromises, I balance that with some of the good things I have done. Some of the great things I've done that made a difference. You just can't have impact in every decision."

Sam decided she wanted to have an impact in everything she did and realized being a clerk even for a year would bore her to death. She'd had enough with boredom. Watts was thrilled by her decision to join his firm.

Sam's first day at Wilson, Smith & Watts was uneventful. Watts wasn't there. He was on the Hill meeting with some senators about a foreign investment deal for the IMF. Janet was with him. Sam adored the way Janet and Watts mixed business and pleasure. Janet loved to tell Sam how she and Watts would negotiate a deal all morning, take lunch breaks in their hotel room making love, and return to the negotiation table that afternoon. Janet thought it was the perfect diet; she'd lost fifteen pounds in two months by cutting out lunches. When Sam had lunch that day with a few of the other new associates, she couldn't get the image out of her mind of Watts and Janet enjoying their own special repast. She'd have liked to try that with Ben, but Ben was never an afternoon man. The evening or morning was fine, but noon was for work and debate.

The work at the firm was interesting but not terribly challenging. Mostly corporate stuff. Nothing that really pushed Sam. But the firm appreciated her writing ability and spared her the drudgery of a lot of library time researching cases and finding support for positions taken in briefs or opinion letters. Some of the associates complained to one another about the favoritism Sam received, particularly from Watts, but no one had enough nerve to speak up—typical in law firms. No one spoke up to management. The firm held all the cards, and the road to success and partnership was to keep quiet and do the job assigned. Law firms generally did not appreciate original thoughts from associates. Wilson, Smith & Watts was no exception.

Sam continued to hone her skills in corporate law and began spending considerable time with Watts on some of the lobbying efforts of the firm. She found that part of her job to be the most interesting, yet most frustrating. Moving state, much less federal, bureaucracy was a monumental task. Competing interests always tore at one another, and the compromises usually accomplished little of the goals either side hoped to achieve. So Sam and Watts usually went on to the next lobbying effort, measuring success by small victories, each a step to the ultimate goal. As the adage goes, it was a marathon, not a sprint.

The inefficiencies frustrated Sam. Worse, it was common for Watts to ask Sam to keep some of her opinions to herself when she would have preferred to openly express her concerns to a senator or congressman. When she got too vocal despite Watts's admonitions, Watts would punish her by not taking her to meetings for weeks at a time until she came to him and promised she'd behave. They both knew she wouldn't change in the long term, but at least Sam would be under control for a few weeks after each mini-exile. She was learning to compromise. Throughout the process, she was also learning how politics worked at every level. By the third year with Wilson, Smith & Watts, she was running many of the meetings, although Watts never let her do it alone. He was always there, quietly watching and adding his opinions when he thought it was appropriate. They made an effective team, and the clients were happy with the results. Most progress left Sam wanting more, but that was the nature of compromise.

What Sam didn't like about working at Wilson, Smith & Watts were the long hours. Her home life changed dramatically. She was no longer there for all the recitals and important family dates. Saturday night dates with Ben became the exception rather than the rule. Her schedule wouldn't allow it, and Watts was not an understanding man. Watts believed service to clients came first, and personal sacrifice was necessary to succeed in private practice. There was no mommy track at Wilson, Smith & Watts. At times she thought of quitting and finding a cushy corporate job or part-time arrangement at one of the more enlightened firms. But she was flourishing as an associate and increasingly gaining respect among her clients and colleagues, even bringing in some clients of her own. With time, she knew she could become a rainmaker, and she liked the idea of having the kind of independence a partnership would bring, believing it would give her more personal control over her family life and allow her more freedom. And with the rush she got in developing new business and the respect and power it gave her in the firm, there was no turning back.

Ben continued to be Sam's salvation. Unlike Sam, he controlled his daily life, balancing his chores as a professor at Georgetown and a personality on ABC *Nightline* every few weeks. He took care of the recitals and runny noses. He loved joking that he had become Mr. Mom. At best Sam was a part-time mom, finding it impossible to balance her business life with a home life. Jeremy seemed fine with it, but Amanda had some difficulty. Ben and Sam talked about the balance many times. It was those years at Wilson, Smith & Watts that Ben saw Sam mature as a lawyer and powerbroker, but suffer with distance from the family. She was convinced she could make a difference.

She knew she'd have to sacrifice to pursue an activist role professionally and eventually publicly. That kind of sacrifice starts out slowly, grabbing beliefs and dragging you into an abyss, albeit a pleasant one for those who find balance. As Sam pursued that journey, balance proved to be more difficult than she expected.

Chapter Twenty-Six

Reginald Powers grew up in poverty. Crime was simply a part of his life. The police were his enemies. As far as kids growing up in his neighborhood were concerned, you either took care of yourself or others took advantage of you. Drugs were just another commodity that let you escape the poverty by either doping your mind or lining your pockets with cash. Reginald Powers became a user so as not be used by others. Then he chose to line his pockets with cash and became a pusher. Now his defense attorney wants you to be gentle with him because he's just a survivor. He really had no choice. He had to sell heroin and crack to eight-year-olds. He had to show young addicts how to rob liquor stores to support their habit and his lifestyle. It certainly wasn't his fault kids killed or died as a result of the drugs he sold. Don't be fooled by such a sympathetic argument. Reginald Powers is a pathetic man. He is the worst of the parasites that prey on our youth and keep crime on our streets. Find him guilty and let this court send him where he belongs.

Summation to a jury, October 19, 1996.

December 25, 1999
Crownsville, Maryland

Christmas was always a special holiday in the Price family, particularly to Sam. Ben always joked Sam lived her life around one day: Christmas. He was convinced she never stopped believing in Santa Claus. Ben always made sure Christmas was special, with extravagant presents and family gatherings.

Christmas 1999 was no exception. Sam, now a shining star in the Bowling Green commonwealth attorney's office, was becoming as popular in the community as Ben, despite his celebrity from *Nightline.* To the press, they were the ideal power couple, regulars in the gossip columns of the local newspapers. Jeremy had just started in his final year at the US Naval Academy in Annapolis, en route to his dream of becoming a pilot. Sam could not have been prouder that Jeremy was carrying on a Price tradition of military service. She laughed with Ben that her father was rolling over in his grave at the thought of a Price going into the navy and not the army. Indeed, Jeremy didn't even apply to West Point; the army didn't have planes. And the air force was out too. They didn't have any aircraft carriers, something Jeremy yearned to fly from.

Sam and Amanda were having problems, but Sam and Ben wrote them off as mother-daughter conflicts during Amanda's teenage years. They thought Amanda's often combative independence was just a part of growing up near the Washington beltway, where kids matured faster. What neither one of them appreciated was Amanda's sense of loss when Caitlin returned to Belfast just after Amanda turned fourteen. The following string of misfit nannies was a disaster. At fifteen, now with no nanny, a brother who no longer lived at home, and absentee parents most of the time, she felt mostly alone. A latchkey kid in sleepy Virginia. Nothing could have been more boring for Amanda.

But Amanda coped. She had her close set of friends, mostly theater types. Amanda loved the arts and never lost an opportunity to go to a museum opening or new exhibit. Sometimes Ben went with her, and she enjoyed that. Amanda wished her mother would go with them too, but that rarely happened. When her mother did go to museums and theater, she most often went with friends. Amanda wasn't invited.

As always, Christmas 1999 was celebrated in Crownsville at Sam's mother's home. Douglas Sanders and Elizabeth spared no expense in making the experience of Christmas memorable. Ben could see why the holiday was so important to Sam whenever he saw how Elizabeth made the day so special for Jeremy and Amanda. He knew the Harrison tradition of Christmas was secure in the next generation.

When dinner was finally served, the conversation, as usual, turned to politics.

Sanders started the discussion. "So Sam, how do you find your career as one of the most celebrated district attorneys in the state? You must be very proud of yourself, and deservedly so." Douglas Sanders never repressed his pride in what Sam had accomplished and felt his own sense of reward in having helped in a small way in getting her started.

"Doug," as Sam now called him, "we're actually called Virginia commonwealth attorneys, and to tell you the truth, it's overwhelming. I'm not really sure if I'm as good as some say I am. In truth, I'm lucky to have a staff of talented and hungry prosecutors. It's really their success that has worn off on me in the press. I wish they'd get more of the credit."

"Well said, counselor," replied Sanders with a smile. "I think you are more the politician than you know. But I've always said that. So how true are the rumors of a run for Congress? The idea has your mother in a daze. She can't stop telling me how she only wishes your father could see his daughter today."

But he can't, can he? He's dead.

A reality painful to Sam.

Until her recent time in the limelight, Sam resolved politics was something she disdained. Now she wasn't sure. What would her father have said? She needed advice and wanted to know what Sanders thought.

"A few of the party regulars are pushing me, Doug. My old firm, Wilson, Smith & Watts, is very active in politics, and Zachary Watts, one of the senior partners, has been putting on a full-court press of late. To tell you the truth, I don't know what to do."

Sanders leaned forward, as if ready to give some very special advice. "Let me tell you what my mother would have said in this situation. Obviously you didn't know her, but she was a painfully honest and practical old broad, if you'll pardon the expression. She was always optimistic and later in her life became an avid reader of Norman Vincent Peale's books on the power of positive thinking. Personally, I never read any of the stuff. It seemed too close to door-to-door religion to me, but my mom made sure a good deal wore off on me. I think a lot of my success was because I always looked on the bright side of things, never dwelling on the negative."

Sam was confused, "I'm not sure where you're going with this. Are you telling me you think I should run for Congress or what your mother read?"

Sanders leaned back, disappointed Sam didn't get his point. "Right. Hell, Sam, how should I know what you should do? But I'll tell you this. You have a gift. You're special. I don't know what makes one person different from another. I only know that occasionally you meet someone with something special, something you can't understand, usually because you don't have the gift yourself. But you can certainly see it in someone else who does. And you have that gift. My mother would say it's destiny. Your destiny is not to remain the best damn prosecutor in Virginia. Politics is your calling. Who knows? Maybe you could be the first woman president."

"I think you've had too much wine, Doug."

"I haven't had a single drink, Sam. Don't dismiss the comment so lightly. Someday there will be a woman president, and I believe it will be in my lifetime. That woman is somewhere in America right now, reading a book, attending a mass, or not celebrating Christmas at all. Or maybe she's sitting in front of me. There is no reason that woman couldn't be you."

Sam smiled at how confident Sanders was of something Sam believed impossible.

For now I'm going to worry about putting some of the grime on the street in jail. Maybe I'll consider Congress. The presidency is just a bit too much. Really.

The crash in the kitchen instantly broke the moment.

As Sanders and Sam rushed into the kitchen, they came upon her mother sitting on the floor, complaining of pain in her left arm. The dirty dishes, now broken, lay all around her, food scattered on the floor. She was pale and sweating. No one needed to tell anyone what was happening.

Sanders called 9–1–1, and the ambulance quickly arrived. Sam wanted them to take her mother immediately to Johns Hopkins. The ambulance driver explained they couldn't do that. They had to first take her to the nearest hospital. From there, a transfer to Johns Hopkins would happen if it made sense, depending upon her condition.

The paramedics immediately gave Elizabeth aspirin, gently putting her on a gurney. They connected her to oxygen. Electrodes, in contact by radio to the cardiac specialist on duty at Crownsville Hospital, were added to the array of apparatus. All of this happened in a matter of minutes. The orders of the specialist were relayed via walkie-talkie to the scene. It was high tech. By the time Elizabeth was being wheeled to the ambulance, the specialist had ordered nitroglycerin and instructed she be taken directly to Johns Hopkins, where more sophisticated equipment was available. Sam would later learn when the paramedic told the doctor on staff who they were transporting and what Sam had said, the destination was changed.

Sam went with her mother in the ambulance, despite the objections of the paramedics. No one was going to stop her.

Memories of her father's death, which she could barely remember, flooded Sam's head. "Mom, you'll be OK. Just hang in there. You haven't even opened your presents yet." Somehow, Sam knew her attempt at humor was hollow.

Her mother's eyes begged for solace. "I'm scared. I don't think this is going to work out. Things inside me aren't working. I know it."

"Stop it. You're not going anywhere."

Things inside you? What does that mean? Is that what happened to her father? Things inside him just stopped working? It can't be that simple. There has to be a way of saving the last vestige of childhood I have left.

The paramedic, following orders from an unseen doctor, injected something into the intravenous tube that made Elizabeth jump a bit, regaining some of her color.

Thank God, she's going to be fine.

Elizabeth now looked comfortable, able to speak but with a tremor in her voice. "Listen to me, Sam. I'm so proud of you. So is your father. I know that. Be yourself and follow your dreams. Be the success you want to be."

Suddenly, Elizabeth's body jerked as she let out a breath covered with pain. The paramedic, listening intently on the walkie-talkie, injected something else from his supply of bottles. Again some color came back, although less than with the last injection.

No. This can't be happening.

Sam could not hold back the tears and fear on losing her mother. "Damn it, Mom. Hang in there. We're not far from the hospital. Please don't die on me now. I need you."

Elizabeth's body lurched again and became still. Sam backed away as the paramedic tore the intravenous from her arm and started pounding her chest, yelling orders Sam could barely understand through her distress—except when he ordered her to move away and placed two paddles on Elizabeth's chest. He yelled, "Clear!" Elizabeth's body virtually flew off the gurney. He waited a moment while he held his stethoscope to her chest, having torn away her blouse, leaving her chest totally exposed, now reddened by the burning of the paddles. He yelled, "Clear!" again, and the body jumped again. He did it a third time. Sam could smell the odor of burned flesh. She wanted to throw up. Then everything was silent, and the ambulance seemed to slow down as if the driver knew it was over.

Somewhere on a Maryland highway on that snowy holiday, Elizabeth Price died, her daughter by her side.

"I'm sorry. I did everything I could." It was then Sam noticed the paramedic couldn't have been more than twenty years old. A young volunteer whose chance to be a hero had passed unfulfilled.

Sam didn't know what to say as she straightened her mother's blouse and gently kissed her forehead.

"It's OK. I know you did all you could. Thank you."

Within days Sam resigned from Morgan's office, and on January 1, 2000, announced her run for Congress. As the years passed, Sam and Ben grew distant from Sanders, seeing him on fewer and fewer occasions. Even Alex stopped coming by for the holidays. He had his own family to care for as he moved from one place to another. He chose to stay close to home. Christmas never took place in Crownsville again, and Sam lost all desire to go there; Christmas became a time for Sam to reflect on the sad memory of her mother's death. Ben tried to make it better, but there were always long silences when everyone knew what Sam was thinking about. Amanda missed the celebrations and always thought Christmas should have been something more. She never could forgive or understand why Sam prevented it from being what it had once been.

Chapter Twenty-Seven

The purity of air we breathe, the water we drink, and the food we eat must be protected at all times. The fight against pollution and global warming is one that must unite the entire world to a single cause—the protection of our environment. We cannot do it alone. We must not ignore the pleas to stop polluting the air and water with our industrial waste and corporate polluters. Indeed, we should set an example for all to follow. For that reason I will introduce legislation to stiffen the criminal fines for pollution, even allowing jail terms for those who continue to pollute despite warnings. If we fail to take this decisive action, we endanger not only ourselves but generations to come.
Campaign speech, October 17, 2016.

November 7, 2000
Fredericksburg, Virginia

No one ran against her in the primary for Congress. Some had said the fix was in, but she never believed that. The truth was there was no fix. John Smith had put out the word that Sam was his choice and she was the rising star of the party. No one wanted to mess with John Smith.

Throughout her first campaign for Congress, Sam often thought about Robert Morgan and how he so loved a campaign, particularly a down and dirty one. Sam was surprised how she'd come to love her first campaign as well, but never with Morgan's bloodlust. She knew she had a weak opponent. The Democrat Party was resigned to the reality no one could beat Samantha Harrison, so it put up a lackluster political nobody to oppose her. Sam entered public life on a silver platter, ready to face whatever challenges lay ahead. Her first taste of political victory was enough to whet her thirst to drink whatever Kool-Aid Watts served up next.

With the primary behind her and a smooth campaign, on November 7, 2000, Sam was elected a junior congresswoman from Virginia. She won by a landslide. She began assembling a staff, looking forward to her January swearing in.

Ben quit ABC since the party decided it would be inappropriate for the husband of a member of the House of Representatives to express his opinion over a national network on matters that might be before Congress. Ben missed it but found comfort in a new role he found at Salomon, his criticism of junk bonds vindicated. There was even talk President Bush might appoint him to a cabinet post as head of Treasury, but it was all talk. Bush had already made all the promises he could on cabinet appointments.

Sam started tackling her new job with a vengeance. Having been given a relatively small office, she and her staff were crowded. Her crew was among the youngest in Congress, and the cramped quarters didn't seem to be of any concern. Sam and her staff simply wanted to make an impact and help her constituency.

Watts was always there to help. He showed Sam the ropes early, and whenever she crossed the line, he quietly mended the fences. It wasn't long before both sides of the aisle grew to respect Sam, not just for her intellect, but also for how she handled herself. She knew when to listen to her advisors, even though she didn't always agree with the advice. While at times brash and aggressive, in the end she usually followed the rules.

It took little time for Sam to find causes of particular interest to her. She was appointed to the Judiciary Committee and the Intelligence Committee. Crime was clearly important to Sam, and her reputation as a prosecutor gave her a respect usually earned over many years. Foreign assistance to Eastern Europe was another. Fighting terrorism and supporting President Bush in those efforts was paramount. Sam strongly felt the United States should give massive aid to the former Soviet Union and the newly independent Eastern European states. While she wouldn't admit it to anyone but Ben, her good looks also got her some choice appointments. Most of the old guard of Congress are dirty old men anyway, and Sam learned quickly how to make that work for her.

What took a toll were once again the hours and time away from home. They were worse than her years at Wilson, Smith & Watts. Sam often regretted she hadn't moved the family to the district. More and more she found herself making excuses for not being home for dinner. The travel for campaign fundraising kept her away even more. The telephone became the primary way she communicated with Ben and the children.

None of that seemed to bother Jeremy. He was at flight school after graduating with honors from Annapolis and always had Ben when he needed to talk. Amanda, however, missed her mother, finding it difficult sometimes to turn to her father. As time passed, Amanda's emotions increasingly turned to suppressed anger.

Amanda was more mature than her age. At fifteen she had already had two sexual partners and had briefly experimented with marijuana, but she gagged when she inhaled. Despite all the school systems' and media's efforts, teenagers in 2000 were using drugs and engaging in sex—usually safe sex in Amanda's case—in unprecedented numbers. Amanda was not as stupid as some of her friends. She was sensible enough to say no to the harder drugs readily available at school or from her friends. It humored her that neither Ben nor her mother had any idea how experienced she was. She took pride in her ability to keep her private life hers, despite the lonely feeling it sometimes gave her. But as long as her grades stayed high and she was home at reasonable hours, Sam and Ben let her pretty much run her own life.

Whenever Sam brought up the idea of moving to Washington, Ben wanted nothing to do with it. With the increasing media coverage on the two of them, he felt rightfully concerned life in the district fishbowl would be too much for Amanda. Fredericksburg was a place that assured them some anonymity. He wanted that to be preserved above all else. It made for some uncharacteristically tense discussions between Ben and Sam. Watts always tried to keep his distance from the topic, fearful of backlash from both of them. In truth, he preferred the separated family. It made it easier for him to control Sam's days in Washington. It also left dinners free where he could review a day's activities with her without outside interruption.

"I'm worried about Amanda," Sam injected into their conversation over dinner at the Jockey Club on a night Watts had intended to be focused on health care. "I think she may be starting to hate me. The affection she used to show when I returned home is gone. She seems cold toward me. I know Ben is doing his best, but Amanda needs a mother's influence. I just wish I could think of a way of getting Ben to come to Washington. The family would be together more, and I would be with Amanda."

Watts did not like these diversions from his agenda. He never knew where they might go. Sam was headstrong and loved her family enough to be willing to sacrifice all she'd accomplished in politics if she thought it would be best for Amanda, Jeremy, and Ben.

"Sam, you know Ben will never agree to come to Washington. As it is you're down in Virginia every weekend you can be. Maybe you should consider bringing Amanda up here on the weekends you can't make it to Virginia. Or take her with you to fund-raisers." Just what he needed to worry about, thought Watts, babysitting Amanda.

"Ben will never go for that, Zach. He'd never agree to let Amanda loose in Washington or expose her to the media in this swamp. Nor would I. Ben thinks this town is a cesspool, and the more time I spend here, the more I think he's right."

"That's his problem, Sam. He's never given the district a chance. If you insist, he might just go along with it."

Watts knew Ben wouldn't. And Watts knew Sam would never ask.

Chapter Twenty-Eight

Organized labor brought this country out of the sweatshops with child labor horrors and into the twentieth century. The collective bargaining system deserves our support and encouragement. While I am not going to stand here and say I will always support labor unions, it is clear from my record I support labor. When I refuse to support unions, it is usually because a position will hurt our ability to compete in the world markets and cost jobs, not save them. At times labor unions, not unlike politicians, can't admit the future is now and the workplace is undergoing a dynamic change. We must all come together and take labor unions and management into the twenty-first century with cooperation and realism from both sides.

Campaign speech, September 14, 2016.

March 1, 2004
Baltimore, Maryland

When Ben had his first heart attack in March 2004, it was something Sam thought must be a terrible misunderstanding. Certainly the doctors were wrong. Ben was strong and in excellent shape. As far as Sam knew, he didn't have a single vice and led a life that should never end up with a heart attack. What Ben never told Sam was that heart problems ran in his family, and he was long overdue by that standard.

It was not a serious heart attack, and the doctors at Johns Hopkins Hospital pronounced Ben ready to return home only a few weeks following the incident. They suggested he cut back on his work schedule for the next few months and prescribed Lipitor and low-dose aspirin.

Sam felt Ben was never quite the same. A sense of mortality took hold, contrary to his typically optimistic way of looking at life. Suddenly he was planning for retirement and a more relaxed life.

His timing couldn't have been worse. Sam had reached a stride, and Watts feared Ben might hold her back. A choice between Ben and her political career was one Watts didn't want Sam to make. He knew Ben would win. Some of the local gossip in Washington spread the word that Sam's problem was predictable. After all she did marry a man quite a bit older. The quiet attacks behind her back hurt and began to strain her relationship with Ben. He had heard them too, and his reaction was as Sam would have expected: complete indignation. He rejected Washington life as hypocritical and refused to come to the district for any further public events. While he was always willing and pleased to privately be with Sam in Washington, he had nothing but disdain for the Washington scene. Watts tried to explain to Ben that his attitude might hurt Sam's career, but Ben was unmoved. After all, he told Watts, someone had to remain at home to give Amanda some semblance of a normal childhood. Ben always made is clear to Watts and Sam he would never let Amanda live in the cesspool on the Potomac.

After the heart attack, Sam's relationship with Ben became weekly grist for the gossip mill. Even the tabloids occasionally ran photographs of Sam's latest escort to an event with bold assertions he was the latest love interest of the sexy congresswoman from Virginia. Of course it was all untrue and dutifully denied, but there was nothing Sam could do about it. Watts controlled it as best he could. They decided to simply ignore the gossip. Trying to answer it only gave it more credibility and fed the rumor mill even more. Ben, however, was anything but silent. When asked about the rumors, he was first to say they were hogwash and just another example of the Washington mentality of destruction. Ben's public tirades were sound bites both Sam and Watts knew helped no one but reporters looking for a salacious spin to the news.

"No wonder the government is so gridlocked," Ben would tell the hungry tabloid press. "Everyone is concerned more with fictitious happenings in nonexistent bedrooms than they are about health care, corporate growth, or international relations."

After an incident in September, just six months after his heart attack, Sam and Watts finally persuaded Ben to cool off on his public comments to the press.

It was Labor Day weekend. Amanda looked forward to the fireworks display at the Anne Arundel County Fair. Going to the fair had become an annual family event when Sam's mother was alive. This year—as was all too often the case as far as Ben was concerned—Sam was giving a speech at a picnic in Norfolk before the United Garment Workers and was scheduled to march the next day in Washington's Labor Day parade. So she decided to beg off on the fair. Originally Ben had agreed to forego the trip as well and reluctantly accompany Sam to the picnic as her politically proper husband. But Amanda was so insistent and her disappointment so apparent at the prospect of missing the fireworks, Sam and Ben agreed to split for the day. Watts, who accompanied Sam to the picnic, suggested that Janet go with Ben since she hated political picnics and loved fireworks just as much as any kid.

As luck would have it, the *National Enquirer* had a crew shadowing Ben, and they followed him to the fair. It delighted the reporters to find Ben and Amanda out on the town with Sam's campaign manager's girlfriend. Their cameras caught Ben and Janet sitting together at a diner for burgers before the show, conveniently making sure the photos in the diner didn't show Amanda. Later, paparazzi shot the two walking arm in arm on the field where the fireworks display would light the sky and one of Janet playfully hugging Ben as she reacted to a big boom, all to the amusement of Amanda. And of course Amanda was cropped out of the shot, but other photos made the three look like one happy family. The paparazzi's photos went to the highest bidders.

To no one's surprise, the rag sheet headline, splattered all over the supermarket checkouts, characterized the evening quite differently than Sam, Ben, Watts, or Janet intended. The headline on *National Enquirer* read, "Campaign Manager's

Girlfriend Latest Love Interest of Ben Harrison. And Amanda Loves Her Too. Exclusive Photos Inside."

The Washington Post's gossip columnist called Ben the day the article hit the stands to see what he had to say. He had a lot to say, most of which appeared in the *Post*:

> In speaking to Ben Harrison, he told this reporter he was outraged by the tabloid stories, particularly the one in the *National Enquirer*. As Congresswoman Samantha Harrison's husband put it in an exclusive interview with the *Post*: "Crap like the *National Enquirer* is an example of how the First Amendment is abused under a pretense of reporting news. That rag, and all the others that ran photos and lied, had no right to spread libel for the sake of stealing a few cents from imbecile supermarket shoppers getting their jollies off on the private lives of my family. As far as I'm concerned, a good dose of gasoline and a match to their printing presses is what that garbage for a publication deserves. And I wouldn't shed tears if its readers were in the pressroom when it went up in flames." When I asked him if he thought the three million readers of *National Enquirer* would really fit in the pressroom, he answered, "At least that would be a start."

Watts was in Washington on business when his office faxed the *Post* article. He'd already seen the *National Enquirer* article. It was making the usual rounds in Congress. When he called Ben, he didn't bother to guard the tone in his voice. He was sure a firm reprimand was the only way he could convince Ben a one-man attack on the press never succeeds.

After a few perfunctory pleasantries on the phone, Watts got right into it. "So I read the article in the *Post* with your quote about killing readers of the *National Enquirer*. What the hell got into you, Ben? When are you going to get it through that academic skull of yours that you can't take on the *National Enquirer* or the gossip columnist from the *Post*? All you've done now is feed more lies into the public's eye. You've got to stop, Ben. While I know you mean well and I don't fault you for defending you family's integrity, your attacks on the press don't help. Worse, you've just told the world you're ready to incinerate three million of Sam's voters. Not a good idea, Ben."

Ben, not used to being the person lectured to, didn't respond well to Watts's harangue. "You seasoned political weasels seem to have the thickest skins alive. I believe the public needs to hear the truth, not just hogwash and muck. And when my kids are involved, I refuse to stay quiet. What do I say to Amanda if she sees the paper in the supermarket or if someone brings the rag to school, as I'm sure they will. I really don't care what you think I should do. Have you even spoken to Sam? Are you trying to tell me Sam wants me to stay quiet, too?"

Watts now regretted his tone and decided to back off. "I'm not sure Sam knows about either article, Ben," replied Watts, knowing she probably did. "She's been in committee meetings straight for the last three days. All I'm asking is for you to understand attacks in the press are going to get exaggerated or quoted out of context. It's the way it is, and you're not going to change that. With all due respect, Ben, it would be better for everyone if you stopped trying."

You political worm. The day hasn't come when I'll take advice from you.

"Zach, let me make this simple for you. I'll stop trying when Sam tells me to shut up. Then I'll listen. If she really thinks my comments are hurting her or some of her precious voters, let her tell me. That's not your job."

Watts gave up on trying to convert Ben to reason and tried a more respectful tone. "I should have known I'd get nowhere with you on this call. You and I are too much alike. The only difference is you can get away with the kind of shit I'd like to try but have never had the balls to pull off. My frustration is I can't get you to even sympathize with my role. I'll talk with Sam and let her try to convince you. And if the two of you still don't agree with me, I'll get you on *Nightline* to tell the whole story." Watts regretted it as soon as he said it. He could hear the light switch go on in Ben's head.

Nightline! What a great idea.

"Thank you, Zach. For once you've given me a great idea."

Watts hoped to get to Sam before Ben called her. But Sam had an office rule. If Ben called, she took the call or called him back first if she was out or in a meeting that couldn't be interrupted. Ben knew Watts would try to get to her first, so Ben called the private line immediately, even though he assumed she was still in committee. To his surprise, she was in the office and picked up the phone.

"Hi, babe. It's your loudmouth lout of a husband calling. How're you doing?"

"I'm fine, and I'm happy you called. I just got out of a terribly boring committee session and hearing your voice makes the boredom vanish. Is everything OK?"

"Everything's fine. So I guess Zach hasn't gotten to you yet, and you haven't read the morning rags."

"Damn, Ben. Now what?"

Watts made it to Sam's office just after Sam started her conversation with Ben. He quietly picked up the extension. She did not object. Throughout the conversation, Watts passed notes to Sam. For the most part, she followed his cues.

"Our favorite paper, the *National Enquirer*, took some pictures of Janet, Amanda, and me at the fair last week. I guess they kept the ones of all of us naked in bed for next week's issue."

Cut it out, Ben. Your humor isn't working, and this is no time for levity.

Watts passed her a copy of the paper. She began scanning it.

Ben continued. "Anyway, let me be the first to tell you Janet is my new love interest. At least for this week. I'm thinking of hitting on a nun next week."

Stop it, Ben. This isn't funny.

Sam took up the conversation. "Ben, don't you see this will never stop? At least no one with a brain believes what that rag says. Certainly no one we care about. Who was it that said, 'This too shall pass'? What else is there to do?"

Watts's note read, "Nothing."

"Really, Sam? Well try this on for size, how about talking to the *Post* and being misquoted, suggesting all readers of the *National Enquirer* be cremated alive?"

Watts passed a note that read, "True."

"Please tell me you're kidding, Ben. Now I hope you're really trying to be funny."

"I'm afraid not, Sam. Zach already scolded me, so you don't need to. I just refuse to stand by reading lies and saying nothing."

Watts's note: "Make him stop. NOW!"

"I don't like it either, Ben, but it goes with the territory. I'm sorry you and Amanda have been dragged in. When I was a prosecutor, the papers kept the insults, innuendoes, and lies directed at me and kept the family out of it. I guess the stakes just get higher the more you pursue public office. The higher you go, the easier the target, including your family. What did Zach think we should do?" Watts was caught off guard with her question to Ben. Didn't Sam believe him?

Ben reported, "Zach wants me to just shut up, but I've got a better idea. Let's you and me go on *Nightline* and tell the truth. I'm sure it can be easily arranged. I still know most of the producers."

Watts's note to Sam: "NO NO NO!"

Sam was getting annoyed with Watts's note passing and gave him an expression with a clear message to stop. She didn't need coaching, particularly when dealing with her husband.

"Ben, how much control will we have? I wouldn't want to be blindsided by some question I'm not prepared to answer. Not now. And besides, won't an appearance just get the *Enquirer* more interested? They'll probably assign a reporter to each of the kids. Maybe even Janet. I'd hate to see that happen. Can't we just let this one go and not make any big deal out of the next one? I really believe the more we ignore these maggots the sooner they'll get bored and go away."

Ben didn't like Sam's response to his suggestion and wondered if her reaction would have been different if he had told her *Nightline* was Watts's idea.

"Come on, Sam. They're attacking our family and using photos of our child. Even you can't suggest we just grin and bear it."

Yes I can, Ben. Because if you don't, it will only get worse.

Sam decided to make it more of an argument, hoping to get Ben to back down. He hated arguing with Sam. He always won in reasoned debates. But when it came to a good down and dirty argument, Sam had the advantage. "What do you mean, 'even you'? You don't think it hurts me when I read garbage like that? I just think I know a little about the media and how it works. And I'm telling you sometimes silence is better."

Damn it, thought Ben, *how could Zach have gotten to her so quickly?*

"Ben, please listen to me. A smart media strategy is to pick the right moments to hit the issues that attract voters, not alienate them. If you were quoted suggesting voters be burned to death, it will most certainly be a main focus of attention on *Nightline.* The bigger you make the issue, the longer it lasts. After you've put gas on a fire, you need to walk away and let it die on its own. Why don't we just let this go and get on with our lives?"

"Why, Sam? Next week there'll be another article. More lies. How can we let this go on without a response? The voters can't be that important."

Yes they are, Ben.

"No, Ben, the voters aren't stupid, but every one of them is important. I'm sorry, Ben, but I won't go on *Nightline,* and it would upset me greatly if you did. If you want to issue a press release, that's fine. But anything more is a mistake."

You have to trust me on this, Ben. Please stop resisting.

Ben's resolve started to wane. "So we do nothing, Sam?"

"Right, Ben. We do nothing."

I'm so sorry, Ben. But I know I'm right on this.

"Sam, someday you'll see you're wrong. But you're the one in office with the fancy media experts, so you get to make the call. Consider me gagged. So will you be home for dinner?"

Ben's crisis past her, Sam's response was routine—almost dismissive. "I'm afraid I'll be here all week working on new immigration legislation. Please tell Amanda I send my love. Maybe the two of you can come up on Saturday and we can spend some time on the Mall." Sam knew what Ben's response would be.

"A nice idea but Amanda has the usual stuff here at home over the weekend. Sports, parties, you know the routine. Let's try and call one another. And I promise I'll be a good boy. You can tell Zach he won this round. I suspect he's sitting right in front of you." Ben abruptly hung up, taking Sam by surprise. She would have liked to say good-bye.

"Thank you, Sam. You did the right thing," Watts said.

Fuck you, Zach. Whatever is between Ben and me is none of your damn business.

That's what she wanted to say but knew better. "Ben's under control for now, Zach. But I don't intend to make him a eunuch. If he has something he wants to say, then he's got a right to say it."

"I know, Sam. I just don't want unnecessary comments hurting what you're trying to do."

Sam knew Ben's attitude toward the press and Washington was a serious problem. She knew there would be more incidents. The problem was Ben was an emotional man. She understood Ben didn't care what Watts thought was best for her. Sam reminded herself in the end, she'd support Ben when things got tense.

"Zach, you need to understand without Ben I don't care about whatever it is you think I'm trying to do." Sam's tone was ice cold.

With that remark, Watts knew it was time to leave. At that point, he wasn't sure what to say if Sam asked him what it was she was trying to do.

Ben had a tough time explaining the newspaper articles to Amanda. She saw them in school and was taunted by some of the kids. He wished Sam had been there to help calm her down. When Sam called Amanda the next night and asked her how she felt, Amanda said she was fine, leaving Sam with the empty feeling of having no connection to her daughter. Sam asked herself the question that occupied her mind more and more—have the sacrifices of her career cost her Amanda's love and affection? Sam chose to dismiss that notion yet again. She concluded Amanda was simply going through the throes of puberty.

Chapter Twenty-Nine

No politician likes to talk about taxes. No person likes to pay them, including myself. But all responsible citizens know taxes are the only way to support valued governmental needs, from defense to education. It therefore flows that taxes are not inherently wrong. They are only wrong when applied arbitrarily or without a defined plan. President Obama's approach is arbitrary and lacks a defined plan. So Congress should vote "no" to this budget. Where does he expect to find the necessary money to pay the countless billions needed for his plan? It would certainly not appear to be by cutting government waste. Any of the cuts in this budget are illusions, intended to mask the fundamental problem of a government unable to account for itself. When the president proposes an honest budget, he will get my and the public's support. Until then, Congress should not vote for such illusions.

Appearance on Face the Nation during campaign for governor, March 15, 2009.

November 2, 2004
Washington, DC

No other Republican dared run against Sam in her 2004 reelection campaign. She even joked about running on the Democrat primary ticket. And while she didn't, exit polls showed she got at least ten percent of the Democrat votes, a decidedly embarrassing moment in Virginia political history for the Democrats. Watts could not have been happier.

The 2004 presidential election was a sleeper. The media pushed lightly for Sam as a possible vice president, but it was too soon, and she and Watts could only fantasize at the possibility. The Democrats were in too much disarray to make any difference. Bush won reelection without much effort. The truth was the growing deficit didn't matter much in the grand scheme of global economics, but it made for juicy press. The North American economy was growing while the remainder of the world was slowing down. But no one seemed to notice. So someone everyone thought was a one-term president in 2000 easily won reelection in 2004. Some said it was his leadership after 9/11 and success in keeping terrorism at bay on American soil. The fact was John Kerry was simply too aloof and disconnected to voters and never really had a chance. So Kerry went off to lick his wounds and clip the coupons on his bonds.

Throughout Bush's presidency, Sam remained an enigma for Democrats. If it were not for her poise and command of the facts, Democrats were convinced she might alienate important supporters if the public fully understood how conservative she was. But voters liked to look more than listen. All they ever listened to were sound bites. Sam agreed with Watts that the Democrats feared she was in the Republican wings for the vice presidency—or maybe even the presidency. Watts convinced Sam whoever the Democrats put up against her in Congress, they'd never be her match in debates. Many political pundits agreed, claiming she was a possible presidential candidate in 2008.

Despite the absence of Ben at her side and his occasional run-ins with the media, Sam's popularity in Washington continued on a steady rise. It seemed she could do nothing wrong, and the media fell in love with her. She managed to separate herself from the furor of some of the controversial stands she took, particularly on abortion. And when the media pressed her on the tough issues, she parried like a pro, manipulating the media focus onto some of her projects in foreign affairs and criminal justice, two areas where she was concentrating most of her time, and to good cause.

She even managed to stay out of Bush's malaise on the budget and war in the Middle East. Instead, she attacked Democrats who failed to support the Patriot Act or the Iraqi War. She fervently believed there were weapons of mass destruction in bunkers under Saddam Hussein's control. While she supported former president Clinton's peace-keeping policies in the wars in the former Yugoslavia, she wasn't shy to make her views clear that the Clinton administration's concern over blond-haired and blue-eyed Serbs was hypocritical, or worse, when Clinton virtually ignored the ethnic cleansing among blacks in Somalia and elsewhere in Africa. In Sam's eyes, Clinton refused to help where he should have. The inconsistency upset Sam and she never lost an opportunity to tell the media precisely how she felt about the Democrats' polices. She was as ardent a Republican as conservatives could hope to find.

Hard stands on national defense were good fodder for Sam. If pressed on the budget or health care, she deflected the issues like an old pro. It was what the party regulars regarded as business as usual. The thing Sam found comforting was her belief that it would have been much different if Gore or Kerry had been elected—all for the worse.

Sam continued quietly moving her own agenda. Hearings on foreign affairs, many of them closed sessions, were a continuing education for her. And as always, she learned quickly. It was typical with Sam—once she identified herself with a cause, she attacked its enemies with a vengeance. The wars in Iraq and Afghanistan and combating terrorism were causes with which she became obsessed, assigning her staff to provide her with research some believed the president didn't even have.

It didn't take long for the media to contrast her with the other women politicians of Washington. Feinstein and Boxer of California made some early news, but Sam saw them as media clowns, not legitimate leaders. So it was with most other women in Congress and the Senate. Sam seemed to rise above the party stereotypes and gain the image of a true leader, a middle-to-right-of-the-road Republican with a few controversial stances. What perhaps made her particularly popular in those early years in Congress, however, was her continued honesty with the press. While Watts's expertise was sometimes needed to save her from potentially embarrassing situations, on the whole Sam controlled her agenda.

It was the World Trade Center attack on September 11, 2001, that forged her views. She understood Washington and New York and how terrorism would affect such cities. She knew there was no way to police cities so dense and diverse in any meaningful way. She knew it was just luck the 1993 World Trade Center bombing did as little damage as it did, at least in terms of lost lives. Those were amateur terrorists. The same luck held true for the ring collected by the FBI planning additional bombings in New York. Except for the informant the FBI persuaded to turn on his cleric, those bombings were just days away from happening. Sam always believed it was just a matter of time before a serious terrorist slipped through the cracks. She resolved America needed to eliminate the root of the problem.

In her second term in Congress, Sam began holding private meetings with key congressmen, senators, Pentagon officials, and law enforcement. Her group became known to insiders in Washington as the Harrison Caucus, a collection of powerful Republicans and conservative Democrats who yearned for the kind of presidential bravado so often displayed by Ronald Reagan. While they supported Bush and his wars, they were not convinced enough effort—covert or otherwise—was being used to rout out Al-Qaeda. The Harrison Caucus wanted to see Osama bin Laden brought to a swift—and preferably ignoble—death. She and her cronies were relentless in urging more aggressive action. The media loved it and kept Sam in the focus of the public eye.

None of this was lost on liberal Democrats. Sam kept rolling on, gaining in popularity and becoming a focal point of the Republican Party and the staunchest supporter of America's conservative pride—something the Democrats couldn't seem to get a handle on. Sam was sure she was a standard topic of discussion between Bill and Hillary Clinton and most other Capitol Hill liberals and presidential hopefuls. In their private moments, she and Ben delighted in playing the Clintons.

"Bill, dear, just what are we going to do about that Sam bitch? She's stealing our limelight. After all, she's not the president, and isn't it my turn next?" Sam would mimic to Ben.

"Now Hillary, dear, you're sounding just like Nancy Pelosi."

It became a regular routine, at least on those few occasions when Sam and Ben could be together without the pressures of Sam's schedule. By the end of Bush's first term, Ben had given up most of his outside activity, except his classes at Georgetown, to have more time with Sam and Amanda. What he didn't enjoy was the ever-decreasing time Washington wedged between him and Sam. Somewhere between visits to Virginia and House floor votes, Sam and Ben accepted the reality and chalked it off as business as usual for the two of them.

CHAPTER THIRTY

Jeremy, wherever you are, I hope you're fine. Your father and I think about you every day and are never without concerns for your safety. I know what you're doing is noble and something you love, but please remember we want you home safely. You don't need to be a hero for anyone. You'll always be a hero in our hearts. Write when you can.

Excerpt from letter to her son, Jeremy, November 27, 2007.

February 7, 2008
Washington, DC

"Sam, it's the president on the phone," reported Pamela over the intercom. Pamela had risen from a temporary secretary in one of Sam's early campaigns into Sam's political assistant, running her congressional office.

"You mean his secretary?"

"No, Sam, it's really him. I recognize his voice."

Sam looked at the phone. The red hold button blinked as if it were warning her not to pick up the receiver.

Why is the president calling me? He wants something. And calling me direct must mean it's something big.

As she raised the handset to her ear, her intuition told her something ominous lay ahead. Her hand shook. Say whatever you want, but a call directly from the president was a decidedly sobering experience.

"Hello, Mr. President. This is Samantha Harrison."

God, I called myself by my full name.

It was the first time she'd done so in her memory.

"Congresswoman Harrison, I wonder if I might trouble you to come over to the White House. Something has developed, and I'd like you to be in the loop. A car is on its way." The tone in his voice was somber, almost fearful. Something was seriously wrong. It had to be. The president of the United States was calling Samantha Harrison, namesake of the Harrison Caucus. Sam knew he couldn't be calling her on a matter of domestic policy.

"Yes, Mr. President. I'll be over immediately."

When she arrived at the White House, security was expecting her. A single marine guard, replete in a stiffly starched uniform and head nearly shaved bald, greeted her after a White House security guard let her in the west entrance. The presence of the marine, even though routine, gave Sam the sense there was something foreboding in the air. It was eerily silent as the marine guard escorted her down the hall toward the Oval Office. It suddenly hit Sam it was the first time she'd ever been in the inner circle of the White House. The occasional state dinner never really saw the true place. The sense of history as she walked down the hall was far more humbling than she'd ever imagined it would be. The wars, the tough decisions, the life-and-death struggles. She suddenly felt sorry for its forty-third resident. She also felt in awe and wished she had called Ben before she was rushed over by the president's private car. Oh, how she wanted him to know where she was. As she approached the final door to the Oval Office, she asked the guard to stop. She needed to go to the ladies' room.

"I'd hate to interrupt the president with such a request," she feebly told the guard.

"I understand, ma'am. It's right over here." She regretted it was so close. She'd have been happy if it were in Siberia.

She stared at herself in the mirror, shocked by what she saw. The reflection was not what the media made her out to be at all. This was no ice woman. It was a fragile person who was about to meet the president of the United States, the most powerful person in the world, to probably hear something of vital importance to the lives of Americans. She felt a crushing sensation at the enormity of the power of the office and the White House itself. She clearly needed to get a grip.

Come on, I'm one of the House's most influential members. Surely I can handle a simple meeting with the president. We're even in the same party. So how bad could this really be?

The light knock on the door dragged her back to reality.

"Is everything OK, ma'am?" came the voice of the marine from outside the door. "The president is waiting."

Damn, I don't want to go.

"I'll be right there."

Sam composed herself as best she could, took a deep breath, and walked through the door with all the conviction she could muster. It wasn't much.

"Well, Sergeant, let's get along, shall we?"

"It's Lieutenant, ma'am. Right this way, please. He's right through that door."

Great. Now I've insulted a marine officer. He probably wants to kill me.

She entered the Oval Office. The president was sitting as his desk while Secretary of State Condoleezza Rice sat on a couch across the office. No one else was there. The room seemed much smaller than she thought it would be.

Both the president and Rice rose as she came in. Bush walked from behind his desk to properly greet Sam, acting as any gentleman would when a lady entered a room. None of that impressed Sam. She had no doubt it was Laura Bush who made sure her husband showed proper respect, and but for her, he would have never gotten out of his seat.

Extending his hand, Bush said, "Mrs. Harrison, thank you for coming."

"Mr. President, what's wrong? I have a terrible feeling about this meeting."

Jesus, I could have at least thanked him for having me over. Instead, I spill by guts and admit I'm scared. Get a grip.

Bush smiled and motioned for Sam to have a seat on the couch opposite Rice. Bush sat in the chair between the two, as if ready to referee a debate.

The president continued. "Mrs. Harrison, I like the way you want to get to the bottom of an issue. Always admired that about you. You're more like a Texan than you might think."

Sam remained mute. She felt a lump in her throat and feared she'd never get a word past it.

"We have a problem." The president handed her a typewritten note, stored in a plastic sleeve to protect it and preserve any fingerprints. She read it:

> President Bush:
>
> Your worst nightmare is here. You have forty-eight hours to free El Sayyid Nosair, Omar Abdel-Rahman, Mahmud Abouhalima, Ahmad Ajaj,

> Nidal Ayyad, Mohammad Salameh, Ramzi Yousef, Eyuc Ismoil, Mustafa al-Hawsawi, Walid bin Attash, Khalid Sheik Mohammed, and Abd al-Rahim al-Nashiri.
>
> If you fail, a nuclear bomb like the one you will find in the convention center in Atlanta will detonate in a city in the United States. The blood will be on your hands. Pra*ise Allah.*
>
> The United Brotherhood of al-Qaeda

Sam said nothing, staring at the letter. Her mind was racing.

What the hell is going on? They're right; this is America's worst nightmare!

Rice's words brought Sam's head up. "Mrs. Harrison, we received the letter this afternoon at two o'clock. Believe it or not, it was hand delivered. The man in custody won't talk. At least not yet. Their list includes virtually all of the terrorists convicted in the 1993 bombing of the World Trade Center and the 9/11 attack."

I know the names on the list, you idiot. And the man in custody has not yet talked? What do you mean not yet? What about all the torture I know you use but deny?

"Mrs. Harrison, are you all right?" interjected Bush.

Am I all right? No, damn it, I'm not.

"Yes, Mr. President, I'm fine. And please call me Sam." Bush didn't respond that she could call him George.

Rice continued with her usual clinical tone: "The device found in Atlanta at four o'clock was a Russian-made one-megaton nuclear bomb. Small, but effective. From its markings, we believe it was originally from the Ukraine. Two months ago they couldn't account for four nuclear devices. Now three."

Bush took up the conversation. "Sam, other than the three of us, the detail we sent to Atlanta, and the army intelligence group responsible for tracking down nuclear terrorism, no one else is aware of this threat."

"Why tell me?" asked Sam.

Bush seemed a little surprised. "Because you're vice chair of the House Foreign Relations Committee, Sam. That's why. And because despite your conservative views, you appeal to both sides of the aisle."

So what? You think I know where the damn bombs are?

Bush moved to the couch and sat beside Sam, his eye contact making it clear he meant what he was about to say. "Whatever I decide to do, I need a united front. I do not want to let liberal Democrats risk American lives as they attack me. And the truth is, I have no ally I can trust in that party. So I need someone who can reach across the aisle but still carry the conservative interests of national defense. And most of all, I respect your knowledge of terrorist activities. Everyone does. Your staff probably knows twice what we do." Sam could see Rice flinch. "So I'd like to know what you think."

What I think? I think you're trying to set me up as your puppet like you did Colon Powell before his speech at the UN convincing the world that Saddam Hussein had weapons of mass destruction when all he had were empty bunkers. Not me. I'm no one's dupe.

Her courage returning, Sam was blunt. "What I think, Mr. President, is we're about to lose an American city. If they have nerve enough to give one back, you can be sure they will deliver on the threat. We need to strike quickly but quietly. Army intelligence will never find the bomb. Secretary Rice, how true do you think the Al-Qaeda identification on the note is?"

Now I'm in command of this conversation.

"We're pretty sure it's them. We figure if they're cocky enough to rub it in our noses like this, they want to take credit. The CIA says the other two bombs are in the Arabian desert somewhere, but they don't know where."

Don't know where? My God, what exactly do the two of you do with the intelligence briefings you get every day? Do you bother to read them?

Sam shot back trying to keep her tone balanced. "If it's Al-Qaeda, their base is likely in the Sudan, Yemen, or Iran. There are only so many places they could be, Madam Secretary. That's if you're correct that it's Al-Qaeda. Don't we have assets on the ground or surveillance that can pick up signatures? What has been the Internet chatter? Do we have some drones we can send in to search for activity? Are there any satellite images that can help?"

Rice remained calm and clinical. "Well, you're partially right, but I don't think we have the luxury of time to debate the point. According to our intelligence, there are a number of potential Al-Qaeda sites: at least three in the Sudan, one or more in Iran, and one potential site in Yemen. Our operatives have ruled out any other locations. Does your intel indicate other terrorist havens that might have the capacity to harbor a nuclear weapon?"

Harbor a nuclear weapon? You've got to be kidding. A nuclear warhead is the size of a duffel bag. A terrorist with a pup tent could harbor one. What's the matter with you people?

Surprised by the question and how it revealed the schisms between the White House and Congressional intelligence apparatus, Sam told Rice the locations sounded right. "Although I'd also be concerned about Saudi Arabia or Syria. The truth is I'm sure your intel is every bit as good as anything our committee has. But I'll check right away."

Your intel stinks, Rice. Just like it did at the beginning of the Gulf War.

"The president's plan is to deploy insertion teams into all three areas," Rice replied. "If there are more sites, we'll insert more strike teams. We can't afford a mistake, so we'll go in everywhere we think a bomb may be. We hope to capture someone who will either talk or who we can use as a bargaining chip. In the meantime, we're doing all we can to alert cities and search where we can."

Sam was curious why Rice and not the president was outlining the mission. She wondered if it was some naive way of preserving deniability. The president could always say whatever Rice said wasn't what he meant.

You're not getting off that easy, Mr. President.

Sam turned to the president. If she was about to become involved in planning a covert operation, she was going to talk to the top man, not his flunky. Sam had a well-known dislike for Rice. She thought she was far too removed from reality and stuck in academic debate to be heading the State Department, but that was the president's choice, not hers.

Sam ignored Rice. "No matter who you might capture, Mr. President, he won't be a bargaining chip. Anyone in Al-Qaeda would rather die than become a pawn in your game. I've sat in more than enough Congressional Committee meetings to know that. No, Mr. President, your team has to get someone who will talk by whatever means it takes."

Bush responded directly to her, now talking as if Rice was not in the room. "Mrs. Harrison, it's quite obvious I am facing something I cannot handle by conventional means. I too have sat in countless meetings. You don't have a monopoly on reality, Sam. In my presidency I have conducted more covert operations than many people know, including you and your buddies on the Hill. Some might have skirted the line legally. But I don't give a damn."

Sam's brief feeling of bravado faded as she again realized she was speaking to the president of the United States.

Bush continued: "I know some people, maybe even you, feel I've made mistakes. And I don't much give a damn about that, either. I know we need to do whatever is necessary to find the bombs and the people who have them. This is my last year as president, and I assure you I intend to do whatever it takes. I don't care how many Al-Qaeda die in the process. Or their families. They murdered thousands of innocent Americans. The blood is on their hands and the hands of anyone who harbors them. This is not about what I need to do. I know what needs to be done. I called you here because I need your help."

Now humbled, Sam raised her chin and as firmly as she could, replied, "What can I do, Mr. President?"

"You have a choice, Sam. I'd like you with me on this, for both political and practical reasons. I need you to control Congress. I am confident you can. Rest assured, I intend to do what needs to be done and not be held back by any congressional rules—or any law for that matter. If you're not prepared to work with me on that basis, go. I only ask you give me forty-eight hours before you crucify me with the press if I don't succeed. If you go public or tell your colleagues before that time limit, you'll accomplish nothing, and I swear I will do everything in my power during whatever remains of my presidency to derail any political career or office you may have set your eyes on, including this one."

My God, the president of the United States has just told me that if necessary, he would break the law and if I interfered, he would destroy me politically. He isn't asking for my support. He's asking me to put my career on the line for what may be an illegal conspiracy. What will this one be called, Nukegate?

Sam knew she was between a rock and a hard place. If she failed to participate but remained silent, her career might be over if it ever came out that she knew and said nothing to her colleagues. She'd lose any credibility in Washington. If she did withdraw and tell, she would face the wrath of a president and all the public support he could undoubtedly muster. If she participated, she may be drawn into an illegal act that could bring her and the president down. If she didn't help, millions of people might die. Sam realized she had just learned firsthand how sly a president she was facing. Bush had obviously thought this out carefully. Only one witness in the room. A witness who was clearly loyal to the president and not about to come to the aid of a distractor or someone not loyal to his cause. In the game of chess, Sam just hit checkmate.

Why did I ever pick up the damn phone? I should have listened to Ben and gone home for dinner.

Sam straightened in her chair. "Well, Mr. President, I guess you've got this whole thing pretty well planned out, at least in terms of my involvement. I suppose you already know I have no good choice to make. For now I'll go along on one condition."

Bush's expression was not a pleased one. "Condition? And what is that?"

"If you at any time make a move without telling me, I'm out, and I go public."

The president relaxed, leaning back on the couch. "Very well. You have my commitment to that." Sam caught the approving exchange of glances between Bush and Rice.

The next eight hours were immersed in planning and debating. One proposal after another was adopted and rejected. The participants were at times members of the Joint Chiefs, the CIA, and the FBI. When Operation Freehand became the name for the exercise, it seemed there was no "what if" ignored. Sam brought in a few loyalists from the House and Senate, including a couple of Democrats. They needed to feel they were consulted, even though Bush couldn't have cared less about what they had to say. It was Sam's job to keep up the illusion he did care. But everyone knows there are always things you never consider. Things you know are there in the back of your mind, but contingencies you never bring to a conscious level, however hard you try. There are always surprises.

The plan was simple in its basic deployment. Special units of Army's Delta Force and Navy Seals would take control of the suspected camps and question the prisoners to find out the location of the devices. The CIA would conduct the interrogations. All agreed that drugs, waterboarding, and any other legal means could be deployed to get to the truth. While no one ever said illegal means could be used as well, everyone knew they would be used if needed to extract the information, provided it didn't "unnecessarily" endanger the prisoner's life. The president's memo, which Sam insisted be written and signed, reflected the basic strategy. The president made Sam initial it as well.

Bush rose from his seat. "Ladies and gentlemen, I think we've come to the end of what we can do as a group. It's time to leave it to the professionals. Godspeed."

Sam wanted to tell Bush the homily to God was a little out of place under the circumstances, but wisely chose not to.

As everyone left, Bush made a point of thanking each participant individually with a few private words.Sam would have loved to be a fly on the wall to hear the private words to each of the participants, feeling a combination of curiosity and paranoia at what Bush might be saying. When it was Sam's turn for the personal whisper, Bush told her he owed her one and that what she'd done would not be forgotten. For a starter, he said he'd take a closer look at her foreign aid package, certain the two could work out an acceptable compromise.

That was quite a concession since it was likely Bush could execute his package with or without Sam's support. While grateful, Sam's main desire at the moment was to go home, shower, and sleep before returning to the White House Situation Room for the operations phase, ready to hear the news of success or failure firsthand. It was going to be a long day ahead for everyone.

Bush looked invigorated, impressing Sam with his stamina and ability to control the situation. He was not as weak a leader as some Republicans had made Sam believe.

Chapter Thirty-One

We missed you this Thanksgiving. I was in church when I suddenly realized this was our first Thanksgiving with you away. It made my heart sink. But then I remembered all the glee on your face that first time we took you to the Macy's Thanksgiving Day parade. Dad and Amanda are fine, and I'm still trying to figure out what politics is all about. I figure if I keep trying, I'll get it right one of these days. We all miss you, Jeremy, and hope we'll see you at Christmas.

Excerpt from letter to her son, Jeremy, November 27, 2007.

February 8, 2008
USS *Harry Truman*

Marine helicopter squadron commander Lt. Colonel Jeremy Harrison, the son of Ben and Samantha Harrison, was relaxing in the wardroom of America's aircraft carrier USS *Harry Truman* when an ensign came in to tell him the captain wanted him in the ready room "on the double." Jeremy, on graduating Annapolis, chose the marines over the navy for his military career as an aviator. He wanted to be on the front lines of any action. *Semper Fi.*

For five weeks now, the USS *Harry Truman* was docked in the Black Sea harbor at Constanta, Romania. One of the largest deep-water ports in the world, the *Harry Truman* was there while navy brass and other politicos tried to convince Romania to allow them to build a US naval base in the port.

Jeremy knocked on the captain's door. It was already opened.

"Lt. Colonel Harrison, sir. You called for me, Captain?"

Navy Captain Herman A. Shelanski had commanded the *Harry Truman* for more than two years. He held a degree in molecular, cellular, and developmental biology from the University of Colorado, a master's degree in electrical and space systems engineering from the Naval Postgraduate School, and a graduate certificate from the Navy Nuclear Power School. He did some training at the Naval War College in Newport, Rhode Island, as well. His career at sea was stellar, including several deployments in the E-2C Hawkeye, the navy's tactical airborne warning aircraft or its "eye in the sky," with the signature radar dish atop its fuselage.

"Sit down, Harrison. It seems the president has cooked up a good one for us. Operation Freehand. Rumors say it also has the approval of your mother, but I couldn't care less about rumors. We received our orders at eleven hundred hours, so I guess they're up late in Washington. Right now they need to know if you're ready to pull off your part in this little sojourn our commander-in-chief has planned for you."

Shelanski rarely hid his contempt for Bush. But when he received orders that the president authorized a covert mission, he approached it without reservations, ignoring any political consequences that would interfere with executing a proper military solution. It wasn't that Shelanski thought the military should make all the decisions; it was just that he regarded sending men to die or suffer in battle to be a decision that should be carried forward only if the soldiers and aviators are given complete support. In Shelanski's eyes, no one is expendable. Everyone needs to return from a mission to label it a success. He had seen too often what it was not to return.

Jeremy led a squadron of six AH-64D Apache Longbow attack helicopters based at NATO's air base in Incirlik, Turkey, roughly two hundred miles from the Iran border.

The AH-64D Apache Longbow is a twin-engine heavy attack and close-support helicopter manufactured by Boeing's Defense, Space & Security division. Each aircraft has a pilot and copilot, one in the front and the other behind the pilot much like a fighter plane. Indeed, the Apache is more of a fighter plane than a helicopter. Capable of speeds in excess of 290 kilometers per hour, the Apache has a range of 260 nautical miles, more than enough for the mission at hand. It is undoubtedly the world's most advanced attack helicopter, proven in combat during the Gulf War. Its armaments include a thirty-millimeter machine gun, called a chain gun. Mounted on a turret beneath the fuselage, it is controlled from a helmet worn by the pilot, known as the Integrated Helmet & Display Sighting System. Wherever the pilot looks, the gun points, ready to fire its twelve hundred rounds at the press of a finger. In addition to the chain gun, the Longbow sported an array of hellfire missiles and seventy-millimeter rockets. The Longbows under Jeremy's command also had the enhanced ability to detect objects (moving or stationary) without being detected. Jeremy particularly liked the high-tech monitor that could classify and threat-prioritize up to one hundred and twenty-eight targets in less than a minute. Best video game $14 million could buy. For all it mattered, each of the Longbows is a battleship capable of devastating destruction in a matter of seconds.

Jeremy was considered among the best command pilots in the region, and for that reason was singled out for the mission he was about to receive. The joint chiefs thought twice about choosing him when they realized he was Samantha Harrison's son but decided against making it an issue since their orders were to use the best pilots available. Jeremy was the best.

Temporarily on the *Harry Truman,* Jeremy was part of larger group of American aviators evaluating the requirements for an air base in Romania. He didn't like living on the carrier and longed to be back in Turkey with his crew. So any mission that got him off the boat suited him just fine. Anything to get him off what he considered a floating hell.

The captain explained that Harrison's squadron would be deployed from their base in Turkey. From there they would fly at low altitude, entering Iranian air space from the north. Their target was about fifty kilometers into Iran. According to the orders, a team from army Special Forces and a civilian would accompany his crews in a Chinook 47F. One civilian would fly in Jeremy's Apache as his copilot, although Jeremy was told not to expect him to know how to fly a helicopter. Jeremy didn't like that idea at all but knew he had no choice. When Special Forces and the civilian were through with their mission—whatever that mission was—Jeremy was to take them and any prisoners out the same way he came in. At that point, air support from F-16 jet fighters out of Incirlik and Izmir was available if they encountered any serious problems. Otherwise, the mission was covert. "Serious problems" meant the brass didn't want to hear about any problems, serious or otherwise. Jeremy knew he and his squadron were on their own.

At other US military locations elsewhere in the world, the same exercise and instructions were repeated to the crews who were assigned their own particular targets.

That afternoon's overcast weather suited Jeremy. It made the flight easier because good weather made pilots less focused, watching the scenery rather than their instrument panels. Jeremy liked to command his wing in bad weather. From the *Harry Truman,* it took an F-16 only an hour and a half from Jeremy's initial briefing to cover the five hundred miles to the US Marine base in Incirlik, Turkey. In Incirlik they picked up the civilian. From there they flew to Diyarbakir, Turkey, where Jeremy's Apache Longbows were waiting.

He arrived at Diyarbakir at 2000 hours, eight o'clock in the evening in the civilian world. Throughout the flight, the civilian, who identified himself only as Mr. Jones, said nothing except an occasional acknowledgment of instructions given to him. That also suited Jeremy just fine. He had no doubt Mr. Jones had another name. It didn't take long for Jeremy to figure out Mr. Jones was CIA. A real spook. All Jeremy could figure was this mission was some quick intelligence effort. Why they needed thirty men on the Chinook from Special Forces was still a mystery, particularly for what would probably be another uneventful covert recon mission into Iran. Unbeknownst to most, many such covert missions were undertaken.

After landing in Diyarbakir, it took an hour to get his Apaches ready. Jeremy and three other Apaches in his squadron were activated for the mission, along with the Chinook. While ground crews serviced the helicopters, Jeremy had time to write a letter home.

At nine thirty the Apaches and Chinook left Diyarbakir, covered by the cloak of an overcast, moonless night. Once again, just how Jeremy liked it.

About fifteen minutes into the mission, Jeremy's squadron entered Iranian airspace, undetected, just as it had numerous other times. When Jeremy let the civilian know they had crossed the border, the spook spoke a full sentence for the first time.

"I understand your mother is Samantha Harrison."

"Yes, sir. That's correct."

This is all I need. After entering hostile airspace when I need all my concentration, the spook wants to chat.

"I really admire her, Colonel. She's got more guts than almost any of the politicians on the Hill. If you ask me, I think she planned this whole mission. Bush doesn't have the balls for it."

"I wouldn't know, sir."

Jesus, what the hell are we up to? Bush doesn't have the balls to do something the spook thinks my mother conjured up?

It looked as if there might be some excitement after all. Jeremy's wing hadn't seen real action for quite some time and needed it to keep on edge. And it certainly didn't bother him that this was a covert operation. It would be the sixth he'd flown, typical for an Apache squadron protecting transports dropping off supplies to Iranian rebels.

Flying at less than fifty feet—known to pilots as flying nap-of-the-earth or NOE—the Apaches skimmed the surface of the desert, approaching the target downwind to delay the point at which the target would hear the engines. While the Apaches were among the quietest helicopters made, no helicopter could be made stealth. The beating of rotors through the air was easily heard from a thousand yards, regardless of the prevailing winds. There was also some disadvantage to the overcast skies. The roar of the Apaches carried further. But it also meant the Apaches were harder to see. Not that any of it really mattered. The time between a target hearing the rotors and the Apaches arriving at the target was no more than thirty seconds, hardly enough time to mount any defensive strategy. To defend against an Apache coming in under the radar, you either needed to be warned ahead of time or be on full alert at that precise moment. Jeremy knew neither would be the case. Iranian security on these covert missions was always tight, and the Iranians never seemed to be on alert.

At about fifteen miles from the target, the direct feed from the satellite positioned above came to life on the display panel on Jeremy's Apache. The latest in detection technology, the Milstat satellite, secretly launched by a space shuttle in 1993, actually sensed heat from targets using infrared sensors. First used in the Gulf War, Milstat was still a closely guarded secret. From Jeremy's display, it looked like a relatively small camp with five or six buildings. The satellite photos indicated six, but they were sometimes off a bit. There were probably about fifty or so men housed there, an easy group for the Apaches and their Special Forces.

The target actually had five buildings and four tents, housing a relatively small group of thirty men and ten women, all of them loyalists to Al-Qaeda, ready to die for their cleric.

"We're just a few minutes out." Jeremy broke the radio silence and ordered the penetration to move ahead and to hover a hundred feet from the compound in an arch around it. In that way, the defenses would be scattered in an attempt to deal with the Apaches. Once in position, the Chinook would fly in and drop the troops. Two Apaches would remain in the air while Jeremy and one other landed. Once the troops were off the Chinook, it would fly off a safe distance and await Jeremy's command to return when mission was over. Jeremy knew any effort by the Iranians in the camp to defend themselves would be futile. Each Apache was virtually bulletproof, and its chain guns were capable of firing hundreds of rounds in the blink of an eye. If the mission required it, the Apaches could annihilate every man in the camp in a matter of seconds. But the orders made it clear that Washington wanted survivors.

At first Ahmed Bahar thought the noise was nothing more than the wind. A desert wind made many odd noises in the night. Unlike the wind, however, the noise grew steadily louder and rhythmic. Bahar realized the noise was the sound of helicopter rotors. He started yelling commands.

To Jeremy's surprise, the target detected them about a mile out, before they should have heard the rotors. Jeremy made a mental note to himself to go over that when he debriefed after the mission. Perhaps the overcast night had a greater effect than he originally thought. No matter. In less than twenty seconds after being detected, the Apaches arrived at the target.

Panic took hold of the camp. No one expected the enemy would find out where they were, let alone attack. After all, hundreds of thousands of lives were at stake if they detonated the bomb. Could it be the United States was willing to sacrifice so many of its citizens just as Islam would for its Holy War?

Impossible. This attack is insanity, thought Bahar.

As the rotors grew to a roar, Bahar rushed to the communications tent. He had to get the message out that they were under attack. While he was fully prepared to welcome his death, he wanted to be sure thousands of Americans died as well. Looking about him, the rest of his comrades disgusted him, running in every direction in panic.

Let them all die.

To his right he saw soldiers leaping from the Chinook, covered by chain-gun fire from the American gunships. He turned to fire on the infidels. That was his mistake. He got one round off from his Russian AK-47, just missing one of the soldiers, before he felt the impact. He looked down just in time to see the second impact explode on his chest. Darkness came painlessly.

As Jeremy suspected, there was little resistance, and the surprise was overwhelming. In fact, the encampment defenses were poor, an unusual fact for an Iranian facility. Jeremy made another mental note.

Chapter Thirty-Two

We are now wasting billions of dollars a year on a misguided healthcare system. While more people have access to doctors and hospitals than ever before in our history, they can't chose the ones they want, and the increased costs are staggering. Studies show there has been little, if any, improvement in our nation's health. Americans continue to die unnecessarily for lack of early diagnosis. The death rate of newborns has remained the same. The deaths of men and women from cancer and heart disease continue in unprecedented numbers. When will we learn? We cannot legislate health. We need to put money in education and helping those who live in places where doctors can't be found. We need to find a way of helping those people afraid to talk about their problems. We need to reach out, not with dollars but with people. For decades we've sent people all over the world to help those in need. Let's take some of the millions in the health care plan and invest in people who will go into our cities and our rural towns and bring the health plan to the people. We need a national health care corps to do for our needy as the Peace Corps did for world peace.

Campaign speech, October 20, 2016.

February 9, 2008
White House Situation Room

While Sam had been present when live feeds came from the field before, she had never been in the White House Situation Room, a cramped 525-square-foot conference room and intelligence management center in the basement of the West Wing of the White House, built in 1961 by President John F. Kennedy. Together in the small quarters were President Bush, Vice President Dick Cheney, Secretary of

State Condoleezza Rice, CIA Director General Michael V. Hayden, National Security Advisor Stephen Hadley, some military brass, and a select number of staffers. Everyone's eyes were glued to a screen covering the wall.

An officer whose name Sam never learned explained what was happening.

"At this point, four of our strike units have come up empty-handed. We're now looking at part of the Sixteenth Air Wing out of NATO's air base in Incirlik, Turkey."

Sam's heart jumped from her chest. "My son commands an Apache wing out of Incirlik. Is his wing part of the mission?" The room froze. The soldier continued.

"We have no way of knowing right now, ma'am. I don't have that information on hand."

"Well can you get it?" implored Sam.

The president interrupted. "Sam, I'm sure if your son is in the unit, he's fine. We'll make it a priority to find out more as soon as we can. But for now we have to get back on with the mission." Sam didn't know whether he was sympathizing with her as a mother or chastising her for interrupting such a grand show.

"Coming onto the screen to your left are the helos," continued the soldier. "To the right, about a foot or so from the edge of the screen, you can see the image of the camp they're about to attack. As they get closer, we'll zoom in and increase the detail."

Sam marveled at this *Star Wars*-like technology. She was overwhelmed by technology at the hand of the president that even she, as a ranking of the Foreign Relations Committee, could not access. She'd heard stories that the president could monitor just about any location on earth at any time, down to the license plates of cars, but she didn't know what was fact or fiction in those stories. It was fact.

"OK," the soldier said, "they're getting close and look as though they're landing and deploying. Yes. They are. That bigger chopper is the Chinook holding the troops."

Everyone held their breath as they watched flashes and images darting across the screen. It was all surreal with no sound. Sam kept thinking she wanted to grab the remote and take it off mute.

After a few minutes, the flashes stopped, and the images of soldiers moving slowed down.

"It looks as though the camp is secure, and the unit members are cleaning up the area and perimeter. Those occasional additional flashes may be more resistance, but it does not appear to be significant. We should know for sure what happened in a couple of minutes."

Suddenly the screen went fuzzy. The transmission was lost.

"What that hell is going on?" shouted Cheney. "What happened to the damn transmission?"

"Sorry, sir," blurted the soldier. "I'm not sure."

"Well, get sure pronto and get that picture back," Bush interjected.

They all sat there for a half hour. No picture. No report. Finally one of the civilians spoke. He did not identify himself.

"I suspect the satellite feed has malfunctioned." Sam wondered if that was the truth. "I suggest we be patient until we get final intel from the men on the field."

And so they sat staring at a blank screen like deer in headlights

Chapter Thirty-Three

Secretary Clinton says I'll destroy the environment by letting oil exploration go rampant throughout our nation. Hogwash. The technology exists to safely extract enormous supplies of oil and natural gas from countless locations right here in the United States. Supplies that could give us energy independence in under ten years. But if you'd prefer to waste money on more wind and solar projects that will fail as so many have in the past, then I guess Mrs. Clinton is right, and you should vote for her.

Campaign speech, October 29, 2016.

February 9, 2008
Iranian Dessert

The terrorists who tried to defend their camp died quickly, victims of Apache chain guns and Special Forces fire. The Special Forces deployed from the Chinook overran the camp in a matter of minutes. One American was wounded, but not seriously. He was taken care of quickly by a medic. In less than fifteen minutes after Jeremy's attack team was first sighted, the target was taken. The efficiency impressed even Jeremy. This was the first time he had joined in a mission with Special Forces, and their precision was breathtaking. Another mental note for the debriefing. The Special Forces Naval Commander in charge obviously knew what he was doing. Add that the Iranians were no more the fighters today than the Iraqis were in Desert Storm, and you had the makings for a quick and decisive engagement.

At Jones's invitation, Jeremy accompanied him into the largest of the buildings with the commander, saying it was the headquarters for the encampment. The commander was carrying one of the AK-47s recovered from a dead defender. Jeremy made a mental note to get one for himself as a souvenir of a successful mission.

There were nine prisoners left—seven men and two women—standing in a line, all shackled together. Jeremy wondered why so many others died in so efficient a raid, but it was not his concern. He'd address that in the debriefing. So far his mission was right on schedule. Within a few minutes, his wing and these remaining prisoners would be on their way to Turkey.

"Mr. Jones, just what is this encampment?"

"A training site for Iranian terrorists, no doubt supported by their friends in Al-Qaeda."

Two Special Forces officers entered the room.

"Commander, we've swept the area. Two nukes found. The rest is clear."

"Excellent. Secure the area, load the nukes in the Chinook, and wait outside with the men for my command." He turned to Mr. Jones. "Mr. Jones, the matter is now in your hands. I think it's time Colonel Harrison left you and me alone with the prisoners."

Two nukes outside and you think I'm going to miss this? No way!

Before Jeremy could object, Jones replied: "That's all right, Commander. I think he'd like to see this. His mother is Samantha Harrison."

The commander was clearly impressed. "Really? Colonel, your mother is one tough woman. But I am sorry, Mr. Jones, I must insist you let Colonel Harrison leave."

The spook turned to Jeremy. "You can go or stay as you like, Colonel, but what we have here is a group of terrorists who have managed to get their hands on four nuclear warheads, two of which we just recovered in this camp. The third was recovered in Atlanta earlier today. The fourth is somewhere in the United States ready to go off unless we free some towelheads we're holding in federal prison because they blew up the World Trade Center, among other things. It's my job to convince someone from this group to tell us where the last bomb is. Do you have a problem with that?"

"I wouldn't know, sir."

What the hell is going on here?

Jeremy had a sinking feeling he was about to be part of a book full of Geneva Convention violations.

And my mother had a part in this?

"So, Colonel, are you staying or leaving? I don't have time to wait."

"I'll stay." Jeremy had a feeling he'd regret his decision. But if his mother was involved, he'd see it through, too.

"Good," replied Jones.

"Damn," said the commander.

The commander unshackled the first prisoner, a woman, and brought her over to the spook. Without asking a single question, the spook brought his .45 Magnum to the side of the prisoner's head and fired, making sure her brains splattered all over her comrades. The suddenness of the act startled everyone, and the level of fear in the remaining prisoners' eyes was riveting. The spook nodded to the commander again, and he unshackled the next prisoner, this time a man.

"No," said Jones. "Leave him. Bring me the next one in line."

The commander obliged and again, without a question being asked, his brains were blown all over the others. Some in the line started praying.

Jeremy could not stand by silently. "I must protest this action, Jones. What the hell are you doing? You are violating the prisoners' rights under the Geneva Convention."

Jones shook his head in disgust. "Colonel, when I want your input, I'll ask for it. You're free to stay, but you might be better off leaving." As much as he wanted to leave, Jeremy stood his ground, frozen before the spectacle, strangely curious about the spook's next move. And just as stubborn as his mother.

Another nod from the spook to the commander. Another man brought to the spook.

This time Jones asked the prisoner a question in his native language. Jeremy had no idea what was said, but the prisoner spit in Jones's face and responded with what was obviously some kind of insult. The result was instant, and more brains were all over his comrades, three of who were now crying.

The spook said something to the six remaining prisoners. One spoke back in anger. The spook calmly walked over to him and emptied a round into his head, not bothering to have him unshackled.

He repeated the sentence. Silence.

Jones walked back to Jeremy and the commander. "Interesting isn't it? It seems our friends here don't know what to do when their own tactics are used against them. Colonel Harrison, did you ever wonder why terrorists never bothered Russians during the Cold War? It had nothing to do with the notion of comrades in arms. Hell, they hated the Russians as much as they hate us now. No, the reason they left Russian diplomats alone was because if they fucked with the Russians, their families were murdered in the middle of the night. There was no notion of hostages or prisoners. It's amazing how knowing death is a real consequence of your acts sobers even the most zealous terrorist. You see, this vermin isn't used to being caught, just being hunted. They never taste the reality of war. To them it's just some religious game. They don't really know what it's like living every day knowing there are people hell-bent on killing you—not because they need anything, but because they're ordered to do it. When someone comes to kill you under orders, he's the most dangerous killer of all. That's why these people who think they're so righteous need to feel the penalty. Without the penalty, they'll never stop killing."

Jeremy stood silently, not knowing how to respond.

The commander took one of the criers from the group. One of the others said something Jeremy took to be an order of some kind. They were his last words. Another head blown open by Jones. Five down, four to go.

The spook put the gun to the side of the prisoner's head, making him kneel in front of one of the other criers. He asked his question. Silence. *Bang!* Dead. Six down, three to go. Next.

The next crier, the one Jones skipped earlier, was brought forward. Before a question was asked, the prisoner started talking, shaking like a leaf. The other woman started to yell at him but barely got three words out before the spook laid a round into her chest from about ten feet. While death wasn't instant, it certainly made her quiet as she lay on the ground bleeding to death.

A few more questions. More answers. It looked like the spook was getting the answers he wanted. The few words in English that Jeremy understood revealed the location of the fourth bomb—Dallas, Texas—and something to do with former president Kennedy.

"Commander, our friend here says the bomb is in the book depository in Dallas. How cute. Call it in. Now."

The commander left as the spook pushed the prisoner back to the three remaining survivors.

"Colonel, I don't like this any more than you do."

I bet you don't.

"But in less than five hours, these lunatics intend to blow up Dallas and kill a million people or more. I have no time for pleasantries. A handful of dead terrorists are better than the entire population of downtown Dallas."

Jeremy was in no mood to argue, still unsure of what he should do. "What happens to the survivors?"

The commander came back, letting Jones know the message got through, and a team was on its way to the book depository. Jeremy could hear the crews outside getting ready, the rotors of the Apaches breaking the night's silence.

The three of them sat silently on chairs, no one saying a word. The prisoners remained shackled as the wounded one who was left handcuffed with them continued to bleed. Her low moans and the crying of the others were the only sounds in the room.

It was a half hour before the commander's radio broke the silence. By then the bleeder was dead, and the crying had stopped. The commander listened intently to his handset, a wide smile eventually crossing his face.

"Mr. Jones, the nuke is secured. Dallas is safe. We succeeded. Congratulations."

Jones showed no emotion. "Thank you, Commander, you can rejoin your men. Colonel, why don't you get your Apaches ready? It's time to go." The commander remained, and Jeremy wasn't going anywhere until his question was answered.

"What about the prisoners?"

"Colonel, get the Apaches ready!"

"The first seven died before you had the information you needed. Now your mission is over, Dallas is safe, and the remaining prisoners are under my control. If you do not—"

Those were Jeremy's last words. The commander emptied three rounds from his souvenir AK-47 into Jeremy's chest. He fell like a rock.

"What the hell do you think you're doing?" screamed Jones, his words unheard beyond the room over the roar of the Apaches and Chinook.

"Mr. Jones, my orders are simple. No witnesses to what you did to get the answers. I told Harrison he should leave. He chose not to. I told you he should leave. You let him stay. The two of you sealed his fate."

"Bullshit. I don't know who you think you are, or who gave you those orders, but you're finished. I have no problem shooting terrorists, but no one has the right to murder an American under my command. Now pick up his body and let's go."

"Like I said, Mr. Jones, no witnesses." Five quick rounds from the AK-47 into Jones's chest put him down. The commander then used his own forty-five to finish off the last of the prisoners. After letting go a few more rounds from the AK-47, he wiped it free of his fingerprints and threw it at one of the prisoners. Only then did he radio for the medic.

When the medic arrived, Jeremy was barely alive. Jones was dead, along with all the prisoners. Jeremy was actually calm. He felt no pain. Another mental note for the debriefing. He'd also have to be sure to tell his mother the truth about what had happened. Certainly she would have never condoned what

Jones had done. But now he was tired, and he needed sleep. He closed his eyes and never woke up.

The report the commander filed was simple. In the confusion, one of the prisoners got his hands on an AK-47 and shot and killed Jones and Harrison before the commander could take him out along with the other prisoners, all of whom were unshackled when the photographs supporting the commander's report were taken. Two Americans dead, and one wounded. Otherwise the mission was a complete success.

Chapter Thirty-Four

Today, we have a choice of over five hundred television channels and can use our TVs to order virtually anything we want. Our personal computers can organize our daily lives with a precision unheard of only ten years ago. Technology has helped cure diseases once known to be killers of countless people. Apps on our smart phones can monitor where we are 24/7. We have choices of more products than any time in history. Our children receive the best education in the world. And above all else, we are still free to speak our mind, however unpopular our views. Yet according to the media, we Americans are unhappy. It is said we are saddened by the poverty and suffering we see each night on the evening news. Saddened to live our lives in fear of the crime on our streets. Fearful of the world we are leaving for our children and grandchildren. Deeply concerned about the economy and the rising costs of health care. But the media is wrong. It is not unhappiness, sadness, or fear we feel. It is our desire to do even better. To make our lives and the lives of others better. Do not mistake our drive and hopes as unhappiness, sadness, or fear. That's how the Obama administration and my opponent want you to think. I disagree. Today we are more hopeful than ever, confident we will lead the world to even greater prosperity in the next millennium.

Campaign speech, September 12, 2016.

February 9, 2008
White House Situation Room

Someone handed Secretary Rice a sheet of paper, which she quickly read.

Rice addressed the president. "Mr. President, the bomb is located in the basement of the book depository. We've sent a team to disarm it. The two other bombs were found in Iran and are under our control. That accounts for all of them. Of the four teams, only one had any fatalities. The others had some wounded, but not badly. Congratulations on a successful mission, Mr. President." Rice's pride was a bit too much for Sam as she sat on the couch listening to Rice's report. She had stopped drinking coffee on her fifteenth cup about five hours earlier. The strike team had stayed awake in the White House throughout the mission.

Sam asked, "Do we have the names of the dead?"

"Not yet. We should have that shortly."

"Do we know what location had the casualties?" asked Sam, her heart beating wildly.

"I'm sorry, Sam. We don't know anything yet," responded Rice.

Bush rose. "Well, folks, I guess we can call it a day for now. There will be no press conference. While the mission was an incredible effort, it will remain a secret. We all deserve credit. Thank you."

A secret? Why? Why aren't we going to find out why the signal was lost?

Sam wondered how many other secret missions Bush had ordered. She yearned to talk to Ben and get some sleep.

"Thank you," Bush concluded, "I do want you all to know I appreciate your support."

Of course you do. You had to blackmail me for it.

The worst part of all for Sam was she realized that in time, once it was all declassified, this victory all but ensured Bush's place in history as a great, decisive leader. The American public loved a winner, and this was a big win for Bush.

Chapter Thirty-Five

There are no evil countries. There are evil leaders. President Bush was right when in 2001 he described Iraq, Iran, and North Korea as the Axis of Evil. While there is a fractioned peace in Iraq thanks to the blood of thousands of Americans, Iran and North Korea continue rhetoric threatening our security and the security of our allies. And other rogue nations seem intent on joining Iran and North Korea as they flood their state-owned media with vitriolic attacks on the United States and democracy. After suffering eight years with a Democrat in the White House, our image and honor around the world isn't any better than when Barack Obama took office. It's worse. This country cannot afford four more years of this same failed foreign policy that pacifies and placates. We need strong leadership the world will respect. I offer leadership long overdue.

Campaign speech, October 12, 2016.

February 9, 2008
Arlington, Virginia

Sam went home and showered. Ben was in Chicago for a meeting at the Federal Reserve. Amanda was sleeping over at a friend's. It was nice to be alone after such a long night.

Somehow she felt dirty, knowing whatever was done to get the information was probably illegal. She convinced herself it was necessary. Never before had an American city faced such a potentially devastating terrorist attack, something the United States could not let happen under any circumstances. As she stood under the warm water of the shower, she wondered what she would have done if she were president. She resolved she would have probably done the same thing. America's security must be protected at all costs, and this group of terrorists had declared war. As far as Sam was concerned, they waived any rights under the Geneva Convention.

To hell with the Geneva Convention when more than a million American lives are at stake.

When she finished her shower, she was wide-awake, probably from the adrenaline over the success of the mission and the constant cups of coffee. She had to admit it was exciting. It would probably be a movie one day. Sam wondered who would play her. Maybe Laura Dern or Meryl Streep. The Pillsbury Doughboy could play the part of the putz president. The thought made Sam laugh aloud, something that made her feel good.

The next ten minutes became a flash in Sam's life. The doorbell rang, and when Sam answered it, she was startled to see President Bush standing there, flanked by his secret service contingent. She immediately knew it was Jeremy.

Bush sounded almost clinical, as though someone had written the speech beforehand. He said he regretted telling her Jeremy was one of two dead from enemy fire while trying to take over their target. As it turned out, it was the target with the remaining two bombs and the one where they got the information on the location of the last bomb. According to the report filed by Special Forces Naval Commander Bruce Baker, Jeremy was killed trying to save the CIA interrogator's life when a prisoner managed to get his hands on a weapon. Before Baker could return fire, both Jeremy and the CIA operative were gone. The president intended to award Jeremy the Medal of Honor—secretly, of course.

She needed to be held, and the president obliged, hugging Sam as she cried uncontrollably, her breath coming is spasms. Bush walked her over to the sofa and helped her sit down.

"Sam, is anyone home?"

"No, Mr. President, I'm alone right now."

"Then I'll stay with you until someone comes to be with you." He motioned the secret service to wait outside. When they hesitated, he told them it was an order. Once they left, Bush sat down next to her as she continued crying on his shoulder. Sam had not felt such torn emotions and loss since her father died.

After a few minutes, she gained her composure and called Ben. She broke down again when Ben started crying, saying he'd be home that night.

"Mr. President, it's OK for you to go. To be honest, I'd rather be alone. Perhaps we can talk tomorrow."

Bush rose and walked to the door.

"Mr. President, when will Jeremy be home?"

"Sam, he's being flown to Washington as we speak. I promise you he'll have a funeral with full honors at Arlington." With that, Bush gently closed the door behind himself.

It was anger Sam next felt. She swore if the United States had been tougher with terrorists, her son never would have died. Instead, the CIA could never find the killers, and when they did, it took forever to convict them. For the first time, she cursed the military. Jeremy was supposed to retire and make a second career in business. How could they let her son die?

Sam called Amanda and asked her to immediately come home.

"Is it Dad, Mom?"

"No, Amanda. He's fine. Please come home, we lost your brother in Iran."

"Jeremy? What do you mean he's lost?" Amanda paused. "Mom, is Jeremy dead?"

Ben arrived late that night. Sam told him everything that happened. Everything she'd done.

The funeral was attended by a small group of congressmen and friends. Douglas Sanders attended, too. It was nice to see him again, and everyone promised to stay in touch. No one did. The heroism of Jeremy Harrison would never be known. He didn't get the Medal of Honor. The president told Sam the secrecy of the mission needed to be preserved to avoid public panic over the possibility there might be another attack. The official word on Jeremy was he died in a helicopter accident while flying over Turkey. At least Mr. Jones got a star on the wall of the CIA.

Five days after the funeral, Sam received Jeremy's last letter.

> Dear Mom and Dad:
>
> I write to you from somewhere in Turkey. I can't say where I am or where I might be going, but I hear Mom may know.
>
> I've got an interesting group with me. My crew is prepared, and we're ready for whatever this mission brings. Discipline and preparation, as you always say, Mom. Special Forces troops look so determined it's almost frightening, but I guess I'd rather have some SOBs like these guys with me than a bunch of GI grunts. The civilian with us isn't talking yet. I figure he'll let me know why he's here when he's ready to. The mystery of it makes it all the more exciting.
>
> Whatever it is I'm doing on this one, Mom, I hear your hand was in the planning. Knowing that, I feel secure and good about it. When I get back (maybe for Easter), we can talk all about the mission.

Until then, Godspeed, and I'll see you soon.

Love,
Jeremy

Sam read the letter every day until it couldn't be read anymore, falling apart from handling and tears. Ben read it once and never mentioned it again.

Chapter Thirty-Six

Terrorism can never be allowed to control our lives or our destiny. We must never give in to its demands. Every terrorist and the countries supporting them must learn they will achieve nothing in these personal wars of theirs. The condemnation and wrath of the civilized world is the only reward they will receive. I lost my only son to terrorists who proved nothing other than their inhumanity. I will not let Jeremy's memory or America's spirit be the victims of such individuals or nations. We will not be intimidated, and we will strike at the very hearts of those who believe we would ever cower before them.

Speech in closed session upon appointment to House Special Task Force on Terrorism, March 14, 2008.

March 28, 2008
Langley, Maryland

In the aftermath of Operation Freehand, Sam became head of a special presidential task force on terrorism. Bush had no choice but to appoint Sam to head the group. If he had appointed anyone else, as he had wanted to, he knew he'd lose the key Republican support he needed on new trade agreements with Japan and China. While not a popular president, Bush had a legacy he wanted to preserve and had no intention of losing his momentum or failing to finish up his legislative agenda before leaving office. He wanted history to show how he rose from governor to bring the United States out of economic doldrums and onto the road to prosperity. Bush was confident he was leaving the country in good hands. He had no doubt John McCain would be the next president. Appointing Sam to the post was one step toward accomplishing his goals. Even though it might give her a platform for a national audience, Bush never felt Sam had it in her for a full run at the presidency.

Sam took on the assignment with her usual zeal. It was terrorists who killed Jeremy, she reasoned, and the best revenge for his death was to track down every last son of a bitch and make them pay with their lives. There was barely a night she didn't have nightmares about the task at hand and the many threats her task force would help thwart. On the one hand, she was intent on staying within the law and not crossing the line, as she believed Bush had done with Operation Freehand. On the other hand, she was resolute in her conviction that had the United States been better prepared, Operation Freehand would never have been necessary. The Ukraine would have received the help it needed, and it would have never "lost" the weapons. Without the lost weapons, Al-Qaeda would have been just another ineffective group of misfits usually destroyed through their own ineptness, posing no real threats to Americans. She knew to be effective, aggressive action was necessary.

That day's meeting was scheduled with Susan Weston, a top analyst with the CIA in its satellite reconnaissance sector. They were reviewing photos and maps of the Sudan desert for possible terrorist locations. Over the past few weeks, it was apparent the Sudan had become a center for terrorist activity, and it looked as though the CIA had turned up at least four new sites.

The satellite photographs were impressive. Sam continued to marvel at the technology available to US intelligence. The photographs beamed from a satellite hundreds of miles away may as well have been taken in your backyard. The focus was sharp enough to make out men from women, and at times even read the letters or numbers on a license plate. To Weston, however, they were just another collection of routine photos. She approached them with an objective precision as she clicked the first slide onto the projection screen.

"See this area here?" Weston pointed it out to Sam with a laser pointer pen. "It shows at least five outbuildings and about a dozen tents. At any one time, we think there are probably fifty or more men and women being trained. They come and go. We don't know enough yet about their weapons, but nothing looks like much more than conventional arms. There are probably some explosives as well. There always are. As you know, we're most worried right now about chemical weapons. While we don't think this camp is making any, we're not always so sure with others. It's probably just a matter of time before they all have a capacity for chemical production. There were never enough controls on such weapons, and they're just too easy to make. So far, however, they don't have an effective delivery system. For that, we're thankful. But that will change in time, too."

Sam asked, "How easy is it for them to go to a new location if they became aware we've discovered them?"

"Pretty easy and quick, but not as fast as you see in the movies or read in spy books. They need some pretty permanent facilities to properly train their recruits. Besides, they figure we'd never try the same thing as Operation Freehand since we have no reason to believe there is a nuclear threat involved. At least after Freehand, none of the groups seem thrilled with the idea of dealing in nuclear. The consequences are too difficult to accept, even by the most hardened terrorist. While they don't seem to mind dying, they want to do it only for the glory of Allah and the virgins in heaven. It seems when we act the way they do, they can't cope. Whatever you and the president authorized for *Freehand* certainly made a lasting impression from everything we've seen."

Sam snapped at the last comment. "The authorization was from the president, not me, and if you believe he authorized something that troubles you, let me hear it now." Sam wasn't sure she really wanted to invite a discussion.

"I'm sorry, ma'am. I have no problem." It was obvious Weston also had no interest in knowing the truth, whatever it was.

After showing a few more slides of other sites with essentially the same configuration as the first, Stein projected a fifth image on the screen. This one showed what looked like a much smaller site. Stein couldn't explain why this site was smaller but was convinced those in it were up to no good. She feared a small site might be used for chemical weapons since no more than a dozen people were needed to man such a site, but she wasn't sure.

"So, Miss Weston, CIA figures there are five sites in the Sudan."

"Correct, Congresswoman."

"OK. What is the recommendation that the CIA would like me to take to the president?"

A man spoke up from the other end of the room, hidden in the darkness.

He wore a soldier's camouflage uniform bearing the shoulder insignia of Special Forces. The uniform didn't display his CIA status, but such status was never displayed on a uniform. Those who needed to know knew it. Sam wasn't one of those people.

He spoke calmly and with authority. "We need to take them out, ma'am. An insertion similar to Operation Freehand should be effective." He sat down. Sam had no idea she was looking at the man who murdered her son. Sam didn't know Baker's orders for no witnesses were from someone he'd never met. Just an order given over a secure telephone. As a good soldier, Baker felt it was his patriotic duty to follow his orders precisely and allow nothing to undermine the success of the mission and the effort his men had put into it. As for his fellow CIA operative, the spook was just another unfortunate casualty. He deeply regretted killing Jeremy and did his best to get him to leave. But in the end, Baker followed his orders and did what he fervently believed was right for America.

"Excuse me, but what is your name, sir, and how long have you been eavesdropping on this meeting?" Sam was obviously surprised by his presence and not happy.

"Naval Commander Bruce Baker, Mrs. Harrison. I was in the strike unit with your son when he died. I'm terribly sorry for your loss. For me it made the success of the mission hollow."

It was the first time Sam had met anyone who had been on the raid in Iran. Baker had not attended the funeral. Suddenly, a flood of emotions overwhelmed her. She had so many questions she wanted to ask Baker about what happened to Jeremy—about how it happened and what he last said. But she knew now was not the time. And part of Sam told her it might be better not to know.

Weston broke the silence of Sam's stare at Baker. "Are you all right, Mrs. Harrison?"

Sam's gaze jerked to Weston. "Yes, yes, I'm fine." She looked back at Baker, regaining her concentration on the issue at hand.

"Well, Commander Baker," Sam went on calmly, "I don't think we're ready to mount another Operation Freehand just yet. We have no reason to believe national security is immediately threatened by these camps."

Sam turned back to Weston. "I want the sites monitored closely. I will brief the White House and see what the president and State Department have to say regarding an appropriate response. Thank you, Miss Weston. Commander Baker, have a good day." Sam walked to the door.

There was something cold about Baker that bothered Sam. She regretted again that she'd probably never know exactly what happened to Jeremy. With the determination by the president that there was no reason to investigate, it all remained closed. And Sam was never given access to the report filed by Baker. So no matter what she thought of Naval Commander Bruce Baker and his role in Operation Freehand, Sam knew she had to put that out of her mind to stay objective.

Baker was not about to give up so easily. “Congresswoman Harrison,” he continued in an almost condescending manner that stopped Sam cold in front of the door. “You can’t let us be unprepared again. If we don’t act now, these camps will simply release another set of terrorists, and more innocent people will die. You can’t let that happen.”

I can’t let that happen? Do you really think it is my decision whether the United States sends in more Apaches and the innocent sons of American mothers to annihilate suspected terrorists because the CIA believes its right? That’s not how it works, Baker, and thank God for that.

Sam’s icy stare sent a clear message. “Innocent people died in the desert earlier this year too, Commander. The president will decide the course to take, not you or me. Is that clear?” As much as she wanted to, Sam could not let Baker know how much she would have liked to annihilate the compounds too. But that was the mother in her, not the way someone in Congress was supposed to think.

“I read you loud and clear, Mrs. Harrison.” Baker rose. “If it pleases you, ma’am, I’ll take my leave now, unless you have any further questions or instructions for me.” His tone was on the edge of sarcastic. Maybe she wasn’t as tough as he’d heard. Maybe that was her son’s problem as well. He resolved to never let her become his commander-in-chief.

As he passed Sam and went to the door, she couldn’t hold back. “Commander, were you there when Jeremy died?”

He stopped walking but didn’t turn around to look at her. “No, ma’am. I came in when it was all over.” He shut the door gently as he left.

Sam thanked Weston again and left to prepare her report to Bush.

On the basis of Sam’s briefing, Bush elected to pressure the Sudanese leadership rather than take military action. She made it quite clear to Bush he needed to tell the Sudanese leadership that if they failed to respond appropriately, military intervention was a serious alternative—one that could come without further warning. Both Sam and Bush understood the kind of popular support a president gains when decisive military action is taken. Only Carter, who botched the attempt to free Iranian hostages, saw a negative impact on his popularity. Since Carter, however, Sam noted that improvements in military intelligence and methods virtually assured popularity. And she knew Bush wanted to be popular. It let him exude a pure confidence in his conviction—a confidence that was not lost on the Sudanese.

Not surprisingly, two days after Secretary Rice delivered the threat, the Sudan was compliant. Patrons of terrorists everywhere knew what happened in Operation Freehand, and no one was particularly interested in challenging Bush. They'd learned presidents were capable of all sorts of aggression—particularly this president. Sam again witnessed the attacks on the compounds by Sudanese forces and understood an aggressive United States was something to fear. As Teddy Roosevelt said, "Speak softly but carry a big stick." Diplomacy spoke softly. Apache Longbows, armed drones, and cruise missiles were all the sticks America needed.

Chapter Thirty-Seven

Our country has always been one to welcome immigrants looking for a new start on their lives. Indeed, we are a country of immigrants. And while we cannot remove the welcome mat, we cannot ignore the needs of those who already occupy our great country and who work hard every day to make their homes decent places to live and proud places to grow. But we do not have endless jobs to offer or housing to give. Our hospitals and schools can only hold so many. Our streets are too crowded with the homeless, and all too many disenchanted immigrants are turning to crime just to survive. Let us first help those who are here. We must put a stop to the mindless, open door to our country Secretary Clinton would like to make even wider. Let's first be sure we can feed and care for those we've let in and identify those we want to throw out. Let's stop hurting Americans who are working and living here, and instead make their lives fulfilling and their loved ones safe.

Campaign speech, October 22, 2016.

May 5, 2008
Washington, DC

Ben and Sam grew distant after Jeremy's death. Ben refused to come to Washington for any affairs and kept his public profile to a minimum. The only good news was even the most pathetic scandal sheets stopped bothering the Harrisons.

Sam knew she had to leave Congress. She feared losing Ben, and that was not a sacrifice she was willing to make. And with Barack Obama possibly in the

White House and Congress at another stalemate, Sam no longer felt effective. She no longer felt fulfilled.

Watts sensed it when he first came to Sam with the idea that she run for governor in Virginia. Sam had ruled out any run at the presidency and needed to make a decision on her next political move. Her reelection would be easy, but her frustrations with Congress grew worse every day. Tim Kaine, then governor, succeeded fellow Democrat Mark Warner. As Watts saw it, Virginians had had enough with two back-to-back Democrats in the Governor's Mansion. Sam was very popular with her record in Virginia as a prosecutor and a congresswoman. In Watts's eyes, she was a perfect candidate.

Watts tried to put it as simply as he could. "Sam, there's no reason why you can't win a race against any Democrat the party puts up. I promise you the Republican nomination is yours for the asking, and the campaign will be fully backed by the party. We'll bring out the votes. There are a lot of people unhappy with the Democrats. But you need to make a decision quickly; we have only until November 4 to declare your candidacy." Sam already knew what her decision would be. She didn't bother to wait for the deadline and announced her candidacy on June 1, leaving her Congressional seat up for grabs.

Watts delivered on his promise with more ease than even he imagined. Sam's popularity with the public and the party was at an all-time high. She had clearly broken every glass ceiling she faced. No one else declared, and she won the nomination by default. No primary was needed. The Democrats, for the first time in twenty years, had a primary between four candidates—former Congressman James Thomas, State Senator Creigh Deeds, former Democratic National Committee Chairman Terry McAuliffe, and former state Delegate Brian Moran. After ripping one another apart in the primary run, Thomas got the nod. By then he was a wounded candidate who played right into the hands of Watts and Sam's other handlers.

The election campaign was as uneventful as her campaigns for the House. It was during this campaign that the national depth of Sam's popularity became abundantly clear. She was openly being touted as a possible presidential candidate. One of her biggest problems with the press was quieting fears she would abandon Virginia shortly after being elected governor. By concentrating on the election and repeatedly denying her aspirations for higher office, she successfully belied those fears.

James Thomas was no match. It was pitifully obvious he wasn't ready for the job. It certainly didn't help when he refused to deny his desire to sit on the Supreme Court when the next vacancy came up. Sam made no mistake by pointing out his stated objectives whenever pressed on her future plans. Thomas and the media played right into her hands. When pushed by the media whether she was seeking the office of governor only for a shot at the presidency in 2012, she firmly repeated her desire to serve a full term as governor. Much needed to be done in Virginia, she'd tell the press, and it was enough of a challenge for the moment. Watts hoped she meant what she said. Even he'd had enough with Washington for the time being and didn't think Sam would be ready before 2016.

On the debating front, Thomas was even worse. He was strangely deferential to Sam, feigning respect. That angered her greatly, seeing it as an affront to her as a woman. The voters saw it, too. It also played well with the press and galvanized the woman's vote throughout the state, where feminism ran high. While Thomas still had solid support in Democratic strongholds in Virginia, no Republican could win the governor's office without getting out the vote of party loyalists. With Sam's appeal, Watts and the party were confident they'd get the vote. And given Thomas's lackluster performance, it was unlikely Democrats would come to the polls in high numbers.

It all made it a little disappointing for Sam. She was itching for a fight. There were real issues between them. She was pro-life; he was pro-choice. She wanted greater controls on illegal aliens; he espoused open American borders. Time after time she tried to get Thomas into a fight, but the fight just wasn't in him. He wouldn't take the bait.

On November 3, 2009, Samantha Harrison was elected the first woman governor of the Commonwealth of Virginia, gaining 61 percent of the vote—another historical landslide on her list of accomplishments. She was on the cover of almost every weekly magazine. Sam was a national figure no one thought could be beaten.

Watts thought she was beginning to look invincible.

For Sam, it also meant moving to the Governor's Mansion in Richmond. In all of Virginia's history, the governor had always lived in the mansion, and Sam would be no different. But she knew Richmond was too far from Fredericksburg and Ben's work at GW. And she knew he wouldn't stand for uprooting the family again. So Sam resigned herself to being a commuting governor, splitting her time between Richmond and Fredericksburg, where Sam set up a second governor's office on Caroline Street in the historic district. While some voters and Democrats in Richmond questioned the expense, no one had enough political clout to stop it.

Chapter Thirty-Eight

Crime in our inner cities is destroying an entire segment of our youth while Washington throws money at the problem without a clue as to why we have the problem in the first place. All the money in the world isn't going to fix our cities until the children of those cities have stable families to come home to. Secretary Clinton likes to say "No Child Left Behind." That's a nice thought. But the reality is the broken homes need to be fixed. The absent fathers need to come home. The churches need to be filled. The schools need to teach. And the police need to care. Money alone won't make any of that happen. Our compassion and love, however, can. So before we approve yet another piece of legislation that throws money at the problem, let's first ask ourselves if the money will go to support families and cities rather than simply satisfy Washington's conscience.

Campaign speech, January 23, 2016.

January 23, 2012
Richmond, Virginia

It was like a nightmare come true. Peter Vasquez was not out of Sam's life.

Sam had been sworn in as governor two years before, barely enough time to get comfortable with the job. Being the first woman governor was a greater challenge than she'd initially thought. Breaking the barriers of two hundred years of male dominance with the state legislature was a daily battle, but she thought she was winning. Even changing the fixtures in the mansion's bathrooms proved to be near impossible when Virginia's historians reeled at any remodeling of the mansion.

Sam had gotten into the habit of arriving at the governor's office every morning by five thirty to avoid the press and others looking for favors. At that hour, she was able to find refuge in her office and have all the unpleasant masses screened before she saw them, if she saw any at all. On January 23, Watts, now her chief of staff, broke that refuge of solace at 8:15 a.m.

"Good morning, Sam." As usual Watts was the first to greet her in the morning. He sat in his usual chair across from the governor.

"Good morning, Zach."

"Before we make any official pronouncements of the day, I think you should know the first execution while you're governor is scheduled within a month. To make matters worse, it's Peter Vasquez, someone you convicted when you were a prosecutor. No doubt you remember Mr. Vasquez."

"How can he still be on death row? I convicted him years ago. He hasn't been executed yet?"

"To be precise, you convicted him in 1997. He's managed to get six stays of execution since. Now his time is up, and his latest round of appeals is not expected to give him any more time."

Everything that tore her apart in the 1997 trial came rushing back. "You know how I feel about the death penalty, Zach. I may have gotten him sentenced to die, but that doesn't mean I liked it then any more than now. I have always opposed capital punishment and cannot condone the state's execution of one man for the sake of revenge while I'm on watch. There is simply nothing to indicate it does any good. Even if there were, I still don't think I could support capital punishment. I'll commute the sentence to life without parole. He'll never be on the streets again." Sam saw the hypocrisy in her own words as contrasted with the vengeance she wanted against the terrorists who murdered Jeremy.

"That's not a choice you have. You can commute his sentence to life, but you can't prevent him from getting parole if the state changes its laws. Right now, he'd serve until he dies, but that can change with the winds in the legislature. Even now, there's talk of bringing back parole. And if such a bill gets to your desk, you'll never veto it. Imagine how you'd feel if you commuted his sentence only to later sign a bill that gives him hope to get out. I don't think you want that, Sam. So Vasquez either dies, or he may someday be eligible for parole. You should also know he's not a model prisoner. Of course, that could change if he ever knew he had a chance for freedom."

Sam felt like the walls around her were closing in. "That animal can never be allowed back on the streets or even have the hope of getting out. Give him time, and he'll fool every parole board. Can't I make some kind of deal with the system or his counsel? Can't I get him to waive any loophole for his life?"

"I don't know. I doubt it, but we'll look into it for sure. But that's not the point. I really think you should reconsider your position on this. The man is a cold-blooded killer. You convicted him. There will be a lot of difficult questions on why you have now suddenly changed your mind. We've managed to keep your contradictory stance on the death penalty quiet. This will blow the lid. Don't forget you ran for Congress just after the conviction, and Vasquez's attorneys tried to get the press to buy a connection between trying the case and your bid for Congress. If he deserved to die in 1997, he still deserves to die in 2012. Stay with the course you set out in the first place."

Sam, now cast into a political furnace, hated the comparisons she had to face between campaigns and convictions. As Watts would tell her, something always needed to be compromised in the name of consistency with minimal damage to her aspirations. Sam could only wonder what was really at play and whether Watts and his political machine had long since taken over her life. She knew it wasn't just her aspirations at stake. Perhaps, Sam thought, she was getting to a point where she'd just as soon leave politics altogether. Ben was not well, and she had lost Jeremy. Amanda barely talked to her. Now she had to condone the execution of someone she'd convicted at a time when she refused to be honest with her beliefs, hiding behind the rule of law and the desire of the people of the Commonwealth of Virginia. The same people she now served as governor.

At times like these, Watts seemed to Sam like a monster. He took on a new look, not of her chief of staff and close confidant but of some kind of sycophant working for the unknown owners of the political process in America—the packagers, motivators, or whoever they were. Sam always regretted she had never really met the people behind the likes of Zachary Watts. She knew she never would. Watts would never allow that to happen and lose his leverage.

"I will go see the family of the girl Vasquez killed. I've forgotten her name. I also want to see Vasquez. When is the earliest possible date for the execution?"

"In all likelihood he'll run out of time in about two weeks, no more than four."

"Fine. Set up the appointments for next week."

"Don't jeopardize your future for some worthless killer, Sam."

"We'll see. And Zach, no life is worthless."

Chapter Thirty-Nine

Yesterday street gangs killed three in Houston, five in New York, and seven in Chicago. In every instance the victims, many of them innocent bystanders, died from gunshot wounds inflicted by unregistered guns. Now some Virginians want to ban handguns. Those who would have us legislate a ban are convinced such a solution will keep weapons outside the hands of Virginia's gangs. They claim these murders are evidence that laws requiring the registration of handguns don't work. They demand a complete ban. They are wrong. It is not the registration requirement that increases or decreases the number of unregistered guns. It's the lack of hope for so many of our youth in the inner city. If they want a gun, they'll get an unregistered gun with or without registration laws. We must show them that if they are caught with an unregistered gun, they will go to jail. No deals, no pleas, and no mercy.

Speech before Virginia Legislature, November 2, 2013.

January 30, 2012
Bowling Green, Virginia

Janie Silvers's parents, Mark and Janet, were just about what Sam recalled. Although now well into their late sixties, they looked older than their years—a lot older.

Janie was their only child, and their lives had been a shared hell since her death. They had not been told why Sam asked to see them, much less why she came all the way to them rather than simply asking them to come to Richmond. The Silvers knew it had to be about Vasquez but were not prepared for the message. They were hoping for an invitation to the execution.

When told by Sam she was considering commuting the sentence, Mark Silvers was the first to react. "I can't believe the prosecutor who demanded Vasquez's death is now asking us if it's all right to let him live! Governor, after years of waiting for the day that bastard would die for what he did, you now ask us to tolerate his living out his life while we think of him every day, sitting in prison, knowing he got away with murder! As far as I'm concerned, I'd just as soon press the plunger on the needle myself. I'd like nothing more than to watch the bastard die a slow and painful death. If what you want is our support, you wasted your time coming here." Mark Silvers was not a diplomatic man. Janet Silvers was pale and began to quietly weep.

"Governor," he went on, "what you see has become my wife's life. My life has been no better, waking up every morning missing the sounds of our daughter. I've been through four jobs. We're both on antidepressants. We ran out of money for counseling last year."

Mrs. Silvers softly wiped away her tears and joined the conversation. "We live every day remembering our daughter. Her innocent peek into our bedroom early in the morning when she was young. Her bright eyes when I made her pancakes on Saturdays. How proud she was when she earned her shield at the academy. But now every day we wake from that fantasy and have to face the truth. She's gone. She was raped, murdered, and cut apart like a piece of meat. How would you like to wake up every day with that memory? You can't possibly think we can find any forgiveness in our hearts for Vasquez and help you give him hope where we have none."

Sam knew she'd made a big mistake. Now she regretted ever coming. She should have listened to Watts. All she'd managed to do was add further pain to a couple that had no happiness left in however many more years they'd live.

Mark Silvers took his wife's hand and looked squarely at Sam. "You have a daughter, don't you? When she was ten years old, did you buy her clothes? Did you take her for her first manicure? Go to her first meeting as a Brownie? Did you watch her grow in school? Play the piano? Go to college? Begin a career?"

Sam wasn't pleased with what her answers would be.

"That evil man killed our daughter. We wish he'd killed Janet and me instead. That's what this did to us. And remember how he rejoiced in his crime to his neighbors and friends? Our pain will never be over. Maybe not even after Vasquez dies. But if you let him live, you might as well sentence us to death because that's what our lives will be like."

Sam, visibly shaken and completely unprepared for what she heard, continued, knowing she was probably only making matters worse. But she didn't know what else to do. "I know I'm asking for great understanding. I'm not asking you to forgive him. No one should forgive him for what he did. That is God's work, not ours. I'm really not sure how I'd feel if it were my daughter, but I wouldn't be surprised if I'd feel the same as you. What happened was without excuse and deserves the most severe punishment a civilized nation can exact. But the death penalty is no more acceptable than a public whipping or castration, punishments still used by other countries we would never want to compare ourselves to. If such barbaric punishments are not acceptable here, how can we condone the killing of even the most heinous of criminals? Such animals should be left in prison to rot for the rest of their lives and never see freedom again. If we execute him, we only bring ourselves to the murderer's level. Is that something we should do?"

Janet Silvers left the room. Mark Silvers shook his head. "I'm not sure why you're doing this or what you're hoping to make out of it politically, but please don't play with our lives. You do what you think is right. Don't ask for our help or approval."

Mrs. Silvers returned and handed Sam a small photograph.

"This was Janie's graduation picture from the police academy. I don't know if you remember how you so boldly defended her at the trial. I cry each night wishing her good dreams and pray she's in a better place, away from her pain. And most of all, I remember your kind words from the trial. Without your support and help, I would never have been able to take the stand or testify. You gave me the strength I needed to face her killer. You felt my pain. Please feel it now. That pain will never go away so long as Vasquez lives. I don't know if it will go away when he's gone, but I do know another chapter in our ordeal will end. Maybe that will bring us closer to understanding. Please don't take that away from us, Governor. Please don't take that away from Janie."

Sam's tears were as real as Janet's and Peter's.

Why did I ever come? How stupid can I be?

She should have known no parent whose child was brutally murdered by a street punk would have any compassion, particularly in a state whose population made it overwhelmingly clear they wanted the likes of Vasquez put away "with prejudice."

Sam wiped her tears and rose from the sofa. "I'm so sorry I've done this to you. I'm sorry I've asked you to help me handle a burden that is mine, not yours. I have insulted you greatly, and for that I will be forever ashamed. I'll take my leave and hope my apology will be enough for now."

Mark Silvers rose and spoke sternly in an even voice. "We don't want your apology, Governor, and we don't want you to be ashamed. Your job is a tough one, and you make hard decisions every day. But you made your decision once, and you said then it was right. Nothing has changed since you told the jury to let him die. All my wife and I ask is that you keep your word to the jury and to us."

Sam extended her hand to Janet to return the photo.

Janet Silvers refused it. "You keep it. If you let Vasquez live, I want you to look at that photo every day and remember Janie. He killed her, and you can either set him or Janie free. If you chose him, then you live with the memory too."

Sam put the photo in her jacket pocket and found her way to the door. There were no good-byes. She cried during the entire drive back to Richmond, looking at Janie's picture over and over again and remembering the trial as if it happened yesterday.

Chapter Forty

Today after the verdict, I went to the police department's memorial service for Janie. The minister said nice things about her. But he really didn't know her. Everyone cried. I know Janie is in heaven. But I cannot forgive, and I hope to see Vasquez go to hell. Thank you for making that possible.

Note to Commonwealth Attorney Samantha Harrison from Janet Silvers, August 16, 1998.

February 8, 2012
Waverly, Virginia

It was the first time Sam had ever been in a state prison. In her days as a prosecutor, she'd been to jails, but never a maximum-security prison.

Sussex State Prison, the home of Virginia's death row, had a notorious, well-earned reputation. While much of it had been cleaned up, it still housed most of Virginia's worst offenders. Vasquez was one of them, waiting his turn to die. He would be the first since Eddie Mays on August 15, 1963. Most Virginia citizens lusted for another felon to face death.

Watts warned Sam about seeing Vasquez. His reputation in prison was dreadful. Now in total isolation, he had assaulted inmates and guards and had no apparent fear of committing any crime he could behind bars. He gloated by saying, "What are you going to do, kill me?"

Vasquez never believed his conviction would be reversed on any of the appeals. While he certainly didn't want to die, he wasn't going to let the guards know his fear or the panic he felt whenever he thought about the needle being inserted into his arm and the icy rush of fluid entering his veins. He had been told the burning feeling caused by the serum was bad, but the minute before dying was unbearable as your body reflexively tried to fight it off in a losing battle. That was his nightmare. Now that he'd run out of appeals and stays, those nightmares got worse every day.

As for remorse, he felt none, even though he told the prison psychiatrist he did. He knew the doctor didn't believe him, but he nonetheless followed the orders of his public defender, a woefully inadequate attorney in way over his head. Vasquez found sessions with the psychiatrist a fun game of deception. But he never let the guards think he had remorse.

When he heard the governor was coming to see him, he was impressed with the impact of his upcoming execution. Confident as ever, he refused to have his attorney—a public defender he considered worthless—accompany him. He knew the governor was his last chance and was determined to handle it alone.

Unknown to everyone and as incredible as it seemed, Vasquez did not remember that the governor was the prosecutor who put him away. Who sent him to die. On heroin for most of his trial and during the years he'd spent in prison, Vasquez did not keep up on politics. He didn't know how to read. When allowed television, he only watched cartoons or MTV. No other prisoner—much less any guard—socialized with him, and no one would read him his mail. He was an outcast in a world of outcasts. He couldn't have been any more alone or isolated.

As Sam went through one prison door after another, listening to their metallic bolts reengage behind her, she began to feel as though she were the one in prison. Something within her told her to turn and go back to Richmond. Another part of her didn't understand why a prison had to be so foreboding and desperate. No one would ever criticize her for walking out. If she did, maybe the tabloids would be kinder to her when telling the story.

They brought Sam to a specially prepared room. It was eight feet by eight feet, divided by a gray metal table running wall-to-wall across the room. No one could get around the table. There was a wall below it so no one could crawl underneath. A thick, bulletproof glass separated the two sides of the table, and each side had one chair. The chair on the governor's side was cushioned. The one on the other side was not. The one on the governor's side could be moved. The one on the other side was bolted down. On the top of each side of the table was a microphone, nothing else. The door on the other side had a glass window laced with wire and a small oval hole at waist height. A hole through which a gun barrel could be pointed but a gun could not be pulled in. Sam's side was reasonably comfortable. The other side was a cage where an animal would be kept.

The extensive security was in place because the governor insisted on meeting with Vasquez in private, an idea no one but she endorsed. It was only through the virtual begging of Watts that Sam consented to the gun hole in the door.

Sam sat down to wait. She twisted her chair, regretting the lunch she had earlier. God how she wished she had a Scotch.

The door on the other side suddenly opened as a guard walked in, startling Sam. As she leapt to her feet, her chair crashed into the wall. In less than a second, the door behind her opened, and two men rushed in—a guard with a gun in his hand and Leon Jenkins, the prison warden. Sam first met Warden Jenkins in one of the meetings preceding her seeing Vasquez. Jenkins made no secret of his disapproval of Sam seeing one of his death-row prisoners. On the other side of the glass, there was no sign of Vasquez.

The guard picked up Sam's chair and let her sit down.

Jenkins, to her right, spoke: "I'm sorry, Governor. We just wanted to be sure you were all right with the setup and to let you get comfortable with the microphone before we bring in the prisoner."

Sam settled into her seat. "That's OK. It snapped me out of a nervous mood and probably did me good. Everything is fine. Let's get started."

The guard on the other side of the glass sat down and spoke into the microphone. "Governor, if you don't mind, may I just say one thing? The other guards of the prison asked me to tell you how we feel before you meet with Vasquez. We can guess why you're here."

"Sergeant Burton, that will be enough!" barked Jenkins. "The governor is not here to listen to you. Bring in the prisoner."

Sam raised her hand in a dismissive manner not well received by Jenkins. "Let him speak, Warden. I've no doubt what he'll tell me, but it's better I hear it now than read it in the newspapers."

Burton looked uneasily at Jenkins.

"Warden, please leave the room," Sam directed, "and take the other guard with you. I want to speak with Sergeant Burton alone. And if I hear the sergeant is disciplined in any way for asking to talk with me, you will have served your last day as warden of this or any other prison in Virginia."

Jenkins grunted and left the room with the guard. Sam and Burton were alone.

"Go on, Sergeant."

"Governor, life here for prisoners and guards is hard. We don't mind that. It goes with the territory. The toughest part of guarding these prisoners, however, is listening to them brag about how they beat the system. About how they have more power than we do. About how they run this institution and the cellblocks. For the guards, it's hard to live with the knowledge that most of these inmates couldn't care less about stabbing one of us with a self-made knife. Every time they come back from a hearing or court date, they gloat as though they won another round. A prison guard listens to this on the inside, and then listens to the media on the outside telling tales of our abuse of prisoners and poor performance. We can't seem to win inside or outside."

Burton looked nervously at the blinking camera mounted on the wall.

"Don't worry, Sergeant, I'll make sure any film of this conversation is destroyed, and if anyone is behind that camera, I order you to turn it off *now*." The blinking light went out. "Please continue."

"Governor, if you let Vasquez off, he'll be a king in this place. He's a man who has no fear of dying. He dares the state to carry out the sentence despite the delays his lawyers win. He thinks nothing of assaulting other inmates in ways I don't think appropriate to describe to you."

Sam did her best to be stoic and show no emotion. Sam could see it was making the guard uncomfortable. "What's your first name, Sergeant?"

"George, ma'am."

"George, people call me Sam. You can, too. I promise you, George, that this is simply a conversation between you and me. It will be reported to no one and never be used against you. So I want you to be comfortable and to tell me whatever you'd like to."

Sam's words elicited a sigh from the guard as he relaxed a bit and continued. "We know the death penalty is a tough issue. But the jury was clear. Hell, you even asked for this animal to die. Why give him hope? Why undermine our security and respect even more, particularly for a man no one can show any compassion for and a man who shows no remorse for what he did?"

"I understand, Sergeant. This is not an easy decision for any of us. But as governor my duties are different than when I was a prosecutor. So I have to fulfill the obligations a governor just as I did when I was a prosecutor. Do you understand, George?"

"Yes, ma'am."

"Good. Please bring in Mr. Vasquez."

Sam was growing tired of being reminded of what a hero she was when she convicted Vasquez to die. She felt she was anything but a hero. More like a hypocrite. She was tired of hearing arguments that ignored the sterile statistics that the death penalty deterred nothing and revenge was no way for a society to behave. Now they wanted her to send a man to his death so guards could have more respect.

The door opened.

Vasquez was dressed in a light-blue pullover prison shirt with dark-blue prison pants. His name was stenciled on the left breast of his shirt. He wore Nikes without any laces. His hands were shackled and his face unshaven. His left eye was swollen and his lip badly cut. Sam didn't need to be told how that probably happened. As a former prosecutor, she knew all too well how prisoners were sometimes disciplined. Even with the glass partition, Sam could smell his rancid body odor.

"Please uncuff Mr. Vasquez, Sergeant Burton. My instructions were specific."

"Sorry, ma'am. I can't do that."

"I see. But you can leave us alone." The guard obliged and left the room. No sooner had the door closed than the barrel of his gun peeked through the hole in the door. Sam knew nothing would have pleased Sergeant Burton more than to pull the trigger.

"Please sit down, Mr. Vasquez."

He sat down slowly, knowing he had seen this woman before but not quite placing the face.

Both were silent for the first minute or so. Vasquez stared with a look that cut right through the bulletproof glass, trying to figure out where he'd seen Sam before.

"Mr. Vasquez, I imagine you know I am the governor. And I also imagine you know why a governor would visit a man about to be executed."

"Why do I know you? Where have I seen you before?"

Sam was shaken by the questions. No one, let alone Sam, had thought of the possibility that Vasquez would not remember her from the trial. She chose not to answer.

"Mr. Vasquez, I'm here to talk to you about your death sentence. I have it within my power to commute your sentence to life with the recommendation you never be given parole. I'm here to ask you why I should let you live rather than die."

"Were you my parole officer before? I know I've seen you before."

"Mr. Vasquez, are you paying attention to me? As governor I'm your last hope of a commuted sentence. Unless you convince me you deserve to live, you will be executed within the next forty-eight hours. It makes no difference now if you've ever met me before!"

"Whether I deserve to die? That's it! You're the fucking prosecutor. Now you're the governor. What's the deal? You change your mind, bitch? Holy shit, you're the lady prosecutor who said I deserved to die and is now asking me to cry that I want to live so you can flush the shitty guilt outta your system. Fucking unbelievable."

"I don't need your help, Mr. Vasquez. I have no guilt. You can think whatever you wish about what I said years ago. Today it's not relevant. If you want to die, that's fine with me." Sam rose to leave, and the door opened behind her.

As she turned, Vasquez spoke, the bravado in his voice gone.

"What do you want to hear?"

Sam turned back and told the guard to close the door. She sat down again.

"I want to know why I shouldn't let you die."

"Look, I'm sorry for what I did. It was wrong. I can never be forgiven. But to be sent to death for what I did only lowers all of us to my level. While I never expect to be free again, killing me serves no lesson." He had the speech down pat, rehearsed a thousand times. They were clearly hollow words.

"Please Mr. Vasquez, there's nothing legitimate in that. It's all rehearsed. And it's not good enough. There's no a psychiatrist here, and I don't believe for one minute you mean what you just said."

Vasquez turned in his seat, unsure of what to say next. "OK, it's not enough to say I'm sorry. Fuck you anyway because I'm not sorry for what I did. The only thing I'm sorry about is she died so fast. There was so much more I wanted to do with her."

Sam's expression showed total shock and elicited a broad smile from Vasquez. She knew she should get up and leave. Instead, she stayed at her seat, determined to see this through.

"I picked up the bitch at the park around eleven in the morning. I remember her cute little uniform and shiny badge. She was so willing to talk to me. Just another cop on her way home after a hard day chasing scumbags like me. But that was all good. She wasn't my first."

Sam stiffened. "What do you mean? There were other times?" Sam's mouth was dry, and she barely got the questions out.

"Why, you want to kill me more than once? Or maybe you want to convict me for another murder so we can have these little meetings each time you lose your nerve when my executioners are ready." Vasquez just stared are her.

"How many other times, Mr. Vasquez?"

"Twice. One girl, one boy. I like both kinds."

Sam was sickened. Somewhere there were families whose lost children were dead at the hands of this animal. Sam wondered if their nights and dreams were as crushed as the Silvers's.

"I only got to fuck her twice, once when she was alive and once when she was dead. She just died too fast. Would you like to know how I tortured her? How I cut her arms and legs? And when she screamed, how I cut her tongue out? I think that's how she died. The little bitch choked on her own blood. How about how I cut her in pieces and scattered her everywhere? I hear they still haven't found all the parts. How much do you want to hear, Governor?"

"I just want to know where the other bodies are." Sam wasn't sure he was even telling the truth. This was the first time Vasquez had ever mentioned others.

"Fuck you. You commute my sentence first. Then I'll tell you where the others are."

"I won't do that. Unless you give me proof, I have no reason to believe you."

"Go fuck yourself, bitch. You don't have the guts to let me die. I've heard about you, and the talk in the prison is no one will go to the chamber while you're governor. Maybe, maybe not. I figure my best bet is with you, a chicken cunt. So fuck you."

Sam rose. "When I came in here, I hoped you'd give me some reason to spare your life. A life is precious, even yours. But you give me no reason to believe you are any different from the day you were convicted. You're not. You're the same worthless animal."

Vasquez's kept grinning at Sam.

"The only way you have a chance to postpone your execution is to tell me the truth about the others. And I want to hear the truth now. Otherwise you will be dead in two days. I will personally attend your execution and see justice done as the poison is injected into your arm and you feel the coldness of death coming upon you. The last thing you will see is the sight of the last person who could have saved your life. The one you told to go fuck herself; the one you called a cunt. Well, this cunt is going to let you die. The only thing you can do is buy a little more time by telling me the truth about the others. Otherwise you die the day after tomorrow, and you Mr. Vasquez, are the one who can go fuck yourself."

Vasquez said nothing. The grin faded from his face. Sam called for the guard and left.

Two days later, Peter Vasquez became the 109th person executed by the Commonwealth of Virginia by lethal injection. Sam chose not to attend. In the end he begged to call the governor, claiming he had something he needed to tell her. Something she wanted to know. But neither the warden nor any of the guards granted his request, gleefully reminding him it was the governor, not the condemned, who had the privilege of the last call.

Chapter Forty-One

There will always be injustice. In a free society, we cannot be so perfect as to prevent it. But our judges, above all others, must lead the way in preventing injustice. They are the guardians. If they continue to put criminals on the streets with short sentences, they do nothing but contribute to the injustice around us. I cannot accept the release of the convicted because our jails are overcrowded with prisoners when our streets are even more overcrowded with criminals.

Campaign speech, October 2, 2016.

February 11, 2012
Richmond, Virginia

Sam was never comfortable with television lights. She always found their glare distracting, and it made it harder to read the teleprompter. This morning the lights were particularly bothersome because she had not done her usual preparation for this speech. Unlike other occasions, she did not let Watts take a look at it before she spoke. Nor did she rehearse it.

She spoke from the Virginia Senate Chamber, as crowded as ever once the word got out she was going to talk about the execution of Peter Vasquez.

The sergeant of arms entered the room and said, "Ladies and gentlemen, it is with great honor I present to you the Governor of the Commonwealth of Virginia."

The usual polite fanfare followed as Sam entered and walked down the aisle to the podium. Those present on both sides of the aisle applauded as she walked in to deliver a special address for which she had asked both houses of the state legislature to hear. The speech was also being broadcast live by all the local stations, and hopes were high for some great drama—particularly since Sam had not officially told anyone what she was about to say. Watts, naturally, was petrified. He assumed, as did just about everyone, that it was about Vasquez. He knew it couldn't be good.

The speaker rapped his gavel as he spoke. "Ladies and gentleman, I proudly yield the floor to the Governor of the Commonwealth of Virginia." The dutiful applause and cheers followed.

Sam settled herself, standing behind the podium, one she had stood behind many times before but never with the weight she had on her heart this day. "Thank you, Mr. Speaker. I have asked for your time today to announce a decision I have made after much deliberation. In my political career, this is perhaps the most difficult decision I have ever made."

Flashes flashed. Cameras focused. The room went silent.

"Two days ago, the Commonwealth of Virginia executed a man for a horrible crime that took the life of an innocent, beautiful woman. A Bowling Green police officer. A woman who in life brought nothing but joy and happiness to her family. The man the state executed never once showed remorse for his acts. Indeed, he bragged about it and taunted prison guards. He was as much a menace in prison as he was on the streets. For many, he deserved to die."

Sam paused, clearing her throat and taking a sip of water.

"As you all know, I visited the victim's parents, and also met with this man just days before the sentence was carried out. My views on capital punishment are not a secret but oddly have never been widely reported. So that there is no further doubt, I oppose capital punishment as a barbaric and unjustified way for society to address its criminal problems. No statistics have convinced me otherwise. More so, I feel it is not our right as a society to take a life—any life. That is a decision for God, not us."

Another sip of water.

"I can only imagine the kind of pain a murder like this leaves on a family. Their lives are never again the same, and the desire for retribution is great and understandable. The grief is unbearable."

Just like mine when fanatics murdered Jeremy.

"I have never before faced such a man. A man who had no moral fiber and who took pleasure and pride in what he had done. An animal, not a man. A perverted mind and a menace to all those around him."

Sam saw the audience was fidgeting, wanting her to get to her point.

"I have never before heard the words of the prison guards on what men like this do to those in prison. How they disrupt security and discipline, and how they view the rights of other prisoners and guards as meaningless. If they know they are going to die, it's even worse. They have no fear. They do not live by any rules."

Watts knew the knockout punch was about to come. Sam was a master at building suspense and crashing the roof down on her audience with her words. "So yesterday, I stayed in my office and allowed the time to pass so this man could be executed. The will of the people satisfied. The family had its retribution, and the guards were free of a menace."

Sam put her notes aside and looked straight at the audience. "Yesterday, the Commonwealth of Virginia, under my watch, committed murder. A murder I allowed."

Jeers began to rise from the crowded chamber. Sam couldn't understand what was being said but knew it wasn't good.

"Someday I will answer to God for my silence. I thought I did the right thing. When I awoke to my terrible mistake, it was too late. I will pray for his soul. But it is not too late for the ten other inmates who are now on death row."

Watts could not believe where Sam was going. He wanted to drag her from the stage. The room again became quiet.

"This afternoon I signed an executive order commuting the sentence of each of these inmates to life imprisonment. As long as I am the governor of this state, anyone else sentenced to death will have their sentences commuted as well."

Watts stormed out of the room.

"I know I will receive great criticism for this action. I know I will lose support, some of which may be critical to my continued success as your governor. But everyone must understand I am first a compassionate, God-loving person. I care more for my family and my personal beliefs than I do for politically correct decisions. I was elected to this office with most people's knowledge of my beliefs in capital punishment. For what it is worth, I am now simply keeping true to my beliefs. Unfortunately, I let a man die yesterday before I did so."

Total silence in the room. Only the flashbulbs broke the silence.

"Thank you." Sam began the long walk out the same way she came in.

The chamber burst into a chaotic combination of applause and catcalls as Sam left the chamber. It was hard to tell which philosophy carried the day, even though it was the same legislature that overwhelmingly passed and overrode the previous governor's veto of the capital punishment bills.

The next day's press was mixed but reasonably balanced. Influential papers lauded her as courageous. Tabloids branded her a hypocrite. The tempest passed quickly. Sam did not hesitate to remind Watts when she could how she knew that would happen. Watts's response was a warning that the telling and retelling of a tale is never over in politics. It always waits for another day when the actions of opponents can be reviewed in a vacuum and twisted for an advantage.

Over the next two years of her term as governor, Sam remained a popular political figure. And with the Washington scene behind her, Ben appeared with her far more often. The country was enamored with the power couple from Virginia. Paparazzi followed them almost everywhere, but were respectful.

Because Virginia does not allow a governor to serve back-to-back terms, Sam relinquished control of the statehouse on January 11, 2014, to Democrat Terry McAuliffe who won with one of the smallest margins of in Virginia history. But the transfer of power to a Democrat did not hurt Sam's image. The race was actually one between three unpopular candidates with McAuliffe beating Tea Party favorite Ken Cuccinelli and Libertarian Robert Sarvis, who many thought cost Cuccinelli victory by splitting the conservative vote. Watts easily handled any criticism that Sam let down Cuccinelli. He adroitly pointed out that the 2013 federal government shutdown, blamed by most Virginians on Republicans in Washington, was too much for Cuccinelli to overcome. So even in a fellow Republican's defeat, Sam came out a winner. In truth, Sam believed Cuccinelli lost because his views were unclear and campaign style too divisive.

The next year went by in a blur.

By April, Watts had planted the seed with Sam to consider running for president and convinced her to form an exploratory committee. He made sure the decision was leaked to the press. National polls showed her to be a viable candidate, but not the shoo-in she was in all her past elections.

In May, Sam kept her national image in front of the cameras as she spoke at a half dozen college commencements and received four honorary degrees. By the end of the summer, she'd lost track of all the events where she spoke or the talk shows she appeared on. Watts made sure there was at least one photo op every week.

In the fall, Sam continued the grueling schedule of speeches and started the classic cat-and-mouse game in answering media questions on whether she'd run for president. Watts had taught her to fend off such inquires by saying, "No decision has been made."

Watts suggested she get on some major corporate boards, but Sam declined, not wanting to be seen as beholden to anyone.

Throughout Sam's hiatus from public office, Watts remained hard at work raising money.

As 2015 got underway, it was clear Watts could raise all the money a serious presidential bid would require—by then nearly a billion dollars. Ben Harrison contributed nearly one third. No one was more astounded than Sam at the fortune Ben had accumulated over the years. Despite all the money, Forbes had missed him on the world's richest list because Ben never revealed any finances publicly. He had never been a public figure. Even while Sam was in Congress and served as governor of Virginia, most of the wealth was never revealed. Everyone knew the power couple was rich, but no one realized how rich until Watts undertook the task of raising serious funds for a legitimate run at the presidency.

On February 9, 2015, Sam issued a simple press release announcing she was throwing her hat into the political maelstrom to become the forty-fifth president of the United States and the first woman to hold the nation's highest office. She decided not to make a public spectacle of her announcement. Hillary Clinton had already declared her candidacy, and Sam saw no need to feed the media frenzy with photo ops. While Watts didn't like the idea of such an informal announcement, he wisely elected not to cross swords with Sam over her decision. Sam knew the media would come knocking on her door. And they did.

Countless talk shows and speeches followed, with Sam still trailing in the polls among Republican voters. In polls pitting her against Clinton, however, they were at a virtual dead heat. While she was popular, it was unclear whether Republican voters wanted someone who appeared moderate. The conservatives wanted someone as far right as they could get, believing Obama had virtually destroyed the very fabric of the Constitution. It upset them that Sam would not take a strident tone and instead kept to the provable facts. While they liked her Reagan-like campaign rhetoric, asking voters whether they were better off after eight years of Obama and the Democrat-controlled Senate, they weren't sure where Sam stood on the emotional issues so near and dear to their conservative hearts.

Sam, on the other hand, had no intention of falling into the trap Mitt Romney did under pressure from the far right. He was clearly a moderate on many levels while governor of Massachusetts, much like Sam was in Virginia. Sam believed that approach was why Virginia's economy remained on solid ground. Romney not only commanded loyalty among the vast majority of Republicans but also represented a real option for conservative Democrats. But Romney changed his colors as his campaign progressed. Eventually, he alienated those on the fence and lost the election. An election many believed was his to win. Sam's analysis was Romney lost because he abandoned the ideals that earned him the nomination in the first place. Sam vowed she would not sell herself to the right wing simply to satisfy its lust for outmoded conservative ideas. Yes, she believed in the Founding Father's notions of government embodied in the Constitution. Yes, she believed Obama had trampled the Bill of Rights. And yes, she firmly believed the economy, tepid for years, suffered because of the liberal fiscal policies adopted by the Obama administration. But correcting those mistakes did not require hysterical ranting by Tea Party supporters and right-wing conservatives. The rhetoric needed to be toned down and the focus shifted to finding compromises and solutions rather than confrontations and stalemates.

Chapter Forty-Two

Democracy is a precious blessing America must never take for granted. We must always be prepared to defend it and, when possible, support those in the world who seek it. As democracy takes hold in Egypt, Syria, Iran, and elsewhere, we must commit our resources to ensure these newly freed countries find their path to democracy as painlessly as possible. That is not to say they will not experience pain or turmoil, for they indeed will. What we and all free democracies throughout the world must do is provide both financial and spiritual support. The alternative is something we cannot even consider. As your state motto so proudly declares, "Live free or die."

Campaign speech, March 15, 2016.

December 14, 2015
Concord, New Hampshire

Concord was its usually cold place—as it always was in the presidential primary season, now pushed up even further as New Hampshire jealously held onto its first primary status. Still the first in the nation, it was a litmus test of a candidate's stamina. If Sam could put up with the snow, the cold, and the brutal directness of New Hampshire residents, she could prove her mettle as a candidate.

The initial polls in New Hampshire gave her no chance to win the primary. While conservative, she was a woman, and while New Hampshire did elect women for statewide office, it was still largely redneck, proudly displaying its "Live Free or Die" motto on license plates and unlikely to vote for a woman for President, even a conservative. Sam confided to Ben that she couldn't understand how a place so physically beautiful and tranquil could be so conservative. The entire state was straight out of Walden Pond, not Wall Street, yet its politics acted more like a parole board than it did an environmentalist's retreat.

Everywhere Sam campaigned, local reporters and citizens were polite and respectful, although at times condescending. It was beginning to wear thin on Sam, and she made no secret of that to Watts. He told her to relax. Given time the media would come around, even in New Hampshire, New England's answer to Tupelo, Mississippi, as Watts liked to describe it. Just push the law and order stuff. That's what they want to hear.

Jack Rines, the mayor of Concord, stepped up to the podium as the Concord High School band concluded their rendition of "God Bless America."

When the song ended, Mayor Rines turned to the band. "Thank you for being such a great band. You make Concord proud!" The applause was noticeably tepid.

If that's all it takes, even I could wake this place up.

"These are difficult times," the mayor droned on. "We face competition everywhere. Our challenges are great. It is at times like this when we need great leaders."

Where the hell did this guy get his introduction speech from, anyway? Difficult times? Great challenges? So what else is new? Maybe the smart thing to do is leave before he finishes.

"The New Hampshire primary first tests our leaders. And here to take the test today is former congresswoman and governor of Virginia and, I might add, one hell of a prosecutor in her time, the honorable Samantha Harrison. Governor Harrison." The applause was not overwhelming.

"Thanks for the kind introduction, Mayor. I hope I can pass this test of yours." Sam was tempted to ask if she could get by with a C, but discretion kept her wits.

Sam looked out at the crowd of New Englanders, knowing it would be hard to wake them up—just like she'd failed to do at every other speech she made so far in New Hampshire.

"I've never been one to shy from a test, and this will certainly not be any different. And by the way, I was a tough prosecutor, but I've also been a tough governor and will be an even tougher president."

The applause that followed was automatic and typical of political rallies. An amateur playing an accordion could probably do better. After all, she had told them what they wanted to hear. It's what the media loved to report, although she knew full well her tough-on-crime message would also include prominent mention of her opposition to the death penalty, something not terribly popular in New Hampshire. Not so long ago, they killed their murderers by hanging them.

"But there is something I want to talk about today that is more important than my experience as a prosecutor or hard line on law and order."

Sam put aside her prepared remarks. On the sidelines, Watts was noticeably nervous. Sam knew she was entering uncharted waters, unsure of how the press would respond.

"My political advisors tell me you want me to talk about crime and how I'll stop it. They're wrong. You already know I'll do that. They tell me you want me to talk about the economy. You might, but that's not what you really want to hear from me today. And you don't want me to tell you how I'll keep the military ready for any challenge either. You've all read every one of my positions in the *Union Leader* and *Concord Monitor* over the past few days. And before this is all over, you'll hear a thousand sound bites reiterating my views on all those issues. No, you don't really want me to talk about any of that today. What you want me to talk about is what all of America wants to hear me answer. So let's get to it. Why do I think this woman should be your president? Is that what you really want to hear?"

A few reacted as if at a revival meeting, applauding and yelling, "Yes! Yes! Yes!"

"OK. Let me tell you why. The reason I should be president is simple. I am the best candidate with the soundest policies. And unlike my opponents, I'll tell it to you straight. And not because I'm a woman. It's because I believe you're smart enough to handle the truth, and because I think telling you anything other than the truth is nothing short of fraud. You have taken too many years of crap from politicians who believe that lying their way into office is an American tradition. Crap from politicians whose first concern is their own neck, not feeding your children or paying your bills. Crap from politicians who cut deals with one another, which means it's more important how powerful your congressman is than how severe the needs of your state have become. Crap from politicians who tell you every year it's time to throw the bums out. It's too bad they don't say that while they're looking in the mirror."

From the laughter, Sam could tell the crowd was warming up, with more of those gathered shouting approval as though the meeting had turned into a church revival led by Billy Graham. Sam loved it, although she noticed the reporters were feverishly writing—not a good sign.

"I admit I'm a politician too. But not one from the new age of liars. Compared to my opponents, I'm a dinosaur when it comes to this game. A dinosaur that has survived, and an angry one at that. A dinosaur who believes in telling you the truth regardless of what it means to my popularity."

Yeah, call me Tyrannosaurus Sam.

"Remember Teddy Roosevelt? Remember Harry Truman? They were dinosaurs too. And you know what they did when they couldn't throw the bums out? They just beat the dickens out of them until they did the right thing. They knew you couldn't get rid of them. Fat politicians financed by big money were as much a fixture in America in 1946 as they are today. And there will be fat cats for the next fifty years too. What this country needs is a president who is not afraid to hit hard when she needs to, and one who will not compromise programs when the compromise does voters no good. The last one who did that was Ronald Reagan. And no one since. Elect me, and what does pass will be laws helping those who need it, not those who can make a buck off the system. Elect me, and I will put some of the political bosses and their cute little chippies right where they belong, tending to each other in retirement homes!"

By now the gathering was beginning to come alive. A small group in the back started chanting "Sam's our man," a clarion call that became the standard bearer of Sam's campaign. Watts wasn't sure he liked it, but agreed it fit the bill and was a perfect sound bite.

"So let's get on with it. You know how I stand on the issues. I'm hard on crime, and I want to end plea-bargaining and increase mandatory sentencing. I know we may disagree on the death penalty, but at least I'm honest with you when it comes to my personal beliefs. We all agree on one thing: criminals belong behind bars in prisons, not country clubs. The victims of crime, not the criminals, deserve our support, economically and spiritually. And the handcuffs should be on the criminals, not our cops. Our criminal system needs a complete overhaul."

Sam went on for another twenty minutes. She reveled in every minute of it. When done, she wasn't entirely sure of everything she'd said, but Sam knew she had spoken from her heart—that was what was most important to her. While her respect for Watts was profound, she was equally determined to remain true to herself from that point on in the campaign, regardless of how it might play in the press. She knew she was not the first politician to tell that story, but she may have been the first to mean it. And people who knew her, including Watts, had no doubt she meant everything she said. Watts was completely comfortable in his role as political minesweeper and media mender, duties he found more interesting and exciting every day. It was hard for him to admit it, but this campaign was beginning to be fun.

The rest of her swing through New Hampshire was much of the same. While at first the media was cautious, they too began to join the "Sam's our man" bandwagon, and the snowball effect was becoming uncontrollable.

Sam got the endorsement of virtually every union in New Hampshire. It was the first time a Republican had ever done so. Both the *Union Leader* and *Concord Monitor* endorsed the candidate—something that was virtually unthinkable given the totally opposite editorial views of the two papers, the *Leader* and its conservative staff versus the ever-liberal *Monitor.* Some press said she'd managed to bridge the conservative and liberal agendas, but Sam knew better. The bottom line was the *Monitor* didn't like the other candidates and their arrogant demeanor. They did not connect with New Hampshire voters. The *Monitor* faced a Hobson's Choice and endorsed Sam as the least of the Republican evils on the ballot. But it was an endorsement nonetheless, and Sam graciously accepted it.

While the *Monitor* saw her as a moderate Republican, she most certainly made it clear in speech after speech that she did not have liberal views. Watts told her being labeled a moderate was a good thing. Voters were tired of both far left and far right. Whether a moderate or not, she wasn't going to lose the Republican vote. But if perceived as a sensible moderate, she might move the dial with conservative Democrats fearful of the far left. Her media persona brought in Democrats on the fence, and no true Republican would ever vote for Clinton. Sure Sam didn't want government to dictate rules for a woman's choice to have an abortion, but Watts made sure everyone also knew she personally thought abortion was an unforgivable sin. While she believed in government programs for the poor, she was far from someone willing to freely hand out dollars, believing those who receive government aid had to earn it and prove a true need. What Sam had mastered was not bridging gaps but articulating and spinning conservative doctrine in less strident extremes. She'd learned how to talk with people, not at them. With Watts's tutelage, Sam had evolved into a master politician. In that she took pride. In the personal sacrifices to get there, she was not as certain how to feel.

She won the primary handily. The Republican Party had found a candidate they could believe in. "America is Listening," wrote *The Washington Post,* a paper that had historically taken Sam to task on virtually everything except her stand on capital punishment.

Following her victory in the Granite State, Sam went on to win in North and South Carolina. Rubio came out on top in Arizona, and Paul surprised everyone with his victory in Michigan. From there, it was a roller coaster ride. By June 7, with the last primaries in California, Montana, New Jersey, New Mexico, and South Dakota, the race came down to three front-runners for the Republican nomination: Samantha Harrison, Marco Rubio, and Rand Paul.

Chris Christie, the odds-on favorite after his landslide reelection as New Jersey's governor, peaked too soon and didn't last long. The *Miami Herald* headline after he came in fifth in Florida's primary—"Christie Loses on His Own Weight"—was enough for him. Because he was on his way to the end of his term as governor and was facing unemployment under New Jersey's term limits, he kept his delegates in his pocket hoping for a cabinet spot down the road.

Perennial president wannabes Rick Santorum, Rick Perry, and Mike Huckabee repeated their losing roles once again and were not legitimate factors after the first few primaries. Santorum and Perry threw their delegates to Paul. Huckabee didn't have enough to matter, so he simply released them to vote as they wished.

Everyone thought Ted Cruz might run, too, until reminded he was born in Canada and couldn't be president under the Constitution any more than Arnold Schwarzenegger or George Romney might have hoped to be. Of course, this heated up the old debate surrounding the definition of "natural-born citizen" under the Constitution, but it was all a sideshow. Cruz had no intention of trying to run with the Canadian flag following him. He decided to stay in Texas where his lock on the Senate seat assured him a leadership role in Congress, which, if the Republicans took the Senate as he hoped, might be Majority Leader.

Paul Ryan played a sore loser, licking his wounds at the voters' rejection. At the outset, the polls had him just behind Christie. But his unsuccessful run at the vice presidency on Mitt Romney's ticket branded him a loser, and his campaign lost steam. His home base *Milwaukee Journal Sentinel* reported that his team simply could not get its act together. Even with the endorsement of Senator Ted Cruz, Ryan lost in Texas, a result seen by media as the primary's biggest upset and what put Sam, the winner, permanently in the role of front-runner. Ben often told Sam that Ryan's policies and ideas were too academic. While other academics understand, folks who earn a living in the real world need simple explanations that tell them how you'll put real dollars in their pockets. As Ben would put it, "That's why Democrat-backed incentives and rebates that put a few dollars into the pockets of working stiffs get votes despite their meaningless effect on the economy."

Shortly after the Texas primary, Ben gave Sam another boost when he wrote a *Wall Street Journal* editorial. "The reason tax and spend and socialized healthcare don't work is simple. Of course, taxing the rich will bring in more revenue that can be spent on government programs. And why not tax the rich? After all, they can spare a few dollars. The fallacy in such policy is that the rich won't materially change their lifestyles. They've worked too hard and are too smart to let their comforts go so easily. Instead, they'll simply cut discretionary spending, most notably in philanthropy and business investments. Charities will get less. Businesses won't expand as employees are asked to work harder. And as for the newfound revenue, it will be spent to increase entitlements and help those on the dole. History has shown time and time again, that those who get the short stick in tax and spend are the middle class. They don't have a cushion for discretionary spending. They're just working stiffs. Yet most of them support the Democrats. Why? Because the Republicans can't explain tax and spend in a way that the middle class understands. Instead, Republicans defend the rich, decry class warfare, and bemoan the problems with entitlements and the deficit. All they give the middle class is lip service. Let's face it, the middle class doesn't care about rich people and don't get benefits from entitlements. Simply put, the middle class isn't listening to Republican rhetoric. Obamacare is a clear example. Even when the costs come from their pockets, the middle class still doesn't listen. Republicans have to change their message and tell the middle class what's in it for them."

It turned out to be quite a race. Sam, with her superior intellect, beauty, and poise versus Paul, with his arch-conservative, often-divisive Tea Party politics, and Rubio with his youthful face and rags-to-riches story. At the time of the convention, it was clear no one had the nomination locked up.

Chapter Forty-Three

Someone once told me a heart has just so many beats it can make and must someday simply stop. But they also told me the spirit lives on and moves to the hearts that still beat. Ben's heart may have stopped, but his spirit lives on in all of us and fills our hearts with love and hope. He will be missed, and it does us well to remember him today. But his greatest concern was always the future, and he would want us to look ahead even today with the optimism he brought to us every day. Whatever the future holds for any of us, we will always be taken to new heights by his spirit, filled with laughter by his wit, and left with a smile in his memory. I will always be supported in the memory of the love we shared for thirty glorious years.

Excerpt from Sam's eulogy given at Ben's funeral, September 5, 2016.

September 6, 2016
Fredericksburg, Virginia

The funeral for Ben was simple and private. For once the media left Sam alone. She was thankful for that and hopeful that maybe there was some compassion in the press, even for those in political life.

The next day back in Fredericksburg, Watts interrupted Sam as she relaxed on the veranda at the back of their home.

"Sam, I thought you'd want to see *The Washington Post* before you go back to your office or hear about it from someone else."

"What's the matter? Has the press decided my mourning period has come to an abrupt end?"

"No. Ben wrote a letter to the editor before he died. The *Post* published it today."

The obituary preceding the letter gave a short biography of Ben. It listed his accomplishments, things that impressed even the most callous reader. That he had made millions through his own financial prowess was not lost on a reader either. The *Post* concluded Ben was a renaissance man. And a loving man. It reported all the rumors about Sam and Ben's relationship being rocky were untrue. The *Post* described the two as truly in love and loyal. Accompanying the obituary was Ben's letter to America.

Dear America:

Please do not take this letter as the last words of some do-gooder trying to pull on your heartstrings to garner a vote for my wife, Samantha Harrison. You have to decide for yourself who you'll vote for. I just want to tell you why I just voted by absentee ballot for Sam. I'm not sure if the absentee ballot from a dead man can count if I die before Election Day, but I voted anyway because it matters for our children and grandchildren that I try to have my vote count as an expression of my views.

I have been advisor to many of the country's great leaders. Throughout my career I have stayed out of politics because of a trait I saw in some who I advised that I knew I would not countenance in myself. Their first concern always seemed to be their reelection and assuring themselves continued power and influence. So long as the needs of our country were consistent with their personal goals, they took my advice. If not, my advice was ignored. It's not that I expected them to always listen to me. God knows I was often wrong. It's just that it never ceased to disappoint me that they couldn't be honest with me. After all, I was advising them, not the country.

My wife, on the other hand, has always been a different kind of politician. No one writes her speeches for her. No one tells her what to say at a press conference. God knows she drives her advisors mad, never knowing what she'll do or say next. But it is proof of the respect they hold for her that she's had the same group of advisors for her entire political career. No one has ever deserted her. Including me.

I voted for Samantha Harrison because it matters. Because she matters. She listens and acts from her heart. She acts from the same place that lies at the foundation of our democracy, the freedom and choice of the people. She's neither a part of the old guard nor a newcomer, wet behind the ears. She is what this country needs, desperately needs now. She and history are crossing at a precise moment that we cannot let pass unfulfilled.

My vote was from my heart and my soul. Make yours the same.

Benjamin Harrison, PhD

Sam, her eyes filled with tears, put the letter in her lap and whispered to herself, "Thanks for the vote, Ben."

"Sam, are you all right? I just thought you should see it first. It's a beautiful letter."

She grasped the letter, stood, and took a deep breath. "Zach, I've never felt better." And she meant it.

Chapter Forty-Four

My opponent believes she has done much for America. And no doubt she is a true American. But what she has done is in the classic mistake of her party—tax and spend. Mortgage the future for immediate pleasures and comfort. Secretary Clinton is not a woman of the people prepared to govern this country, she is a politician bent to the will of the vocal few for fear of losing a precious vote or two. This is where she and I differ. In our democracy, the will of the majority or the vocal few must be balanced with the rights and wrongs of their desires. The test of my leadership is I do not accept whatever is popular for the moment or what will capture votes for the sake of what is right. Make that the test for your vote.

Opening statement, last presidential debate, Los Angeles, California, October 27, 2016.

September 15, 2016
Los Angeles, California

Sam did not look forward to the first debate, barely having time to mourn the death of her husband. She knew Clinton would do all she could to obscure the issues facing the country and dwell on Sam's occasional departures from the will of the people, something Clinton had to be careful about since her record was hardly stellar in that regard. Ordinarily Sam wouldn't care. But the polls were slightly in favor of Clinton. For the first time in her political career, Sam had a real fight on her hands.

Sam couldn't understand why so many Americans polled favored a candidate who tolerated adultery by her husband and served as Secretary of State for a president she distained. Sam kept asking Watts and her campaign staff what exactly Clinton had done to prove her worthy of being president. She'd never run a business, she served only one term in the Senate and one stint as Secretary of State. She was accused of more cover-ups than a baby's ward at a hospital. Clinton was no match for Sam's resume. Watts reminded her while that may be true, Bill Clinton's resume didn't hold a candle to George H. W. Bush's experience, but Clinton won. And while the pro-Harrison media seized on the experience differential, the mainstream media ignored comparative statistics in unemployment, job migration, poverty, and crime as it continued its love affair with the Clintons.

Sam's confusing opposition to abortion hurt her. It put Sam in a constant battle with supporters to explain that her opposition to abortion related only to the government stepping in. It was a woman's choice. A choice Sam condemned if the choice was an abortion. Despite the countless times she tried to explain, the message never seemed to sink in, and the Democrats loved to feed the confusion. The reporting kept her off-balance. Sam's biggest hope was to attack Clinton on her tax and health care plans. Attack her on unanswered questions from Travelgate to Benghazi. Clinton was a classic tax-and-spend Democrat ready to continue the Obama policies, feeding a deficit that grew year after year. Sam's message needed to be that continuing those policies would eventually bankrupt America.

Sam firmly believed that Clinton and the Democrat principles were not good for her country, and continuing the Obama administration failures would do permanent damage. By Sam's reckoning, a Clinton presidency could set economic progress back another twenty years. American workers were tired of tax increases. But the population receiving the free handouts at taxpayer expense was growing every year. So while Sam was convinced what business needed were lower taxes and not the increases Clinton proposed, she was fearful the votes of those who felt the sting of taxes might not be sufficient to override the votes of those who found living on the dole an acceptable livelihood. While the economy had stabilized under Obama, its anemic growth was nowhere near an acceptable rate. But it was growth and something the liberal media and Clinton seized on, warning that Sam would cripple it and put

America back into a recession. Sam wondered if America really understood how an economy works and was constantly frustrated by what seemed to be an impossible task of educating voters. The deficit had grown. But did most Americans feel its impact? If elected, Sam intended to cut programs and government fat with a vengeance, even if it meant she'd serve only one term. That was easy fodder for Clinton and raised fears among all the welfare recipients and senior citizens on food stamps. She often thought of the quote from *A Few Good Men,* "You want the truth? You can't handle the truth."

Sam and her team continually emphasized that the General Accounting Office had thrown up its hands in a report to the Senate Finance Committee. Even the GAO couldn't figure out where all the money was going, between entitlements and secret funds to the military, the CIA, the NSA, and whoever else managed to garner the favor of an influential senator or the president. Under Obama, politics as usual had become the politics of stalemate. While it made for nice editorials in both liberal and conservative newspapers blaming the side they didn't support, the *National Review* put it in perspective for most Americans: voters believed lowering the deficit from its unprecedented heights did nothing to put money in the average workers' pockets. While an admittedly simplistic conclusion to a complex problem, the Republicans supported a deep-cut platform as the only way to keep more of the money earned by voters in the voters' pockets. The only way to do that was to cut spending. That philosophy, as with most proposals supporting fiscally responsible change, was difficult to explain to voters, particularly those in lower income brackets. To them, a cut meant something would be taken away from them. The question was whether enough voters would listen and understand, particularly in a sound-bite world.

The dilemma faced by both candidates was that people had put up with two tax increases under Obama and were not about to take any more. That was where Sam had the edge. She was clearly a cost cutter, not afraid to take criticism from special interest groups. She would end subsidies to public television. Farm subsidies would be cut back. Foreign aid would become more focused and given out only with clear strings attached. Welfare recipients would have to work to earn their benefits. Highway maintenance would be transferred to the states, where tolls—not federal tax dollars—could support the roads.

Clinton was at a disadvantage in other ways. She held true to the party line. The Democratic Party was proud of its accomplishments in health care and touted the anemic growth of the economy as a victory over the Republican polices it inherited from Bush. They dismissed deficit concerns with promises that within twenty years their programs would bring about a balanced budget based upon sound economic principles.

Sam's plan was to let others criticize the Obama administration and the Democrats for what their party had done while she attacked it for what it had not done by failing to rid government of waste and corruption. Democrats increased taxes to support the pork in politics. Politics as usual. Sam was from another school and was convinced America was sick and tired of the lies and games.

But after months of trying to get her message across, the polls still said more American voters sided with Clinton than with Sam. Of course, there were the usual uncommitted—enough voters to swing the election either way. Nonetheless, until the votes were cast, the polls made a difference. And Sam needed to change the trend.

The League of Women Voters sponsored the first of the debates. Sam had hoped the league would be impartial but learned quickly they bent over backward to concede to Clinton's demands.

Sam wanted an informal format for questioning and open-ended follow-up. It would have given Sam her best environment. The League, however, saw it another way. Structured questions with one follow-up question. No rebuttal. No debate. A farce.

Sam and Watts hoped the League would have learned by now from prior debates. Unfortunately, all the League and other debate sponsors had learned was that compromise was necessary to stage a debate. That compromise led to mediocrity, as far as Sam was concerned. She had become a voice in the dark and had no alternative but to put up with the format.

Clinton won the toss and opened with the first statement.

"Before I begin I would like to express by deepest sympathy to Governor Harrison for her loss. We all felt we knew Ben Harrison. He was a man who served his country with great honor, helping every administration he served for the last twenty years. He will be missed. I am also compelled to say I do not want the voters or the media to use this loss as any indication Governor Harrison could not fulfill her duties as president if she is elected. She and I have many differences and views on how this country should be governed, but I have no doubt of her ability to serve this nation as she has so diligently in years past."

Sam barely heard the balance of Clinton's opening comments, caught off guard by her gracious words. While the media would later dismiss them as political niceties to fend off the sympathy vote, Sam took them as sincere. They were the first sincere words she had heard from Hillary Clinton. Suddenly, Clinton seemed human. Sam brushed that off and regained her focus.

After Sam's opening statement, including a heartfelt thank you for Clinton's words about Ben, the questioning began. Other than her thank you to Clinton, the balance of words from both candidates was anything but complimentary.

The first question went to Sam. Just as Clinton had been given the first opening statement, Sam won the pleasure of the first question by luck of the draw before the debate.

"Governor, many people have criticized you for changing positions midstream. You certainly did on capital punishment. How can we be sure you won't change your other positions once elected, even, perhaps, on abortion?"

Watts had seen it coming and prepared Sam for it. Ever since she commuted the first death sentence in Virginia, the media characterized her as prone to change positions. In reality, it was absurd. She never changed her position from denying the wisdom, much less the logic, of capital punishment. But it was too intellectual for voters to understand. Instead, she was labeled as indecisive. Sam wondered if she had let more die, would the media have asked the same question.

Sam once again tried to put her position in context. "Your question is decidedly off the point. I have not changed my position. I do not believe in capital punishment and never have. I made the mistake of letting one man die—a man I was instrumental in having sentenced to death in the first place. After his death, I received neither the satisfaction nor the closure the punishment seeks. And I certainly know his death did nothing to stop other murders. I never changed my mind; I simply forgot my convictions for a brief and costly moment. It will not happen again. And on abortion my position has never changed."

Clinton couldn't resist jumping in despite the rules of the debate. "With all due respect, Governor, you did change your mind—you changed your mind twice." Clinton was enjoying herself, thankful she was not the subject of the probing.

Sam turned and looked at Clinton with distain. "Secretary Clinton, I am not about to debate you on how many times I changed my mind because I never did. The point is I made a decision, reaffirmed it, and will live by it today. You may search all you wish, but you will find nothing more than what I have said. On the other hand, I would welcome an analysis of your record. After all, didn't you say Benghazi was no big deal? Or have you changed your mind now?"

At that point, the rules went out the window, and with every question, the two parried like Olympic fencers, saber to saber.

Sam attacked Clinton on her spotty performance as Secretary of State, intimated she'd done nothing serious as New York's senator, and that Obamacare was as great a failure as her and her husband's failed health plans during his administration. Clinton countered with questions on Sam's perceived waffling on issues, her limited experience in global issues since becoming governor, and her failure to address what Clinton described as old South discrimination in Virginia. All of it was predictable banter but felt, as the *New York Daily News* reported, like a real catfight.

In the hotel that night, Watts said he thought it was a draw. He asked Sam why she let the debate get into a tit for tat rather than staying with the script they had all worked out. Everyone agreed that Watts's plan best assured that Sam would make the political points she needed to for votes. Where was her position on crime? What about taxes? They never even came up. Instead, claimed Watts, she and Clinton acted like caged teenagers ready to scratch one another's eyes out. That made for great entertainment but bad politics. Watts repeatedly reminded Sam that she was behind in the polls going into the debate, and a performance that portrayed her as a crazed woman was giving it away to Clinton. In a draw, Watts believed Clinton won. A draw certainly didn't improve Sam's numbers. She needed to attack Clinton on the issues where she could win. This was not the time to get sucked into hysterics. His words where harsher than Sam was used to, but Watts was too close to victory to diplomatically deal with Sam. And Sam knew he was too close to the truth.

Sam was tired after days of preparation and an exhausting debate. "I'm only human, Zach. It's hard to fight someone who disarms you with her first comment. All of her reputation as a cold, calculating bitch went out the window as she damn near endorsed me. It got angry and all I wanted to do was hurt her. How dare she use Ben's death as a debate tactic? At first I thought she was sincere. I knew that was untrue as soon as she interrupted the first question and turned the debate into a grudge match. To be honest, it caught me off guard. I'll make more of an effort next time to stay with the script. I promise."

Sam knew her words were empty. Somewhere along the way, she had lost her drive, and the mention of Ben by Clinton only took the wind from her sails. She began to wonder if she had lost too much of her own life for the sake of packagers like Watts. When she looked at Clinton that night, no more than ten feet away, she saw an old woman worn out by politics and desperately holding on to the last vestige of victory she yearned to have. While she apparently had a good relationship with her daughter, who else did she have? Certainly not her husband. Sam saw Hillary Clinton as someone surrounded by handlers with no real friends. Sam feared she might be standing before a mirror when she looked at Clinton.

It wasn't that Sam thought Watts was wrong. He had his job and did it well. He had Sam's respect. But he was losing her confidence, and she badly needed to talk to someone with whom she could share her most intimate thoughts. She'd lost Ben. She'd lost Jeremy. Her relationship with Amanda was awful. Her best friend, Janet, was sleeping with her campaign manager. She had no one to turn to.

Am I worse off than Clinton? Am I more alone than her?

The remaining two debates resulted in the same draw. Sam did attack more and tried to stick to the script, but she was no longer the fiery candidate who won in New Hampshire months before. Clinton, however, was no better. Her ego got in the way of a lot of her answers, and the whispered allegations of a promiscuous relationship with a campaign aide didn't help. Sam refused to let Watts run with the allegations though, because she didn't want the important issues clouded with salacious rumors and innuendos. Watts reminded Sam that politics was dirty, and items like Clinton's sex life could guarantee Sam more votes. Sam hid nothing in her closet. Clinton's was full of dirty laundry. But Sam insisted on taking the high road.

Watts tried to engage Amanda, but she still wanted nothing to do with the campaign. The media left the rift in Sam and Amanda's relationship alone and so did Clinton. It was the unstated quid pro quo for Sam letting Clinton's personal indiscretions pass.

Watts even reached out to Jim Black, now a retired octogenarian, at his ranch in Jackson Hole, Wyoming. The former senator and confidant to Ben flew to Cleveland on a campaign stop and met briefly with Watts and Sam, only to have Sam politely dismiss his concerns and thank him for his kind words about Ben. The meeting accomplished nothing. The real problem was Watts didn't realize how little Sam respected Black, despite his power when he held office. He represented the old guard, something for which Sam only volunteered her time when it was a necessity.

As the fall months passed and the campaign wore on, the polls kept close. It was a toss-up. But there was no real excitement among the voters. *The New York Times* said the campaigns were just plain boring, criticizing both candidates for failing to show voters passion for the office they sought. It didn't help that the likes of Rush Limbaugh and Mark Levin harped on Sam's views on abortion and capital punishment. But moderate Republicans had long gotten used to attacks from the far right. Never mind that she toed the line on taxes, health care, and just about every other Republican favorite. Limbaugh, Levin, and their followers couldn't see the forest from the trees and realize that they weren't costing Clinton votes but scaring conservative democrats from voting for Sam. When unity in the party was needed, the conservative talking heads refused to compromise.

Watts knew this was hurting Sam and putting what he first thought was a sure bet into a toss-up. It took all he could to keep Sam focused. He had long since abandoned diplomacy.

"You're letting it slip away, Sam. What the hell is wrong with you?"

"There's nothing wrong with me, Zach. It's just a tough campaign. I said from the start that come November, we'd be neck and neck."

"Bullshit. You're copping out. You know damn well the country is ready for you. God, Sam, you all but had this election in your pocket before you started playing Miss Sadness after Ben's death."

Sam's face turned bright red. "That will be enough, Zach. I don't ever want to hear you talk about Ben that way. I won't deny I lost a lot of my energy when he died, but I still want to win. It's you, not me, who has a naive view of elections. This is for the presidency, not some local precinct race for the House or even the governor of Virginia. The electorate isn't going to buy any of your polls and won't rush from your candidate because she's not bitchy enough. This is not only the first time I've run for president, Zach. It's the first time you have, too. So don't claim to be the know-it-all. It's insulting. We'll still win, as long as America is ready."

"They're ready, Sam. Are you?"

Sam didn't answer the question. She asked Watts to leave her alone, an order she gave with increasing frequency as Election Day approached.

By November 7, 2016, it was clear neither candidate could claim a comfortable lead.

Chapter Forty-Five

It's been a long campaign. Thank you all for the support you've given me and my family. When you go to the polls tomorrow, you have a choice. And while that's an old cliché used by politicians since the Greeks invented democracy, I want to be sure you know the choice you'll be making if you vote for me. First, I am a Republican. There are those in the press claim some of views sound more like a Democrat. They're wrong. Voters agree with me because I speak from my heart and not from a party platform or in lockstep opposition to anything an opposing party might say. But make no mistake, I am a Republican. I reject the agenda my Democrat opponent wants you to accept. So let's make a few things clear. Abortion? It's wrong except in very limited circumstances. But it isn't for the government to pass judgment. God will when the time comes, and I believe his judgment will be damnation. So if you think I am pro-choice, you're wrong. I'm against government substituting its partisan judgment for your personal decisions, however wrong I believe those decisions may be. And I'm against capital punishment even though I allowed a man to be executed who I could have saved. I regret that. That does not make me a Democrat. The truth is I can no more condone state-sanctioned execution of a murderer than dictate standards imposed on women where God sits in judgment. Does that sound inconsistent? It's not. Those acts are for God to judge, not politicians. Taxes? Under the Obama administration, they've killed competition. Taxes need to be cut. So do pet pork barrel programs coveted by many politicians and beneficiaries of government largesse. The past administration promised to end them. Instead, President Obama added more. They've got to go. Subsidies and stimulus? No. They don't work. So I will make cuts, but only where they're long overdue. I will not cut programs that help the truly needy. Welfare is important, but only for those who deserve it. Unemployment benefits are important, but only if they do not create a population of permanently unemployed. The past administration has allowed more than 50 percent of the working-age population to be on the dole. That has to end. No nation can survive under that model. And it will end

under my administration. Nor will I cut any program that ensures our national security. Indeed, I want more invested in our defense. I want the world to clearly know our security is paramount, and we will not tolerate any country that harbors those who mean to do us harm. Education should be left in the hands of the states, not the federal government. Federal environmental regulations are out of hand. We can protect our air, water, and food without volumes of regulations that have no relationship to any logical need. I could go on, but I won't. Just know when you pull the lever or press the button tomorrow, you are voting to put a Republican back in the White House who will put an end to waste and timid leadership, restore pride in America, and end the suffering a Democrat administration has brought upon every American family.

Final speech in presidential campaign, Jefferson Hotel, Richmond, Virginia, November 7, 2016.

November 8, 2016
Richmond, Virginia

The morning of the election, Sam found the media coverage strange. Why was it important to film her going to the polls? Did America think she wouldn't vote for herself? Actually, she thought it very sobering when she entered the voting booth, that moment being a private one in the anonymity of the curtained kiosk. When she saw her name on the line for the presidency, she felt a chill, realizing again the gravity of the office she was seeking. It wasn't that she didn't appreciate it before; it was just when the moment came to cast her vote, the obligation became all too real. She even fancied voting for Clinton as a lark but thought better of it once it came to pulling the lever. Sam voted for Samantha Harrison.

The scene in the hotel that night was not unlike the aftermath of the Memphis convention that started it all. Sam and Watts alone in a hotel room, waiting for room service. This time, however, they watched national election results, not convention delegates.

At ten o'clock, NBC predicted Clinton as the winner. By ten thirty CBS, Fox, ABC, and CNN agreed. Sam was unable to carry critical states in the

Midwest including Ohio, Illinois, Minnesota, and Indiana. Her strength in South, Northeast and conservative West were not enough to hold on to a victory. Even if she won California, as she was not expected to do, she'd be short on the Electoral College votes necessary for election. It didn't matter that the popular vote was virtually dead even. Clinton had won enough states to win the majority of the Electoral College. Victory was hers.

Watts poured them both a stiff Scotch, handed Sam a glass, and sat on the couch beside her. "I'm sorry, Sam. The voters didn't turn out the way we hoped. Only two states were the difference between defeat and victory. But it's clear you're the voice of the Republican Party. Your last speech was a clarion to change. The Republican Party is yours to lead again in four years. Don't give up now."

Sam's feeling of loneliness could not have been deeper.

"I don't think I can do this anymore, Zach. You were right. When Ben died, I lost my drive. I've sacrificed enough. Here we are again, just the two of us, sitting alone in a hotel room watching election results. To hell with it, Zach. My son and husband are dead. My daughter hasn't spoken to me in months. I don't know if she'll ever speak to me again. My privacy has been lost to the media for as long as I can remember. I've given most of my adult life to public service, trying to hold fast to my beliefs, popular or unpopular. I gave my heart to the people. Good people. But right now I can't tell you how much I regret getting into all this in the first place. I lost, and I don't like how it feels. In an hour I have to face cameras again and give a gracious concession speech. The first one I've ever had to give. I don't feel gracious. I feel angry. Betrayed. It's too much. I can't give you any more, Zach."

Watts decided it was best not to leave the argument to another day. His candidate was slipping away, and he wasn't going to let that happen. "Don't come to any final decision in your present state of mind. If you like, skip the speech. I can announce that we're not buying into the network predictions. There are still states that have not fully reported and there are always the absentee ballots. You can give the speech tomorrow after you've had a night's sleep. Or we can even stall it for a couple of weeks."

Sam's expression was disconcerting, almost insulting to Watts as she responded. "You want me to continue this charade another twelve hours? Another two weeks? Keep America in suspense? It isn't worth it. I've given enough. You ask too much of me. Find someone of a higher order than me to be your party's next messenger. I'm done. I've sacrificed enough."

Watts couldn't hold back his anger. He'd put up with the wimp in Sam since Ben's death. He knew he should have taken more control. Instead he listened to his wounded client.

He took a long drag on his drink. "Goddamn you, Sam. Someone of a higher order? My party? I'll tell you what. When you're over feeling sorry for yourself and realize Ben and Jeremy aren't coming back, we'll discuss your future. This is the first time you've felt defeat. You don't always win, Sam. As for Amanda, she's your problem. Why don't you try reaching out to her more like a mother than a distant cousin? Stop feeling sorry for yourself. It does not become you."

Sam kept her composure, more out of fatigue than kindness. "Christ, you don't let up, do you. Didn't you hear me? It's over. No more. Get yourself another candidate."

Watts let emotions he'd suppressed for months spill out. "Bullshit! You are the first principled candidate I have known in my lifetime. And I bought into it. Now you want to quit? You can't. You don't have that right. You're damn right the demands are high. They have to be. The presidency is a trust held for our entire country. Whoever wins, millions of people didn't vote for them. Millions of others didn't even vote. Don't sit there feeling sorry for yourself. If you can't rise above your personal feelings, you shouldn't have gotten in the game in the first place. You could have quit at any time. You wanted it. I didn't package you. That's why it worked. You couldn't be packaged. Don't bitch now and try to blame me or anyone else for your heartache. Now that America hasn't given you something you really wanted all along, you want to run home and hide. Well, you don't have a home to run to, and you can't hide anywhere. When you got into this game, you gave that up. Your home is before the cameras and the voters, and that will never change."

All Sam could muster was a blank stare at Watts. "Please leave."

"What about your concession speech?"

"Just leave!"

Watts did as he was told, telling Sam to call him when she was ready to discuss her future. At that moment Sam didn't see much in that future.

With Watts gone, Sam felt the overwhelming loneliness that had plagued her since Ben passed. Every time Sam thought she'd grown used to it, she again felt the pain. When was the last time she'd cried? She couldn't remember. It saddened her that she couldn't cry now. Completely drained, she couldn't call up any emotion within her. Neither angry nor saddened, she simply felt alone. Abandoned. Not in her loss in the election but in the personal losses over the years she had given to public life.

There was a soft knock on the door. Probably Watts again, thought Sam.

"Later, please."

The person knocked again.

"I said later, please."

"Mother, please open the door."

Sam's heart beat furiously as she got to the door and opened it.

At first the two just stared at one another, not seeming to know what to do or say.

"May I come in?"

"Yes, yes, of course." Sam stepped aside.

"I thought you might like some company other than that old fart Watts."

"Where's Nathan?"

"He's home, minding our palatial Georgetown home."

"Is everything OK at home?"

"It's fine. Please don't worry about me. I'm fine. But how are you?"

Sam poured herself another Scotch and offered one to Amanda. She took it. The two sat on the couch together.

"I've certainly felt better. It looks like I lost. At least that's what the networks say. They believe despite my early popularity, I blew the campaign as we came down to the wire. Listening to them it's as though I gave it away to Clinton. I suppose I could just cop out and say America just wasn't ready for an independent woman president and let the media compare me with the Party-owned Hillary, but that's a waste of time. I lost, pure and simple. Christ, I didn't even hold enough of the women's vote to make any difference."

"I'm sorry."

"It's all right. Now I know what defeat feels like. I probably needed it."

"No, you didn't. You deserved to win. I guess I didn't help with our not-so-private feud. Maybe I should have put my personal feelings aside for the bigger concerns you were trying to solve. Maybe I should have remembered you're my mother and not some distant politician. That's what Dad would have wanted. I feel as though I betrayed you and probably cost you important votes."

"Please don't feel that way, Amanda. There may have been times when you doubted my love for you. I understand. I wasn't there for you too many times when you needed me. Thank God for your father. But I have never been anything other than proud of you for sticking to your convictions, even when I disagreed with them. I like to think I had a little to do with that. Don't ever think you should have done anything differently. I lost this election all by myself. The country just wasn't ready for the likes of Samantha Price Harrison."

Sam lifted her glass and took a healthy belt. Amanda did the same.

"Maybe the country's not ready, Mom, but do you think you might be ready for the likes of Amanda Harrison? I think we could use each other right now."

Amanda put her arms around her mother. They held each other for what Sam hoped would turn into eternity. Each let go of long-held emotions. Loneliness was not Sam's monopoly, and Amanda needed her mother now more than ever before, missing the same loved ones and regretting the same sacrifices. Ben was her father, and Jeremy her brother. Family. While Sam's handlers might have written it off as the price of politics, Amanda knew better. And she refused to accept that the price of being the daughter of Samantha Harrison should bring so much pain.

Sam let go, not wanting to do so. "I have to give my last speech, Amanda. Will you help me write it?"

"Not if it's your last speech, Mom. If you ask me, what the media said is true. You gave the election to that bitch Clinton. So now we face four more years of a withering nation under Obama's legacy. She'll do nothing to change the path he started. If we do this together, we're going to fight hard. If I'm in it with you, you've got to be in it all the way too. I don't want to lose."

"How can we possibly win, Amanda?"

"Mom, it's simpler than you think. You lost not just because you ran out of steam, but because you were too open with your conservative views. Why should you be any more open than the Democrats? Obama won because he came across as a moderate while he hid the truth about his left-wing plans. And Clinton isn't any better. To win, Mom, you have to be a conservative wolf in sheep's clothing. Next time, let's campaign to win and then govern to change."

Sam smiled. It was as though she was hearing Ben mixed with a little bit of her father. She knew she'd found the daughter she thought she'd lost.

Chapter Forty-Six

In my defeat in 2016, I found my best friend: the daughter I neglected for so many years and a woman I love and respect. I thank God for blessing me with someone so special.

Samantha Harrison's Presidential Memoirs, June 6, 2030.

November 9, 2016
University of Mary Washington
Fredericksburg, Virginia

Sam officially lost the popular election by fewer than 200,000 votes, and with California going to Clinton, she lost the Electoral College by double digits. It appeared, however, that the Democrats lost the Senate. So maybe Sam had an impact after all. Clinton now faced a House and Senate controlled by Republicans.

It was five o'clock in the afternoon. A beautiful day as sunset approached. Sam stood at a podium set up on the steps of Monroe Hall at the University of Mary Washington. Sam, Amanda, and Watts had driven back from Richmond first thing that morning, deftly avoiding the media. This was the first time the country had heard from Sam since early election night, well before the polls closed and Clinton was declared the winner.

Sam and Amanda felt at home in Fredericksburg for obvious reasons. They both particularly liked the historic Jeffersonian-inspired campus at the University of Mary Washington. Watts couldn't think of a better place to make her speech—a university named after the mother of the county's first president.

Sam cleared her throat. Flashbulbs lit up the sky despite the sun. "Last night America spoke. She decided on her next president. She did not choose me."

Some of Sam's supporters began chanting, "No, no, no," tears visible on so many faces. In America there is nothing more bitter than political defeat, particularly on a national level. Defeat in American politics was rejection by millions of people and something not easily accepted. How could so many people dislike you so much? It didn't matter that almost the same number of people liked you.

Amanda and Watts stood by her side. Even Sam's brother was on the stage despite his relative obscurity during the campaign. How Watts and Amanda found him and got him to Fredericksburg on such short notice amazed her.

Sam raised her hand to quiet the crowd. "We tried our best to tell America what we thought she needed. Maybe Congress was listening. If not, every one of us must remind them. We can't give up. We must continue the fight."

The uproar was deafening. Despite the small crowd, Sam thought they were even louder than the cheers in Memphis where the journey began. She knew they weren't, but it sure felt that way.

"I let you down. In the last few weeks of the campaign, I lost my drive in my personal grief. Like the media said, I gave it away to Clinton. Tradition says I should congratulate my opponent on her victory, and perhaps someday I will. While I certainly wish her success for the sake of all the people of this great nation, my heart is too heavy to offer congratulations. I cannot repeat the charade of past candidates who put their hearts and souls and the hearts and souls of so many volunteers aside for the sake of civility. I will not be a hypocrite. I never have been. Defeat is crushing, and the honesty I have always had with you prevents me from describing it any other way."

The crowd grew silent as it took in the finality of defeat.

Don't give up on me yet, my friends.

"But there will be another time. In the meantime, let us all keep the pressure on our new president to perform and deliver on the promises America elected her to achieve. Let's all wish her success. Despite this bitter defeat, I also know the nation must come first. We are a democracy, a form of government not without its pain and sacrifice. This is just another diversion for us. After the next four years, we'll get back on course and look for a Republican victory in 2020—my victory if I am honored again to be your candidate. But whoever our party's candidate is will have my full support."

The crowed was reenergized. Their matriarch had not given up. She was not defeated after all. "Sam's our man. Sam's our man," rose from the plaza.

"Over the next four years, I promise you I will earn back the confidence you placed in me when we started this campaign. In 2020, America will be ready for Samantha Harrison. And when I return, it will be to celebrate with you in victory! Thank you all for your support and friendship. God bless you all, and God bless the United States of America."

The cheers continued. The pain of defeat was lifted.

Sam never did call Clinton. She always thought that was a ridiculous exercise.

The next day Sam announced that Watts would remain a consultant and that her daughter, Amanda, would be her campaign manager. The three began planning Sam's bid for Virginia's Senate seat in 2018, then held by Democrat Tim Kaine. This time Sam promised to let Amanda and Watts run the campaign their way. The next day, Amanda leaked Clinton's fling with her campaign aid. She had no intention of seeing Sam feel the sting of defeat again.

Author's Note

This book is a fictional account of a woman—Samantha Harrison—and her run to become president of the United States in 2016.

I began this book in the summer of 1996 when President Bill Clinton was in his first term. While we had previously seen many women run for president or vice president, it was not until Geraldine Anne Ferraro ran in 1984 and Sarah Palin in 2008 that we saw women run for vice president from a major party. Then in 2008 Senator Hillary Clinton made a serious run in the presidential primaries, only to lose to Barack Obama. After the election, Senator Clinton was appointed Secretary of State and stayed front and center in the political arena. She resigned in January 2013. Many believe she is working on another presidential bid for the 2016 elections, and early polls have her in the lead for the nomination should she decide to run. Regardless of what Secretary Clinton does, it is clear the United States is ready to elect a woman to the presidency. Over the years I picked up my drafts, dusted them off, and did rewrites. For whatever reason, I never quite had the energy to complete it. The run by Senator Clinton, however, inspired me to finish *Presidential Intentions* as I realized that the prospect of a woman becoming president was now simply a matter of time.

This is a book fiction. It is not intended to resemble any living individuals in their personal or professional lives. While I use the names of real people who held office or were in the public eye throughout the book, it is with creative license; I do not mean to say the quotes or actions I ascribe to them are true, although I tried to be as historically accurate as I could. My apologies to any politicians who lost an election to Samantha Harrison. No doubt none of them likes losing, particularly to a fictional character.

I hope you enjoy it.

Appendix
Samantha Harrison Timeline

Date	Event	Age
8/14/1957	Born	
10/1/1968	Father's death	11
6/23/1974	High school graduation	16
8/27/1974	Enrolls at Stanford	17
5/19/1978	Graduates from Stanford	20
8/25/1978	Marries Ben Harrison	21
9/6/1978	Begins MBA studies at Stanford	21
2/24/1979	Birth of Jeremy	21
6/5/1980	MBA graduation at Stanford	22
6/16/1980	Begins job at IMF	22
6/26/1985	Amanda's birth	27
8/1/1985	Resigns from IMF	27
8/27/1985	Enrolls in GW Law	28
5/17/1988	GW Law graduation	30
6/1/1988	Begins job at Wilson, Smith & Watts	30
2/3/1993	Begins job as Commonwealth Attorney	35
2/26/1993	World Trade Center bombing	35
2/15/1995	Appointed Deputy Commonwealth Attorney	37
6/4/1996	Jeremy graduates high school	
6/24/1996	Jeremy enrolls in the USNA	38
12/25/1999	Mother dies	42

12/31/1999	Resigns from Commonwealth Attorney position	42
1/1/2000	Announces run for Congress	42
5/26/2000	Jeremy graduates from USNA	
11/7/2000	Federal elections; Bush elected president; Sam elected to Congress	43
1/3/2001	Begins term in Congress	43
9/11/2001	Attack on World Trade Center	44
6/5/2002	Amanda graduates high school	44
11/5/2002	Federal elections; Sam reelected to Congress	45
11/2/2004	Federal elections; Bush reelected; Sam reelected to Congress	47
5/10/2006	Amanda graduates RISD	48
11/7/2006	Federal elections; Sam reelected to Congress	49
2/9/2008	Operation Freehand attack in Iran	50
6/1/2008	Declares intention to run for VA governor	51
11/4/2008	Federal elections; Obama elected president	51
12/31/2008	Ends term in Congress	51
11/3/2009	Elected VA governor	52
11/6/2012	Presidential election; Obama reelected	55
1/13/2014	Ends term as VA governor	56
2/9/2015	Announces run for presidency	57
1/12/2016	NH primary victory	58
7/26/2016	Nominated as Republican candidate for president	58
9/2/2016	Ben Harrison dies	59
9/15/2016	First presidential debate	59
10/27/2016	Last presidential debate	59
11/8/2016	Election Day	59

Made in the USA
Middletown, DE
21 January 2015